*Dear Racha[...]*
*Hope you ha[...]*
*aboard the Audacity.*

*LAURA LOUP*

# The AUDACITY

## LAURA LOUP

Dedicated to Trista Mayes and Zack Loup who climbed aboard
the *Audacity* long ago.

## AUTHOR'S NOTE

You're about to board the *Audacity* and discover a universe imagined by every known past, one highly caffeinated present, and a few optimistic futures.

Douglas Adams (may he smile upon me from Atheist Heaven) said, "Space is big. You just won't believe how vastly, hugely, mind-bogglingly big it is." It's easy to get lost out there. And sometimes amidst boldly going where no one has gone before, you need to curl up on a cozy orange couch and watch some "I Love Lucy" to remember where we've boldly been.

# I LOVE LUCY

The "I Love Lucy" theme song drifted brassily through the alien rocket ship which had been orbiting Earth since the nineteen-fifties.

No one noticed.

No one except the lanky blue alien who watched, for the zillionth time, with a smile which broke open his face like a piñata, the grainy black and white heart scrawl across the screen of a boxy, rabbit eared television.

Lucy was his singular joy in life, and he had been watching it nearly constantly since it first aired. Not all aliens loved "I Love Lucy" as Xan did. In fact, none of them did. None of them had seen it and, as such, had no opinion.

The picture wobbled, and Lucy was caught in a freak snowstorm accompanied by a sound one could only describe as "fuzzy." A literal shadow fell across the TV; a figurative shadow fell across Xan's face. The viewscreen behind him was no longer illuminated by the cheery yellow sun he'd come to appreciate.

He vaulted over the back of the couch and leapt up the orange shag stairs to the control loft three at a time.

Outside, so close he could see the neon orange of the *Audacity*'s hull reflected in it, an enormous ship dubbed the *Peacemaker* blocked his signal. The loss of Lucy was the least of his worries.

"By the thumbs of O'Zeno, she zuxing found me."

*She* was not, in fact, looking for him, but he didn't know this.

He pressed the Button Which Typically Made The Ship Go several thousand more times than necessary. The ship did not go.

The *Peacemaker* was having issues of its own. The flash of an explosion whited out the viewscreen and when it cleared there was a huge gash in the side of the spaceship. An AMC Gremlin shot out of the *Peacemaker* and disappeared into a nearby wormhole. Debris from the explosion pinged against the hull of the *Audacity*, and Xan tried not to think about all the new nicks the orange hull would have.

Something had fallen out of the Gremlin and snagged on a jagged tooth of metal that had once been part of the *Peacemaker*'s hull. Someone, actually. And this was where Xan's day took a turn, because now he felt obligated to help.

He flailed at the control panel, pressing every button he could find, hoping at least one of them was a tractor beam. As luck would have it, one of them was.

# TWO
# AMC GREMLINS

In the event that the human race has ended and you're reading this from a distant planet, it's important to note that old cars don't ordinarily fall from the sky. Yet, across planet Earth, dozens of 1970's AMC Gremlins had done just that.

No self-described sane person who saw it happen was brave enough to talk about it. Saying you saw a car fall from the sky was the kind of thing that made you sound insane and people are typically rather concerned with continuing the illusion of sanity.

There were, of course, those who had no delusions of sanity and they were only too happy to postulate, theorize, and conspiracy-theorize about the cars.

May was troubled by this. Not the cars, that she could handle. The people who wouldn't stop talking about the cars troubled her. Mainly because it seemed as if every single customer she'd served in the past ten hours at the 24-hour Sonic she, for lack of a better term, worked at brought it up. "Hear about them cars?" they'd ask conspiratorially, as if they were about to share with her the gospel itself.

May had shut off the part of her brain that cared if she was asked the same question fifty-seven times in the span of an hour long ago.

"No," she'd say, letting them go on to enlighten her over and over again as she counted their change.

At last, it was midnight on Friday. No, wait, it was Saturday. Sunday? May tipped her phone out of her pocket and was more than a little horrified to learn that it was now Monday. Again? Most people had weekends; May had smoke breaks and a few hours to sleep and rinse off the soda syrup between shifts.

She grabbed the nearest damp towel and rubbed it on the counter, more evenly distributing the germs.

"Going home?" her manager Kathy asked, closing out May's register.

"Oh no, the night is young. I'm going to a wild kegger after this." May pulled out the trash bag, twirled it closed, and slung it over her shoulder, giving Kathy a tired, crooked smile.

Kathy squinted at her. "You're being sarcastic again."

"Yes. Good night, Kathy. Make lots of tips."

Kathy snorted, fiddling with the register. "The only tips I get here are men telling me I should pull my shirt down more."

May pushed open the back door, pointedly ignoring the squelch of her steps as she walked into the poorly lit alley and flung the garbage bag into the dumpster. She released her curly black hair from its sweaty prison under her Sonic cap and shook it out with her fingers. With a groan, she leaned against the dumpster and began the long process of psyching herself up for the even longer process of walking home.

This would require a cigarette. She pulled one from the package in her back pocket and lit it. The first drag helped her hoist herself off the dumpster. The second got her to dig her keys out of her pocket and thread them between her fingers in a make-shift sort of weapon she referred to, cleverly, as "Key Fist."

Finally, she straightened her back, set her mouth in a tight line, and thought murderous thoughts. Thoughts that, May hoped, would seep out of her pores and repel anyone looking for an easy target.

She started the two mile walk back to her apartment, ready to studiously ignore any sketchy activity she might encounter on the way.

The night was cool and quiet. May had the gall, forty-five minutes in, to think that perhaps she wouldn't see anyone at all on her evening stroll. It was a nice fantasy, until she passed a particularly nasty alley-way stuffed with piles of wet cardboard, mysteriously stained rags, and, amid the cardboard and rags, a urine-scented man.

"Ey, watch yerself out thar," the man muttered to a spot about five inches to the left of her head. "Thems Gremlins about town—they been a'snatchin folks naw. Up ta no good, mum."

She winced but tried to morph it into a smile. "I'll keep that in mind."

"God bless," he mumbled.

May walked a little faster. Not that the man was in any state to give chase, she just needed to breathe fresh air again. At last, her apartment loomed darkly before her. The streetlight had been out for months, but the person whose job it was to let someone know about these things hadn't been paid in months, and the person whose job it was to do something about these things hadn't cared in months.

She jammed her key in the lock and wiggled it around for a while until the door finally clicked open. The familiar earthy smell of home greeted her, a sliver of moonlight fighting its way in through the thin window above her front door which accounted for the only natural light in the apartment.

The living room – which was also the kitchen, the library, the ballroom, the lounge, the study, the conservatory, and the bedroom – was dark enough that she didn't have to worry about cleaning it. Atop her mini fridge, in a beam of moonlight, sat May's one faithful companion: Betty, the cactus.

It was a resilient little prickled lump. May had over-watered it, underwatered it, and left it in a box for a few weeks when she moved in. It just wouldn't die. It fed off adversity, as if it got a kick out of taking the punches that life (and May) threw at it.

"Hey, Betty, long day?" she asked.

It slowly converted carbon dioxide into oxygen at her.

May converted some oxygen back into carbon dioxide in return and gave it a mist of water. The massive cloud of oxygen that Betty emanated was beginning to make May light-headed.

Not tired enough to sleep, not awake enough to do much else, May absently pulled another stick from the pack in her back pocket and went outside to sit on the metal steps that lead to the upstairs apartments. She sat on the cold metal, lit her cigarette, and watched a candy wrapper cross the street, aided by a gentle breeze.

The traffic light at the intersection nearest her flickered through its rounds: green, yellow, red. Giving the go-ahead to no one, suggesting to no one that stopping might be a wise thing to consider, and firmly telling no one that they were now law-bound to stop.

The night was quiet, as we've established. It was quiet because the things that typically make noise in the early morning—birds, crickets, drunks—were avoiding the area around May's apartment.

The reason why was about to become clear.

Down the street, past the fruitlessly flickering traffic light, an engine turned over in a car which loitered in the dark space between two feeble street lights. May flicked the ash from her cigarette, leaning her head against the railing to get a better view of the car which had broken the silence. Though she was a self-described sane person, the car made her nervous.

A single headlight turned on, the other winking as it attempted to light before it settled on a dull yellow glow and then blinked out altogether.

Slowly, as if she might frighten the car if she moved too fast, May lifted her cigarette to her mouth. The car began to move. She let the cigarette drift back down again, unpuffed.

She could go inside; the idea crossed her mind, anyway.

But doing that would be both admitting that the car had freaked her out a little and drawing attention to her presence. She decided to instead pretend to be part of the architecture. Nothing to see here, just a bit of railing.

The car moved forward into the light. It was, as I'm sure you've guessed by now, a 1970's AMC Gremlin. What you could not have guessed was that its body work was done out in pickle-green with black racing stripes that swooped nicely upwards towards the back of the car.

What you further could not have guessed was that the car sported two rather large black metal thrusters which had been welded onto its sides in something of a hurry.

May pressed herself further into the stairwell, but she still made rather unconvincing cast iron.

The car completely disregarded the traffic light's suggestion that stopping might be a wise thing to consider, further disregarded the concrete street median that endeavored to keep it on the proper side of the street, and still further disregarded the sickly hedge that surrounded May's apartment complex as it screeched toward her.

Half a second short of turning May into an unwilling hood ornament, it stopped.

May dropped the cigarette.

A sizzling sound came from the car window, a pop, and then, over what sounded like a megaphone, someone shouted, "We have come in peace, Earthlin-"

She heard a thwack, which sounded suspiciously like someone being hit over the head with a megaphone, then a different voice.

"Can I give you a trip?" it said.

"I'm sorry?" May said, more out of the habit of customer service than as a way of actually apologizing for anything.

"Do you need a car? Might I offer you a ride?" The voice was vaguely metallic, and vaguely threatening.

May knew what this was now. This was teenagers. She groaned, stomped on her cigarette, and stood up. "Fuck off," she proposed, doing her best impression of someone you wouldn't want to mess with; it wasn't a good look on her.

From the car: silence. The megaphone clicked on then off, then on, and off again as the bewildered wielder considered their next words.

"No thanks," the voice finally said.

The Gremlin slammed into May, officially making it one of the top ten worst nights of her life.

# THREE

# YOU'RE HERE NOW

Something sharp pressed into the side of May's head. So she was alive; that was good. And really, aside from the sharp ache in her skull just above her ear, she was pretty comfortable.

The air smelled clean, but coppery. She could hear things again as her senses started to slowly peek out of hiding, like forest creatures timidly returning to their patches of grass after a bit of a fright. She heard papers rustling, keys clacking, someone calling someone else's name, and the someone else telling the first someone that they were busy, hold on.

"Hello? Where am I? I can't see," she tested, hoping that perhaps whoever was rustling the papers nearby would offer an explanation.

"Hello, May June July. I'm Dr. Granger. Welcome to the *Peacemaker*. You may be experiencing some darkness right now. I recommend opening your eyes. The procedure is over," said a voice that sounded like a clogged sink.

The word "procedure" stuck to the back of her mind like a fly to fly paper and wiggled there, making her anxious. She was sure she'd shut her eyes for a good reason, but what?

She opened her eyes.

Ah, now she remembered.

May screamed.

It was a proper, horror-movie, damsel-in-distress type scream, and she wasn't sure how she'd pulled it off, but she did, and it helped her feel a bit better about what she was seeing.

She clambered upright, curling her legs into herself for protection, and noticed that she was no longer wearing her old Sonic slacks, but a skin-tight white latex suit. She tried to get a sense of how much danger she was in. She appeared to be in an office cubicle so, possibly, quite a lot.

"Culture shock. It should dissipate in seven to eight Earth years."

The doctor, who looked more like a Jell-O shot stuffed into a wetsuit than a medical professional, held out a slimy yellow-green hand.

"Shake?" said the doctor.

May shook.

"Good girl. Well trained. You'll do nicely here."

The gelatinous Dr. Granger twisted back in her seat towards the small white desk and began shuffling papers again, trying rather transparently to appear busy. Transparently because May could see that she wasn't actually doing anything but shuffling around paper, and because May could also literally see through her translucent, dripping hands.

"Where am I? How do you know my name?" May asked.

The doctor shook her head as if May's words were gnats buzzing around it.

"Now, now. I'm very busy," she said, placing a paper she'd just removed from a manilla folder back into it and removing another paper which she set down on the desk, shifted a bit to the left, hovered over for a moment, then replaced in the folder exactly where it had been.

Before May could interrupt her very important paper shuffling again, a pale young man with messy dishwater hair entered the cubicle. He was wrapped, much like May, in a greyish white latex bodysuit and he was barely old enough to drink.

"May?" He looked at her with one bloodshot grey eye and one black eyepatch.

"Yes, but how-?"

"Follow me." He walked off, his hand trailing behind him in a half-formed sort of come-hither gesture.

May followed, but she wasn't happy about it.

"Excuse me, could you please tell me where we are?" She was quickly running out of patience. That was the last "please" she'd be able to muster for at least a few hours.

"We're here now," he said helpfully. She jogged a little to catch up with him as they rounded corners and passed cubicles identical to the one she'd woken up in.

The enormous building they were in seemed, to May, to be some sort of hospital hub. She was partially right. The place was enormous, and it was a kind of hospital hub, but it was not a building.

They reached a long wall lined with hundreds of human-sized pneumatic tubes which made her feel like a mouse at a drive-up bank teller. Between each tube, the same poster had been copied and pasted.

"You're here now!" it said in cheery blue letters under a stock photo of smiling strangers.

The young man stepped into the tube nearest them and stared at her.

"I'm not getting in there until you tell me what's going on," she informed him.

He tipped his head back as if his neck could no longer bare the terrible weight and sighed.

"I don't know, man. They brought me here, like, five months ago and put a chip in my head that translates everything into German so they can boss me around. The food here blows, and I miss apples. That's about it. Would you please get in here? I'm supposed to take you somewhere."

He looked desperate, so May joined him in the tube. The doors whooshed shut in a zippy sort of science-fiction-movie way that Earth elevators hadn't quite gotten the hang of yet, and they shot into the ceiling at a speed Earth elevators would never get the hang of.

"I'm August, sorry." He held out a hand. "If we're going to be bunking together you should probably know that."

Nothing about the way August held his hand out to her made her want to shake it politely. She shook it politely.

"May," she said.

"I know."

"I know, you know. Where are you taking me?"

He sighed, chewing his lip in a way that was both gross and disconcerting. She was standing on the eye-patch side of him so she couldn't see the haunted look in his eye, which was probably for the best.

"You don't want to know."

She hated when people said that because ninety percent of the time, she did. She liked to be prepared.

The pod stopped, and August exited, but May did not.

"Tell me where we are." A "please" tried really hard to push itself out but she grit her teeth against it.

"We're at the labs. We have to go, come on." He reached for her arm, but she backed away.

"What happens if we don't?"

"Something along these lines!" He pointed to his eye—or lack thereof.

May found that reasonably convincing and exited the tube.

## FOUR
# UNMENTIONABLE

Within the *Peacemaker,* a healthy dozen or so miles away from May and August, the physical form which contained the languishing spirit of a long-forgotten chaos demigoddess sat cross-legged on a black and white checkered floor.

Standing, she was a full eight feet of muscle and glistening deep purple skin. Silver hair rippled into a high mohawk atop her head and cascaded down her back, pooling on the tiles beside her.

Sitting, hunched as she was, she resembled a very angry purple swan. Still majestic, still terrifying, but slightly ridiculous. The kind of ridiculous only the extremely brave or incredibly stupid are wont to point out.

Her looks weren't unusual for a Rhean, and nothing about her was particularly *unmentionable,* except for her eyes. Her eyes were of an unimaginable color and intensity. They hadn't always been this way, but being possessed by the spirit of a long-forgotten chaos demigoddess did funny things to a body. Starting with the eyes.

13

The physical form called herself Yvonne, and she was becoming quieter by the season as Chaos' consciousness soaked into her body like an unmentionable liquid soaking into a dry sponge.

Before her, on a white square of what could pass for linoleum, stood a blown glass figure of a puntl, a kumquaty sort of horse-like creature.

Chaos sighed with Yvonne's lungs, and rested her head in Yvonne's palm. Billions of orbits ago, she would have been able to transform this tiny figurine into a sulpoosian cocktail with a decorative paper umbrella stuck through a twist of llerke rind by simply remembering the salty smell of a beach. Now, even convincing the snout to succumb to entropy and devolve into sand made her horridly mortal head ache.

She glanced upwards. Above her, behind a field of glistening glass spikes, the *Peacemaker's* Stardrive boiled away.

An entire demigoddess-consciousness took a lot of energy to sustain. Roughly a small star's worth of energy. Coincidentally, the massive starship *Peacemaker* also required about a small star's worth of energy to function. And so, the travel-minded Tuhntian engineers who built the *Peacemaker* had siphoned the energy from a distant white-dwarf in a desolate corner of the galaxy into the compact Stardrive with a shockingly elegant little device. The details of this device are not important to the story and, as such, will remain unexplored.

This had, at first, been a nuisance, to the chaos demigoddess who called the star home. But she soon found that living in a massive, planet-destroying warship had its advantages. Namely, the ability to possess its captain.

Chaos had been compacting Yvonne's soul like trash in an overfilled bin for a little over a thousand orbits now, and she was finally really getting the hang of it. She was so confident in her host body's allegiance to her, that killing the pesky Chief Engin-

*No!*

Ah, Yvonne's favorite word, thought Chaos. It was

practically all she could get out nowadays. But coupled with the searing chest pains and debilitating ache in her limbs, it was enough to keep Chaos on something of a leash.

Destroy a few planets here and there, sure. Murder a few of her best scientists, why not? Try to off the engineer and this body threw a fit.

She needed someone to kill, though. To keep her mind off her limitations.

Chaos waved a hand over her BEAPER, summoning some unimportant conductive track in her circuit board who could take the brunt of her frustration.

The intershoot doors opened, almost apologetically, to admit Doctor Granger. Her gelatinous green face dripped nervously and with good reason. Few who were called to Yvonne's chambers left as much more than a puff of ash.

"Ah, Doctor Granger." Chaos smiled neatly from Yvonne's mouth.

"Yes, ma'am?"

"I'm experiencing some medical distress. I'm glad you're here." Yvonne rose to her feet in a way that was uncannily like a cloud of steam rising from a manhole.

"What seems to be the trouble?" Granger wrung her hands wetly.

"Every time I think about killing a certain someone, this body tries to incapacitate itself. Why is that?"

"Oh," Granger bubbled uncomfortably. "Perhaps, you don't actually want to kill her-them!"

Chaos shook her head slightly, her silver hair glinting from the light of the Stardrive like the edge of a freshly sharpened knife. "No, it's not that."

She pulled from her belt a small, sharply tipped plasma zapper and turned it on the doctor who promptly disintegrated into a puff of ash.

Again, she waved her hand over the BEAPER on her wrist. "Medical unit? Assign a new head doctor and send them to me. I need a second opinion."

# FIVE

# LOT IN LIFE

May, again, found herself sitting in a brightly lit cubicle. The being that poked and prodded at her now looked like Dr. Granger, but hadn't introduced themself. Dr. Granger could've been a candy striper in comparison.

They were harmless, thought May, as the creature took notes, murmuring under their breath. A bit rude, but harmless.

Harmless until they lunged for her face, forced open her mouth, and yanked out a back molar with one surprisingly powerful tug.

She screamed, first out of surprise, then pain, and reflexively punched the oral interloper in the face. Her fist sunk into their slimy flesh, but didn't seem to bother them in the slightest, which bothered May quite a lot.

"Report to Food Service Facility 8A in one rotation. Leave," they said, turning their back on May and typing something into a holographic screen.

May was only too happy to oblige; she slipped out of the cubicle and ran. Or, at least, she tried to run. August caught her by the arms and put a bit of a damper on her running. "Woah, hey, calm down."

Never in the history of spoken language has the phrase "calm down" ever calmed anyone down. On the contrary, centuries of anecdotal evidence prove that it does the opposite.

"I have work in the morning. I want to leave," she said, wiping the blood that had dribbled from the corner of her mouth with the back of her hand.

"Well, you can't."

"Why?"

August ran a hand through his long hair, somehow making it messier than it had been before. "If I told you, you wouldn't believe me. I'll show you if you come with me. They should leave us alone for a while."

Her mouth was filling up with blood and she toyed with the idea of spitting it out on the floor, but couldn't bring herself to. She swallowed it and shuddered.

"Fine."

August took her to the tube again, which pulled them downwards and deposited them in what looked like an indoor hallway in a dingy motel. The carpet was a low-pile abstract affair in shades of green and pink that were not on speaking terms, the walls dripped steadily from brown stains in the wallpaper, and rows of numbered doors lined the walls.

May followed him down the corridor to a small alcove. She half expected to see a vending machine when she turned the corner. What she saw instead through a large porthole in the wall was a bit of a shock to her.

It is likely, dear readers, that since you're aware of the premise of this book you've guessed by now what May saw. I'll describe it anyway.

May saw a digital billboard which read "Forbinated Moringarg: For the distinguished ch'stranda," and showed a high-res looping video of a creature akin to an over-sized ferret licking something from a bowl.

May looked back at August, confused.

"Hold on, it'll move."

It did.

"Oh, I see," she said.

"Uh-huh."

"Is that...?"

"Yep."

"Oh. I see."

May watched a blue, white, and green marble spin slowly, lit on one side by an enormous yellow dwarf star and on the other by a round hunk of reflective rock.

"Come on, our room's just around the corner. You can take the bed."

A strange amalgamation of items decorated the room August brought May to. It looked as if someone had ransacked five different three-star hotels. On one wall hung a poorly rendered painting of a parrot in a chipped gold gilt frame. Another wall hosted a large but unplugged TV and two paintings of palm trees, which were identical in every way but one. What the difference was, exactly, May couldn't say.

It occurred to her that she ought to think she was dreaming. Everyone in books and movies always thought they were dreaming when something this unusual happened. She thought for a moment, asking herself how she knew she wasn't. Then she decided that if she *were* dreaming, she wouldn't have the capacity to think that she was dreaming. Which wasn't strictly true, but it made her feel better. Or worse.

She definitely wished she was dreaming.

August fell into a densely stuffed chair beside the bed and closed his eyes. Or at least closed the one. May hoped he still had another eye to close under the patch.

Slowly, May explored the bed. It was a plastic-covered brick of a thing with a single pancake-thick pillow and no sheet, twisted at an odd angle from the bamboo headboard. She poked it; it crinkled at her.

"Report to the cafeteria," said a voice from the ceiling that sounded like milk poured over Rice Krispies.

August groaned dramatically as he stood. "Damn aliens don't fucking sleep," he mumbled. "Come on, it's time for work."

"Work?" May asked, following him as he left the room. She didn't know what else to do at this point, since running away was out. Running in space was impossible for many reasons.

"That's why they brought you here," August said as he walked. "Needed another server."

The cafeteria looked like a Jim Henson-brand sex dungeon.

Monstrous creatures she had only seen the likes of in cheap sci-fi films, slight yellow-green beings that were uncannily human, Amazonian beings which came in varied shades and hues of purple and with various numbers of eyes, arms, and legs, creatures that looked almost entirely like cicadas in sausage sleeves, all stood in a meandering line or sat, eating quietly, at tables. Each was Saran wrapped in the same white latex.

August towed her along by the arm now, noticing that she had paused to gape, and brought her to a narrow doorway at the back of the cafeteria which led to the kitchen. And it was a kitchen. Just a normal, boring industrial kitchen like the one May had wasted a solid forty hours a week in on Earth.

She'd rather be wasting her time there. No one here had asked her to sign a W-2, and she doubted she would be compensated for her time.

Someone who looked an awful lot like a grey-haired grandmother from Minnesota handed May a ladle and patted her shoulder apologetically. "Down at the end, honey." The woman hobbled out the door they had entered through.

"Take it easy, Fanny," August called after her. "Go on, I've got to take care of something in the back." He tried to walk away, but May stopped him with a ladle to the shoulder.

"What are they paying us?" she asked. August snorted a derisive laugh, pushed the ladle off his shoulder, and went to the back without a word.

Aside from the ache in her jaw, the unusual appearance of the customers, and the persistent knowledge that she wasn't on Earth in the back of her mind, this was all oddly familiar. Standing, serving, smiling. The smiling was awkward. She couldn't really turn it off, but it didn't feel at home on her face right now.

She hadn't eaten for quite some time, and she sensed a distant need for food, but she wasn't hungry. Whether that was as a result of the stress, the pain in her jaw, or the food she ladled out, was unclear. Likely all three played a role.

I'm sure you've read enough descriptions of things that are poor excuses for food, so I hope you'll forgive me if I simply say that the food was quite a few times blander and more like soggy cardboard than anything you've ever had described to you before.

At last, the line dwindled. Her final customer was a relatively short, plum skinned woman. She was still an impressive foot-and-a-half taller than May, but short in comparison to the other purple bipeds May had seen.

She had what May considered the proper number of arms, legs, and eyes, but one of her arms gleamed silver in the harsh cafeteria light. The arm moved with impeccable grace to accept a tray from May. The woman paused, looking at May with a slight tilt to her head.

"You're not Fanny. This must be your first day here, is that right May June July?"

May nodded, wondering how everyone knew her name but not daring to ask the tall figure.

"General Listay," she said. "I oversee military operations onboard this vessel. Here."

The General reached into a pack attached to her thigh and produced something shiny, purple, and orange. She set it on the counter and twirled it like a top on its convex side.

"It's a llerke fruit. Welcome to the *Peacemaker*." The General walked away and May watched her take another fruit from her pack as she tossed the tray of food-like glop into a disposal slot.

With no one left to serve, May set down the ladle and hopped onto the counter, picking up the fruit to give it an experimental squeeze. It felt fleshy inside, like a soft mango. Peeling a bit of the skin away from the knot at the top, May found juicy, yellow meat.

Briefly, she considered the dangers of eating a mysterious fruit given to her by a mysterious stranger on a mysterious ship which was, also quite mysteriously, not on Earth. It was a bad idea. Decidedly.

Still, hunger commandeered her frontal lobe and she pulled away more of the skin and sank her teeth into the thing. And it was good. Really and truly the first good thing that had happened to her since...well, she couldn't remember really.

If it killed her, so what? She didn't have much to live for at this point. She took another bite. It was ripe, sweet, and tart and had a lingering aftertaste like the cherry syrup from Sonic. Or maybe a real cherry. Yes, probably more like an actual cherry.

August appeared just as she finished the fruit, a little damper than he had been when they arrived.

"Looks like you met Listay," he said, nodding to the fruit pit which she tossed into the empty pot of whatever she'd been serving.

"It would appear so."

"Hot, isn't she?"

May blinked at him, but he had begun walking and didn't notice. She never really noticed when people were hot and always had to be told. She wondered if August was hot but doubted it.

"If you're into that sort of thing," she offered.

"What, plum chicks? Yeah, I guess my standards have gotten messed up out here. She's nice, though. That helps."

May made a noise of agreement, and they walked in silence back to their shared room.

# SIX

# ROCKETPARTY

After perhaps an hour of fitful sleep, May awoke with the feeling that something wasn't quite right. What *was* it?

She sat up against the bamboo headboard and tried to reason with her surroundings. She was in a hotel—right? Not a chance, said the mismatched palm tree paintings. Okay, well, on Earth at least. She *was* on Earth. Again, her surroundings disagreed with a humming buzz. She folded; there was no getting around it. She was in space.

August was asleep on the chair beside her, snoring so loudly she was surprised she'd slept through it. Moments later, she realized that she hadn't, in fact, slept through it.

She knew she'd seen Earth from a distance, stars that were not twinkling because there was no atmosphere to make them, and a billboard advertising some sort of alien pet food. She *knew* this but she didn't believe it. Not entirely.

She slipped out of the room and found the window alcove.

Yep, there it was. Space. All black with little not-twinkling points of light. The spinning blue marble continued to spin without her.

"Hey, I wouldn't go wandering off alone if I were you." August startled her.

"You should not be here." Someone startled August.

May was getting extremely tired of people telling her what she should and shouldn't be doing.

In the entrance to the alcove stood a periwinkle-skinned woman who might have been related to a bamboo shoot. She wore an immaculate double-breasted coat, she smelled of molten metal and plastic, and her violet hair jutted out in a way that perfectly framed features as sharp as a Russian Constructivist propaganda poster. Her eyes were like two pools of recently expired milk, white and wispy.

August found his voice before May even started looking for hers. "What are you going to do about it?" he said with terribly unconvincing bravado.

The alien blinked her two empty eyes slowly, considering. "Nothing," she decided. After a moment of stillness, her lips turned up slightly as if she just had a very pleasant thought. "I am leaving. Would either of you like to join me?"

Leaving? Leaving generally meant not only going away from a current location but also turning up in a different one. The question was about this second location. Was it better than where they were currently? Or was it worse?

"Leaving, here?" August pressed, evidently on the same train of thought May found herself aboard. "Like, as in leaving this alcove or leaving this spaceship?"

"I am leaving the ship. I can drop you back off at Earth, if that is what you would like. Earth is on the way to Rhea."

"How?" May asked, muscling August out of the way.

"Are you insane, May?" August turned on her. "She's a Rhean. She's not going to help us. She wants to torture us or something," August whispered harshly to May in a voice she was quite sure the Rhean could also hear. His visible eye was wide as he turned to the periwinkle woman. "My apologies, ma'am, we'll get back to our room now. Sorry for the disturbance."

He grabbed May's hand, but only succeeded in further convincing May that she was better off with the stranger.

"I want to come with you," she said, shaking August's hand off her own as if it were a fruit fly that had unwittingly landed on her.

"Let me see your arm," the Rhean said and offered her hand to May. May obliged, placing her hand in the Rhean's. May hissed through her teeth as the Rhean yanked her arm closer, turning up the soft underside and rolling back her spandex sleeve. With a long, white fingernail, she traced a vein in May's arm. May looked over at August, but only got a silent sort of I-told-you-so look.

"Do not scream." She plunged her nail into the soft brown flesh of May's arm. May slapped her free hand over her mouth to keep herself silent as the alien plucked out a small black chip.

"This is a tracker."

May stared at it like it was a German Cockroach corpse in her soup. The Rhean pulled May's sleeve back down to cover the blood and let her go. May leaned against the wall and held her arm to stop the bleeding.

The Rhean looked to August. "And you?" she asked.

"Hold on, Ms. Whats-your-name. Why should I trust you? There could be poison or *dirt* under your fingernails, you could be leading us to our deaths, you could be-"

"An opportunity to escape! How many escape offers have you turned down since you've been here?" May asked him defensively.

"My name is IX, Chief Engineer. As you wish, August. Come along, May. We are going."

May stood. "How does everyone know my goddamn name?" she whispered.

IX ignored her.

"Wait! Where are you taking her?" August's voice went up an octave or two. In the five months he had been here, no one had just offered to show him out. Then again, he had never asked. This deeply, deeply disturbed him. Could he have asked to leave all along?

"I am dropping May off on Earth before heading back to

Rhea," IX said patiently. "Would you like to come?"

"Ye...yes," he stammered. IX nodded and snatched his arm, performing the same gruesome operation on him. The alien then crushed the trackers under her heeled shoe.

"Act like prisoners," IX murmured in their ears and slipped pairs of suspiciously glowing handcuffs around their wrists. They followed; they didn't have much of a choice.

"Why are you helping us?" August whispered.

"I want to leave, and you want to leave, so we will carpool," she answered as if it were obvious. The word she really used was closer in meaning to "rocket party," but the translators in May and August's heads took great pride in their work and if there was a suitable translation for the word, by golly, they would find it.

IX led them back through the corridor to the intershoot bay and pushed them into the tube. May suspected she would never get used to the feeling of plummeting through a pneumatic tube. She was wrong, of course. Everyone gets used to it eventually.

The tube stopped in a dark cavernous space low in the ship. The trio popped out, May and August stumbling after the graceful IX.

A football field is generally the largest form of spatial measurement humans use to colloquially describe things that are big. A docking field, for some reference, is a few hundred football fields long. This particular docking *bay* spanned roughly twenty docking *fields* and was filled, end-to-end, with AMC Gremlins.

"Why-" May began to ask but IX shushed her. They had to act fast now in order to get out without being noticed.

IX stepped onto a moving platform and pulled her prisoners along behind her. She typed a set of numbers and letters equivalent to an American license plate into the control panel and they were off, rocketing by the largest collection of cars May had ever seen.

It would be inaccurate to refer to them as cars at this point, though. AMC Gremlins were never a terribly popular mode of transportation on Earth, but they lent themselves so well to the modifications needed for space travel that they were an ideal and inexpensive machine to build a short distance fleet with.

They stopped in front of a mustard yellow ship with some interesting green racing stripes along the side that gave you the idea that someone had had a bad time on a road trip. IX removed the handcuffs from the humans and motioned for them to pack in. The pair scrunched themselves into the backseat and IX took the wheel.

She revved the engine, making an uncomfortably loud noise in the quiet bay, then revved it again. Then once more. She sighed, removed the key, then surprise attacked the ignition. This time, it sputtered to life and began lifting off the platform.

An alarm sounded. IX whispered an alien curse that was easily translatable but not for the faint of heart and slammed the gas pedal. The ship went shockingly fast for a decrepit old car.

May struggled to find her seatbelt; it was jammed so tightly into the crease between the seat and the door that no amount of force, willpower, or frantic begging could loosen it. August attempted to help her, but the ship's acceleration pressed him back into his chair.

A crackle of light shook the ship, ripping May's door off the car. May clung to the seat in front of her as if it was the only thing keeping her in the car. And, at that point, it was.

A line of Gremlins followed them closely, beams of destructive laser light followed them even closer.

"Hold on May June July. If we make it out of the bay, the oxygen field will turn on and keep you inside the car." IX drove them toward a solid wall, blasting a hole in it with the lasers that had been retrofitted to the front of the car and spun through the hole into the vastness of space.

"May!" August grabbed for her hand as she lost her grip, his fingers catching the edge of her spandex suit.

The car cleared the enormous ship, but May did not. She felt her suit catch on the jagged edge of the hole, she felt the icy cold vacuum of space, she felt a warm beam at her back...and then she felt nothing.

## SEVEN
# CANNED CORN

"Fuck, fuck, fuck," May chanted under her breath, her eyes shut tight to keep her from seeing whatever horrible things you see when you die, waiting to run out of breath. "Fuck, I'm dead."

"You're not dead, May June July."

"Oh, you would say that."

"I would?"

"What are you, God? If you are, I've got some complaints to file."

"I-uh...no. Not a deity, sorry. Xan of Tuhnt," someone said, fairly close to her it sounded like. A hand was outstretched in her direction, but she didn't see it.

She opened her eyes and rubbed them to try to clear the grey fog she appeared to be swimming in but only succeeded in getting an eyelash in her left eye that would bother her off and on for a good hour to come. "May," she said.

"I know, it's on-"

"How does everyone know my name?" she shouted. The stress had finally poked enough holes in her veneer of politeness to allow a good, angry shout to come through.

"It's on your suit," he answered.

May looked down at her suit but saw nothing. She supposed it must be there, though.

"Sorry, stress. Okay, tell me exactly who you are, where I am, and give me an itemized list of your intentions with me. Please." The shout had helped, and she had a "please" or two to spare again. She hoped she hadn't wasted it.

A heavy hand landed on her shoulder, and, though she wouldn't admit it, she jumped slightly.

"Xan, as I said, of Tuhnt. You're on the Audacity, which is a Class 20 Racing Rocket. And my intentions were to keep you from asphyxiating or worse in the unforgiving vacuum of space. But now that that's taken care of, who knows! We could get ice cream." His hand left her shoulder. "Once I get the ship working again," he added in a mutter.

May blinked, shook her head, and started to get colors back. They came back with a vengeance. Was it common, she wondered, for experiencing the vacuum of space to short out the cones in ones eyes? It wasn't common to experience the vacuum of space at all, so probably not.

What looked like a living room out of a 70's magazine wrapped around her orangely. She half expected a silky-haired couple to slink forward from a back corner and try to sell her matching jumpsuits. For a moment she could almost believe she was back on Earth, having gone through some sort of spatial and temporal shift.

The enormous half-round window across from her told her otherwise. More stars, sans twinkle.

The tall blue-skinned thing hunched over a control panel in a raised loft to her right also told her otherwise. Blue wasn't exactly the best descriptor of his skin; it was unlike anything May had seen thus far. It was the color of the sky but with low batteries. It was the color of a blueberry milkshake with far too few blueberries in it. It was the color of an albino Smurf. And his hair was orange, but proper orange. Just orange.

His clothing wouldn't have looked out of place in the glam-rock scene of 70's England. May had the sinking suspicion that the BBC was behind all this.

She left the round metal plate she'd been on and waded through the thick orange shag carpeting to sit on the side of an old couch which faced an even older Earth television. "So, how much time do I have?" May asked.

"I wouldn't know, I'm not an actuary." Xan hopped down from the loft, ignoring the stairs and perching on the back of the couch beside her. "You look pretty healthy, though. Pretty young. I'd guess four-and-a-half thousand orbits?"

"What? No, I mean how long before you turn me in? I was trying to escape." She rubbed her forehead as if she could rub away the events of the past day.

Leaning back a bit, the alien blinked his eyes in sequence rather than in unison. Whether this was an alien thing or a him thing, May was unsure. She knew with certainty, however, that it was unsettling.

Xan thought for a moment, his intent stare now refocused on a dingy brown stain in the orange shag. "Do you think there would be some kind of reward for bringing you back? Like a bounty? I mean, when you say 'escaped' are we talking wanted criminal escaped, or is Yvonne running some sort of alien abduction probing campaign?"

"The latter, I think. Unless I've broken some heretofore unknown Space Law. Who's Yvonne?" May leaned her head back on the couch, trying to remember the last time she paid her Space Taxes to the Space Government. If there was a Space Tax, she was behind.

"Last I knew, Yvonne had command of the Peacemaker. Good way to check!" Suddenly, his hands were in her mouth, gently prying apart her jaw.

"Hey!" She swatted him away, standing up. "Ask before touching, alright?"

"Oh, sorry." His hands floated uncomfortably in front of him for a moment. "Can I, uh...can I look at your teeth?"

May squinted at him. "As long as you don't touch me."

"Right, no problem!"

She opened her mouth and he peered into it curiously.

"Eugh, don't they have dental hygiene nanobots on Earth?" he asked.

"I've had better things to think about than dental hygiene lately." She closed her mouth self-consciously and ran her tongue over her grimy teeth. "Also, no."

"The missing tooth—recent development?"

"Yes," May nodded. "I think they were trying to figure out what I was."

"What are you?"

In the absence of television, May had been pretty reliant on the public library for entertainment back on Earth. During her pulp sci-fi phase, she'd picked up a few terms that she hoped would be useful out here. "Terran is probably what you'd call us."

A violent shiver racked Xan. "Don't say that about yourself."

"What? That I'm a Terran?"

He winced. "Okay, sensitivity training lesson one. No idea how it works on your backwards planet, but out here that's a slur."

"What, Terran?"

His head shook almost imperceptibly. "Yeah, stop saying that."

"I'm a human," she said. "From Earth in case that wasn't clear."

"An Earthling? No kidding? Okay, first things first. Lucille Ball is too good for Ricky—am I right or am I right? Lucy deserves the world. The entire Earth, just for her. Any human she wants. The TV signal is awful out here so I haven't-" May cut him off.

"Lucy? From the old TV show? I've never seen it," she said.

He smiled at her like he knew a sinister secret she didn't.

"Why are you smiling at me?" she asked.

"We. Have. So much to talk about!" He was uncomfortably close to her. Whatever species he was obviously wasn't big on personal space.

"What happened to turning me in for a reward?"

It occurred to her, then, that this alien probably wasn't terribly smart. It further occurred to her that by reminding him that there was a possible reward for her return she herself was not terribly smart. She shook her head, wondering briefly how forgiving the term "intelligent life" was.

"Er..." He looked behind himself. "It's fine. It's just gem, right?"

May shrugged. "I don't know, is it?"

"Yeah, well, that was rhetorical. It's fine."

It was difficult to tell whether he was trying to be nice or if he was terrified of something. The language chip in her head could not translate body language, apparently, and his was distressingly alien.

May relaxed a bit regardless. "Did you see what happened out there? What happened to the people I was escaping with?"

"They were on the Gremlin? Umm..." He squinted at the ceiling, searching for a tactful way of explaining. "They flew into a wormhole. Which means one of two equally interesting things happened. Either they've popped out somewhere incredibly far away and are well out of danger. Or—and here's the rub—they've been torn into obscenely gory confetti by something utterly horrific. There's just no telling with wormholes! Part of the fun, I guess. And the horror."

May bit her lip and had the distinct feeling that she had been entirely too lucky. This was followed by the suspicion that all of the good luck allotted to her in this lifetime had been completely blown on that one rescue. A life of unluckiness, just to survive being ejected into space. It seemed a poor trade-off.

The alien either didn't notice her pensive expression or didn't care. Leaning back, he threw his boot-shod feet atop a rickety wooden coffee table.

"So, what do you want to do?" Xan pressed. "I've got a virtual reality deck that's only virtually malfunctioning— the reality part works perfectly. There's a quarantine bay with some questionable packages that we shouldn't open for another four orbits, but zuut, we can live on the wild side. There's the hover-swivel chairs. Oh, or my personal favorite, all the lost rubber bands in the Universe are sucked into a wormhole that empties into my basement!

You can do a lot with all the lost rubber bands in the Universe. Too much, actually, I've had to send a few back."

May leaned into the couch arm and rubbed her temples. "I don't want to do anything, if that's alright." She glanced at him, desperately trying to get a read on his sanity level.

To her relief, he nodded and headed for the pneumatic tube. "Rest it is, then! You just make yourself comfortable. What do humans need for sleep?"

She smiled, but it came out as more of a grimace. "Do you have water in space?"

"What's water?" Xan asked, to May's horror. "Only joking, only joking. Of course, I've got water! Need it for the coffee. Anything else?"

*Food,* thought May. The llerke hadn't lasted long, and now that she had a moment to think about it, she was starving.

"Do you have any Earth food? Anything that won't kill me?" she hazarded.

"There's no telling what's in the basement. I'll see what I can dig up! Oh and, May," he said. Suddenly his tone shifted, and his eyes became a darker shade of green. "Don't go wandering off," he warned. "Unless you really *really* want to."

With a hand gesture that was almost like a finger gun but not quite, he disappeared down into a pneumatic tube that ran through the floor.

May closed her eyes. She played with the idea that she had died after all and that Satan was an off-brand Looney Tune. Picking at the ripped latex of her sleeve, she found she missed her comfortable, if ugly, Sonic uniform polo shirt.

She surveyed the room again, now that her eyes had adjusted to the offensive color. An ancient TV squatted in front of the couch, something else that could have been a 70's landfill find. Numerous cable adapters spilled from the back of it and atop it sat rabbit ears so elongated they looked like the antennae of a beetle feeling around for scraps of signal.

Her eyes fell on a stack of magazines on the floor beside

the couch. A pamphlet advertising something called a Space Race, a travel brochure from Eroticon VII, a molding copy of Jane Austen's *Pride and Prejudice*, loose sheets of paper covered in mathematical formulas and graphs, and a user's manual with an artistic rendering of an intensely orange rocket ship on the cover. When she picked it up, the manual opened to the table of contents. Most of the nouns in the text were completely untranslatable; she could almost hear the translation chip in her head grinding and sputtering to keep up. She put it down, worried that if she kept at it the chip might decide to make a break for it.

A terrible sucking sound announced Xan's reappearance in the tube. He carried an armful of cans and a mug. The plexi-glass door to the tube creaked open about an inch. He stuck the toe of his thickly-soled boot into the door and coaxed it open with his elbow and shoulder.

Setting the mug down on the coffee table where it would leave a lovely white circle in the wood, he dropped onto the couch and it creaked louder than the walls of a pay-by-the-hour motel under his weight. "I have Blorsh, Glorf, forbinated Moringarg, unforbinated Moringarg, and corn. Take your pick!" he said, spreading the cans on the couch between them.

The corn was a bit of a shock to May. There was nothing inherently shocking about the canned corn itself; the label was verdant, with an image of golden kernels traipsing away from the homey look farm they were allegedly raised on and a nicely designed name-brand logo that May felt she could trust. Contextually, though, the innocuous can of corn seemed almost sinister.

Still, she was hungry.

She took the corn.

"Thank you," she said hesitantly, popping the cap off the corn and, after staring at it for a moment to be sure it wouldn't jump up and spook her, tipped a few kernels into her mouth. Corn indeed. Nearly absent of nutrients, but it would do.

Xan stacked the rest of the cans on the table,

presumably for her to enjoy later. "Sure! There's got to be at least twenty cans of that stuff in the basement."

"From the wormhole?"

"From the wormhole!" he confirmed. "So, tell me about Earth. What's it like? Tons of people down there, I bet. Must be fun."

"Not particularly," she said. The thought occurred to her that perhaps he would take her back there if she asked. Back to work. She needed to get back to work or she'd be fired. She had a shift coming up. Or had it past? She had probably missed her shift. She began trying to piece together a reasonable excuse that didn't involve alien abduction, but her neurons limped along, not so much firing as they were meandering.

"And the Earth clothing!" continued the alien who had draped himself casually over the back of the couch, the arm of the couch, and the coffee table. "It's so loose and baggy. What are humans hiding?"

"Genitals, I guess," she said hazily. The couch was becoming comfortable, she sunk into it a little more.

"Genitals, eh? Hm." He paused to consider this, but only for a moment. "Oh, and the grammar! Insanely complex, right?"

"For which language?"

"There's more than one?" He was excited about that. "May June July, that's a rather long name for an Earthling isn't it? I always thought there were only two individual names, the second being stolen in a vicious rite of passage."

May chuckled, closing her eyes now because keeping them open was a great deal harder than it ought to have been. "Not quite. Just call me May."

"Right, of course! May, I've got to say it's nice to have someone to-"

May was asleep.

# EIGHT

# MATTERS OF LOVE AND DEVOTION

Reasonably civilized demigods have a bit of an unwritten but oft-discussed rule: don't meddle in matters of love and devotion.

Chaos was not reasonably civilized. She was, as far as demigods go, something of a barbarian. As such, she was only too happy to meddle in matters of love and devotion and this she did with wild abandon.

Now, however, she was beginning to see the wisdom in not.

IX was not only the *Peacemaker's* brilliant and beloved Chief Engineer, she was Yvonne's brilliant and beloved Chief Love Interest. And she had, in innumerable ways and with varying degrees of murderous intent, done everything in her power to keep Chaos from possessing Yvonne's body.

When Chaos schemed to start her own religion, IX launched a ship-wide campaign regarding the warning signs of cult-formation. When Chaos endeavored to turn the medical wing into an arid desert-land, replete with stinging microscopic bugs and stinking misanthropic bogs, IX convinced the service bots that Yvonne was, in fact, a large purple stain that needed prompt removal. When Chaos targeted an annoyingly bright planetoid for disintegration, IX re-wired the anti-matter cannons.

But Yvonne loved IX, and IX loved her back. And this was a problem.

A problem which IX had, by leaving of her own accord, neatly solved for Chaos.

Another problem now arose, though. Yvonne's consciousness, so distraught at the loss of the last vestige of her old life, rampaged. If her body had a self-destruct button, she would've gladly used it. As it was, Chaos could feel Yvonne tearing at her very sinews in outrage.

If Chaos didn't overpower her soon, the vessel would be lost. The plan would be in shambles. Meddling in matters of love and devotion would've been her downfall.

Ah, but in the poison, thought Chaos, the antidote was found.

Somewhere onboard, and likely not very far, a well-built general was in love. With Chaos.

"General Listay," Yvonne spoke to the BEAPER on her wrist, "please come to my office." Her voice was impressively smooth and sultry for an ancient goddess waging an internal battle with her homicidal host.

As expected, the rapid thumping of footfalls echoed from the corridor outside. Listay had been loitering.

"Yes, ma'am." General Listay stood impossibly short for a Rhean, but impossibly tall for a human. What she lacked in height, she made up for in strength. The extra foot she was missing on top had gone straight to the muscles of her arms and thighs.

Her dreadlocked hair, stocky build, and no-nonsense style were unusual. Nonsense was popular with Rheans. Despite her lack of style, or perhaps because of it, she was the ideal candidate for Chaos's plan. It helped that Listay was as dedicated to Chaos as Chaos was to the unmitigated degeneration of the cosmos.

Listay was, unlike IX, a supportive partner. From the moment Yvonne hired her, she had done everything in her power to cater to Chaos's will.

She'd been the first to dip her toes into the new religion, offering to take on the mantle of historian. She'd wholly supported the idea of a desert wasteland in the medical bay, provided the bugs and bogs were properly inventoried. And she did agree that the annoyingly bright planetoid looked out of place in that sector of the galaxy and would be better off disintegrated; she'd even begun the arduous process of filing planet removal forms.

"Listay, as I'm certain you're aware, IX has deserted her post. I expect the Senior Engineer to take on her duties. Please inform them."

"They have already stepped up ma'am." Listay replied, glancing at those unmentionable eyes and feeling, for just a moment, that her brain had simultaneously caught fire and frozen over. She looked away, her eyes searching the floor for the smidgen of sanity she had just lost. Ah, there it was. In the crack between tile number seventy-eight and seventy-nine.

"Listay," Yvonne's voice was smoother than a ride in a brand-new Class 987 Rocket (No money down, 0% interest, latest models, contact Dan's Motors today! 55-899-DAN).

Yvonne cupped Listay's face and traced a scar on her jawline with her thumb. That scar had earned her the title of general. Not that the scar itself had really done much to get her there—it was *how* she got that scar that had impressed Yvonne.

General Listay had single handedly destroyed a legion of seventy-five rebel Rheans. Literally single handedly. In the battle, she'd lost her right arm.

Yvonne smiled like the mythical wyrntensil staring down its prey, and Listay's cheeks flushed a tell-tale mauve. "I trust you will be able to improve upon our dismal progress now that the traitor is gone."

Yvonne bent down close enough for Listay to smell her sweet breath.

"I want the nearest inhabited planet under your thumb

within three rotations. Do not involve me; I do not exist. Hold the people in an iron grip and allow them nothing but work and sleep. I want soulless slaves stripped of all individuality." Her eyes grew more unmentionable by the second as she spoke. "I want them to cry out for spontaneity and find nothing but spreadsheets and forms and policies. I want each building to be the same, each block to be the same, each city and country and continent on that planet to be molded from exactly the same blueprint. Squeeze their very souls from their bodies and then fine them for not applying for a soul-release license. Do you understand?"

Listay nodded, trying to keep the excitement from spilling out of her. There would be spreadsheets; she'd been hatched for this moment.

Chaos blinked Yvonne's eyes slowly, carefully, as if she could fly out of her body and expand to fill the universe if she blinked too recklessly at this point.

"Naturally, you will be rewarded for your hard work." Yvonne's unmentionable irises flicked down pointedly to Listay's lips and back up.

Listay swallowed, trying to keep her pulse at exactly fifty beats per beoop, no more.

"Anything for you, ma'am."

"Lovely." Yvonne patted her head. "You're dismissed."

Listay hadn't been this pleased with the loss of prisoners since the wretched smelling and foul mannered Huntitcherion from Galaphoo had perished in their sleep. She felt as if the artificial gravity had been tampered with as she floated away. But the minute the doors slammed behind her, the gravity turned back on with a vengeance and the task ahead of her weighed on her shoulders like a library full of reference books.

That was one nasty piece of baggage taken care of, Chaos thought...but there was one still to go. She eyed the brilliant speck of orange on her monitor. Yvonne's voice repeated a chant in the back of her head. *No*, Yvonne thought. Over and over.

Yvonne was always telling her no.

*Don't kill IX*, Yvonne thought. *Don't kill my zoup-nog ex*, she thought. *Don't kill...*

Blah, blah, blah. Yvonne was really opposed to killing certain people. Perhaps Chaos' life would've been easier if she'd followed the unwritten rules of the more civilized demigods, but she so enjoyed meddling in matters of love and devotion.

# NINE

# THE ROBERT

Dear readers, at the risk of being blunt, I feel it's time to tell you: IX and August survived their trip through the wormhole. This is how it happened.

"August?"

"Yes?"

"Are you alive?"

"Yes?"

"Am I alive?"

"I would assume so."

"Good," IX said, feeling around the dashboard of the Gremlin. Or, at least, what was meant to be the dashboard.

The Gremlin was in poor shape indeed. The front end had smashed into a slab of copper ore, the clock had frozen, and the engine sputtered desperate pleas for the merciful escape of death. IX obliged, turned the key to cut the engine, and twisted around to fix August with her white stare.

"You lost May," she said.

"I did not!" August sputtered for a moment as his brain tried to spin the situation. "She fell. There wasn't a thing I could do about it."

"You were next to her; you could have grabbed her." Her colorless eyes chilled him more than the metallic-smelling draft from outside. "It smells like we have landed on a copper deposit. What can you see?"

August poked his head out of the gaping hole in the car's side. His depth perception had been a little off ever since the gloopy green alien "doctors" took his eye. He was told they would replace it with a better one, but he insisted that he liked the one he had just fine and that he would prefer to have it back. They laughed at him. He supposed humor was not their strong point. Removing integral bits of his anatomy, however, seemed to be.

The horizon was vast and flat. The only thing between them and the dark void of the night sky was a greening shack made entirely of copper that, due to August's poor depth perception, was either a few miles or a few feet away.

Fortunately, it had a sign. Unfortunately, the translation chip in his head wasn't quite up to the task of reading it.

"Khaninagaharatchiyarta Chroosantooackagatgunst Junkers?"

"Oh, you mean..."

IX proceeded to pronounce Khaninagaharatchiyarta Chroosantooackagatgunst correctly but typing it out here phonetically would be a hassle and you, dear reader, would skim over it anyway. So the correct pronunciation will remain unknown until the screen adaption. In the interest of saving time I'll abbreviate it to KC from here on out.

"Sure."

"Well that is something. KC was destroyed five years ago. The wormhole must have moved us in time and space. That is good."

"How, exactly, is that good?" August was beginning to panic. He was not on Earth. He was alone with one of the creatures that had been his captor for half a year. His arm hurt. And, worst of all, he was cold.

"If we have truly traveled backwards in time, I have

more time to work out what to do about Yvonne. Firstly, though, we must repair the Gremlin." She climbed from the car and motioned to August. "Come along, I will need help carrying parts back from the junker."

The numerous vast wastelands and deserted landfill planets in the Universe offer a particular kind of person a particular kind of living; the delightful job of cosmic recycling or "junkering." A good junker would carefully sort through mounds of garbage to recycle precious metals, easily fixable automatons, and appliances. Each piece would be tediously considered; would the price it fetched be worth the five or so seconds spent tossing it into the ship? Often the answer was no, but occasionally a junker would come across the kind of trash that could make a person rich.

By occasionally, I mean exactly twice in junkering's long history. Once, it was a very small Queen who had accidentally been thrown out with some old linens. The Queen's country paid a handsome reward for her safe return. The second time, a junker stumbled across a ghost planet upon which every living being had suddenly died and left a mighty fortune unclaimed. While these instances were rare, millions of otherwise intelligent beings decided to make junkering their trade, clutching the hope of wildly good fortune to their underfed chests.

The junker outpost on KC was nothing to write home about. In fact, it had never been written about in the history of the universe until now and, even then, just coincidentally. Passing travelers were often so put off that rather than rate it a whole single star on the Universal Review, they would simply erase their memories of the place.

There were piles of doors surrounding the building, but none of them had been able to find their way to the door frame which gaped open. The pair approached the place where a door should've been, and August knocked on the frame.

"Well howdy!" A creature that couldn't be said to be male or female, but *could* be said to be thoroughly coated in green dust, greeted them from behind a desk. "I've a fine selection of recycled bots, Fidobots, chauffeurbots, huntin' bots, and some frisky little bedroom bots if you catch my drift." The creature winked at August and, with some help from the translator chip in his head, August did in fact catch the drift. He would've been very pleased indeed to catch that particular drift. But IX's determination to get off the copper planet triumphed over August's curiosity.

"I need to repair an Earth 1975 AMC Gremlin with a 709 Plasma Rocket Engine. Do you have 12-volt halogen headlights?"

The creature blinked. "Uh, huh...well you can look around. Anything's fair game except the register." It tapped a metal box that squatted toad-like on the edge of a desk. "Oh, hell, name a price and the register's yours!"

August eyed the bots; they were the only items in the store that were neatly arranged. Everything else was in piles on the floor that seemed to be sorted by color and not much else. He tried to call IX over to ask a question but realized he had forgotten her name. He was sure she said it at some point...oh, it was too late now. It would be too embarrassing to ask; he'd have to wing it. Eventually she would have to introduce herself to someone else and he'd be there to hear it.

IX felt around the store and dubiously collected a few tubes, some wires, and a drill. "Do you accept Rhean currency?"

"Pff! Funny gal you got there," the creature addressed August. August blinked in reply; he wasn't sure that was true.

IX sighed. Fifteen years ago the Rhean dollar had gone off the Crystal Standard and plummeted to a universal low. The most affluent Rhean at the time was Daag Narmiroust whose thirty-seven billion Rhean dollars could hardly buy a spool of thread outside of Rhea. Since then, their economy had been on the upswing. But her Rhean money wouldn't be of much use in the past.

After a few moments of tense silence over which only the quiet oxidation of the entire planet could be heard, August took charge. "I know how this works," he sagely lifted a hand to the shopkeep and secured eye-contact. "You will accept anything we offer you as payment," he said, summoning all the Hollywood drama he could muster.

The shopkeep hesitated, entranced by the human's display. As if in a dream it slowly shook its head back and forth. "No...no I don't think I will," it intoned.

August laughed nervously. "Really? Because I felt I was pretty convincing."

The creature pulled a dangerous looking object from some fold of its anatomy. "I think y'all better leave."

"Of course." IX began to walk out the door, her haul still in hand. The shopkeep jabbed the dangerous looking object in her direction and beset August with a tense stare.

"Tell her to leave that stuff where she found it, kid," it sneered.

August blubbered unintelligibly, fear and confusion warring for control of his brain.

"August, come along. We have work to do,"

"Okay, right, but...it's got a gun!" August tried to press himself against a wall but ended up tripping on a pile of rusted metal hands.

"I know, ignore it." IX continued walking away, she was nearly out the door. August scrambled after her and ducked as he heard a blast from behind him.

"Get back here!" Another blast sounded, but nothing came of it.

"Won't it come after us?" he asked her.

"It cannot. That is a floosoon—a holographic employee. The only defense it has is to threaten."

"I'll have the intergalactic police after you!" (It wouldn't.)

"My wrath is inescapable!" (It wasn't.)

"You'll be sorry you ever came to-" They were out of earshot.

They walked back to the wreckage, materials and tools in hand. IX explored the hole in the side of the car with her precise fingers. "I think I can add onto this a little. We will need shelter and somewhere to rest. Earth people sleep fairly often, correct?"

"In relation to what?"

"Rheans, of course. Oh, and I will have to feed you something. What manner of nutrition do you require?" IX asked.

August shook his head at her. "Don't bother. I'll find myself some place to stay on this godforsaken penny." With that he went off, his white spandex clad feet sending up little puffs of green dust at every step. He expected at least a bit of a fight from her, but she seemed not to care one way or the other. He supposed he wasn't exactly a prisoner now, though. He didn't know where he was going but figured if he walked far enough something would appear. Right? He kept walking.

The shack and the wreckage were out of sight now. In front of him, a small ball of reddish light began to rise, turning the sky a pale green. It was easier to see now that things were properly lit. An improvement. Soon, however, he bemoaned the sun as it began to reflect off the copper ground and turn the planet into an oven.

Fortunately for August, the days on this planet were extremely short. Mere minutes after the sun had attained its utmost height in the sky it was behind him again, and soon it was gone entirely. This happened three or five more times: the hot, the cold, the hot, the cold...then, a discovery! Something was rising over the horizon that wasn't the small, cruel ball of heat.

August's spirits lifted and he began to jog. Soon, he slowed to a speed walk, then to a normal walk, and finally a crawl. It was the Gremlin. He had explored the entirety of the planet in just under an hour and came back around the other side.

"Let's get out of here," he sighed and started to help IX put the machine back together.

"I knew you would eventually come around," IX gave him a wry smile, but August didn't catch the play on words. She would never try to be funny around him again.

"What's Robert?" He pulled out a sheet of metal from the pile. It read "Robert" in big, bold letters. The "o" and the bottom of the "b" became two eyes in a smiley face below the logo.

"Robert is a brand of wet ch'stranda food in a can," IX replied. "But the panel is in good shape, and we can always paint over it."

"No, I like it. Robert was my grandfather's name. Let's call this ship the Robert."

"But it is a Gremlin."

"That's what it is, not its name! We're calling him Robert and I'm not helping," he said defiantly.

"I think you mean 'or.' We're calling him Robert *or* I'm not helping," IX corrected as she continued to work on soldering some loose wires.

"I know what I said, and I don't need a German lesson from an alien."

"We are not speaking German, August, we are speaking Rhean."

August sighed. "Fine, you're speaking Rhean, I'm speaking German, and someone for some godforsaken reason is reading it all in English right now. I'll help if you drop the matter."

"Robert it is," IX replied and bolted the metal siding over a gouge in the car.

## TEN
# CIGARETTE

"Good morning starshine!" rung loudly from somewhere above May. It's never pleasant to be caught, no matter how momentarily, between the world of dreams and the world of reality. It's even less pleasant when you're in an unfamiliar location on a strange, lumpy couch, in a pile of worn blankets, with white latex sinking so deeply into your ass it could perform a colonoscopy.

"Uhh?"

"It's a song! From Earth, I thought you'd like it."

"Uhuh..." The first neuron of the morning was a lively one. It fired right into the part of May's brain that dictated how stressed out she was at any given time and it had a singular purpose.

"Work!" May shouted, sitting so quickly her consciousness almost didn't keep up. She was late, she was who knew how far away, she didn't have her uniform.

Xan had been idly spinning in the pilot's hover chair, but now he was standing, the word "work" had made him anxious. "What about work?" he asked.

"Could you take me back to Earth, please?" May twisted around towards him. "I might still have a job if we hurry."

"Oh." He deflated a little, almost imperceptibly. "Sure! Where on Earth?"

"The Sonic on the corner of State Street and MLK Jr Boulevard. Do you know how to get there?"

Xan panicked. "Of course, I know!" He did not know.

"Would you please take me there? I'm going to try to make myself presentable. Do you have a mirror?"

"Uh, um..." Xan shuffled through a pile of books and magazines at the base of the stairs until he found something shiny. "This came off the Audacity a while back." Tossing her the round plate of metal, he leapt up the stairs to the control panel. He began by pressing a few buttons, flicking a couple switches, considering a few read-outs, and cursing at a stuck toggle.

May attempted to comb through her matted hair with her fingers. Would she be hours late? Days late? Would she arrive back just a few minutes after she left? How did time work in space, anyway?

This is a much-contested point. Most of the discovered universe has agreed to a standardized time format based on the planetary movements of Estrichi. Estrichi, being a planet used exclusively for time measurement, is a hotbed of time-centric tourism and produces the finest hourglasses, which instead measure a single beoop, in the universe.

Time, therefore, worked exactly the same in space. Give or take a few blips.

"Minor problem," Xan called to her. "Ship's stuck."

That sounded like a major problem to May. She joined the alien at the control panel, ready to suggest things in a helpful voice that would turn out to be entirely unhelpful. She glanced over the field of doodads, looking for a toggle, perhaps, that was labeled "Stuck" on one end and "Unstuck" on the other.

Nothing to that effect jumped out at her.

"Have you tried the parking brake?" she offered in a haphazard sort of way. In her pre-Sonic days, she'd had a fifteen-year-old Ford Fiesta with a faulty parking brake. It had become something of an inside joke with herself. She didn't really have inside jokes with anyone else.

"Oh, uhm—heh." Xan covered his embarrassment with a guilty laugh and kicked a lever on the floor. "That was it!"

Relieved to have her engines freed up to do what they were meant to do, the *Audacity* shot off towards the blue, green, and white marble of Earth.

Relatively speaking, they weren't terribly far. They were a great deal farther away than it is from New York City to Istanbul, and a bit farther than it is from Montana to civilization. But relative to the entirety of everything that ever was and ever has been, they really were just around the corner.

The ship set itself down, wobbling a bit, in the Sonic parking lot. "We're here! Stand on the teledisc and I'll send you down." He motioned to the circular, metal depression in the shag which she had been standing on when she first arrived. She hesitated before stepping onto the metal.

Having your atoms ripped asunder here and haphazardly mashed back together there by a teledisc isn't a fun or recommended pastime. Is the teledisc practical? Extremely. Safe? A gaggle of lawsuits would claim otherwise. Enjoyable? No. Not even a bit.

May tried to get her bearings and failed miserably. Her head swam, her bones vibrated, and her skin undulated. Her surroundings were wholly off as well. She saw pieces of landmarks she recognized, like a half-finished jigsaw puzzle, as if the city had glitched out the moment she was gone. She recognized the Sonic sign and a low billboard across the street, but as far as she could see everything else was rubble. It was silent and still and far too bright. Her feet carried her forward because they felt obligated to.

Xan had never actually been on Earth before; it was far too dangerous for extraterrestrial life on Earth. He had heard the horror stories whispered in hushed tones: unattainable beauty standards, golden waves of deadly grain, and something called mosquitos awaited him on Earth.

But, in the hullabaloo, he had forgotten his trepidation and landed on the planet whose media he had admired from a distance for so long. Visions of old west shootouts, mansions owned by hillbillies, and luxurious boats upon which every single passenger found a life-mate tempted him. He stepped on the teledisc, took an altogether unnecessary breath, and rearranged his atoms on Earth for the first time.

"It's—" It was grisly, it was gruesome, it was really very much not good. "It's lovely!" he said. "I can see why you'd want to get back here in such a hurry."

May stood with her back to him, studying a pile of bricks. Xan joined her.

"Is this your work?" he pointed to the pile. "Well done. That is one immaculate pile. You must be so proud." His smile was so tight it was a wonder it didn't crack.

"Everything is gone. How long was I in space?"

"About the same length you are now, give or take a bit on account of the microgravity."

"I—wha—never mind." May, finding nothing which inspired her to keep standing at this point, knelt down for a moment.

Xan joined her in a squat. "Yvonne's really made a mess of the place." He reached down and picked up a charred chunk of brick to frown at.

May stared ahead at nothing. There used to be something there. She couldn't remember what, but there should've been something.

"What about my apartment?" May asked. "Do you think it's still there?"

"Eh...." He didn't want to say no, but he didn't want to lie, either.

"I want to go. I have to know for sure." She hefted herself up, brushed off her dusty knees, and began the familiar walk that was now *hauntingly* familiar.

"May, there's no point," Xan called after her as he stood and reclined against one of the *Audacity*'s fins.

"You don't have to come," she flung over her shoulder.

"Wasn't planning on it." He crossed one foot over the other as if to prove it.

With a curt nod, May continued onward. She expected to hear the *Audacity* sputter away, leaving her to explore her personal apocalypse. It did not. She walked a little farther down State Street, trying to focus on visually sorting out the ruins around her. Still, she did not hear the ship take off. Peering over her shoulder, she watched Xan kick idly at an empty Sonic cup.

He wasn't leaving. She didn't care; she wanted to go home.

A pile of rubbish looked like the old pharmacy. It had been closed and rotting away for years, decades perhaps. Seeing the inside walls, in the dark for so long, now lit by an uncaring sun was almost garish. She turned left around it; her apartment would still be a few blocks away.

It was not. There was nothing a few blocks away. A small, distressed noise escaped from her chest. A speck in the distance hurried toward her, a speck she knew.

"Kathy!" she shouted at her manager.

A faint yell came from Kathy, but May couldn't quite hear her yet.

"What?"

"Uuunn!" Kathy shouted again, almost tripping as she sprinted toward her.

"Kathy, I can't hear you!" She began jogging to meet her.

"May, run! Run the other way!" Kathy gasped at her, out of breath. She was being followed by a small floating sphere that produced a beam of yellow light. The sphere caught up with her, the light enveloped her, and she was gone.

The sphere turned its yellow eye on May, and she felt sick. She searched for the bright hull of the *Audacity* between the broken buildings, realizing now why Xan had stayed. Behind her, the beeping of the sphere grew louder, but before her, Xan lounged against the *Audacity's* silver fin.

"Beam us up!"

"Can't! It's a teledisc not a transporter. Also, you need

an anchor," he shouted, pointing to the top button of his suit. To her surprise, he started to run toward her and the deadly metal sphere which pursued her.

The beeping of the sphere became a droning buzz, and a yellow puddle of light glowed beneath her feet. She closed her eyes and launched herself forward with a burst of adrenaline. It felt like she had been smacked by a bag of bricks and torn into a million pieces simultaneously. When the sensation settled, she hazarded a glance around. She was holding onto something. She peeled her face away from the plasticky material it had been smashed against and gasped in relief. They were back on the *Audacity*. The plasticky bag of bricks was Xan.

He jumped up to the console, pressed the Button That Typically Made The Ship Go, and let the ship decide where to take them. Then he turned to May who stood motionless on the teledisc.

"You can't teleport or, uh, 'beam up' unless you have an anchor button," he informed her, tapping the top button on his suit again. "It's linked to the ship's teledisc. Otherwise anyone could get in!"

May stared.

Xan tried to get her attention with a weak wave. "Hey, mun, are you okay, or...?"

May shook her head.

Unsure of what to do, Xan watched her. He hadn't seen her blink in awhile and was fairly certain humans didn't just do that for kicks. "Are you, uh, are you with me?"

She stared.

"May! You're the main character, this novel's not going to get very far if you just stand there staring."

Fourth wall breakage made May extremely uncomfortable; she blinked. "What happened?"

She attached herself to the small control panel on the wall beside the teledisc and started trying to figure it out. Xan dragged her away.

"Woah now. You saw it, the city's kaput! And if I know Yvonne, and I do, it's not just your city. She thinks big— the biggest, in fact. Earth is her all-you-can-eat buffet now and she's not above second and third helpings."

"Yvonne? You mean the person that captured me destroyed the Earth the moment I left? Why?"

"She's got her hobbies," he shrugged.

"Why can't we stop her? Don't you have laser guns or plasma cannons on this ship?"

Xan barked a laugh. "Even if *Audy* had weapons, the *Peacemaker* can comfortably dock five hundred rockets this size. Besides, Earth's doomed. A lost cause, over and done with, out of commission-"

"Stop," May said.

He did.

She thought of her apartment and how very late the rent check would be this month. Could she be evicted from a pile of rubble? She thought of her poor cactus, Betty, the only joy in her shift-to-shift life. She thought about the feral cat that had made a home in the dumpster out back. She hoped he was okay; he was tough enough to outlast an alien invasion, right?

Her mom and Kathy and that one really sweet bus driver...all of them gone.

When she tried to think about all of it, her brain stalled like her old Ford Fiesta. She cranked the engine which hiccupped and sputtered but didn't really get anywhere. A short break. She cranked it again—nothing.

May drifted to the couch and collapsed on it like a tower of Jenga blocks. Xan perched on the arm of the couch and watched her, concern, or the alien approximate, pulling his eyebrows together.

A thought occurred to her. Less a thought, more a desire. Less a desire, more a terrible yearning. It was not for her bed, her apartment, or anyone she'd known on Earth. She wanted—no, needed—a cigarette.

"Do you have tobacco in space?" she asked Xan wearily.

"Tobacco? What in Blitheon's name do you need that for, are you trying to off yourself?"

"It's not going to kill me," she said. "Anytime soon," she amended.

"Look, I know you're upset, but don't do anything you'll regret. Maybe you just need sleep. Humans sleep a lot, right?"

"I need a cigarette," she whined.

"Oh, a *cigarette*, is that all?" he laughed. "I wondered when you'd ask for one. So, what are they for? Do you need them to survive or something?"

"What? No, not necessarily. They're just nice. How do you know about cigarettes?"

He tapped his temple with a knowing glint in his eye. "Lucy. They smoke them all the time in the show! Never could figure out why exactly. Is there tobacco in those?" he said, more than a little horrified.

May nodded. "Yeah. It's not poisonous to humans—or not very, at least. It's addicting though, and I really do need one."

Xan sighed. "Alright hop to." He stood in the intershoot. "If there are any cigarettes on board they'll be in the basement. All sorts of things have ended up there. Videos, magazines, single socks. Never pairs," he mused. "They must get so lonely."

May squished into the intershoot beside him. The door closed with some forceful kicks from Xan and propelled them down into the bowels of the ship. The basement was freezing, black, and suspiciously noisy. A whooshing sound like an old box fan emanated from one dark corner, a tender cooing sound came from another, and the distinct chirp of cicadas echoed from somewhere above.

Xan loudly tripped over a few things before finding a ball chain that hung from the ceiling. It lit up a dingy yellow light bulb that illuminated about five feet around them. In that five feet alone, May saw a rubber duck, something that looked like an alien sex toy, a taxidermy jackalope, a birthday card written in a language so ancient it did not translate, a sprinkle of dried macaroni bits, and an enormous scarf. There might have been a pack of cigarettes in that mess, but she was sure they'd never locate it.

Xan crawled around a pile of garbage and knelt down, speaking to something May couldn't see.

"Good boy! Fetch cigarettes," he said. A small square robot burst through the pile of garbage and puttered off into the darkness. Xan stood and stretched, kicking over a few objects as he waited.

"What was that?" May asked

"Oh, just a Fidobot. They're cheap but extraordinarily useful. They were originally built to collect samples for miners or something, then junkers started rehabilitating them to find scrap, now everyone uses them. They really are useful little buggers."

Moments later the square bot returned with a box clutched between its metal teeth. The brand was unidentifiable, the packaging faded. Better than nothing, May thought. Refusing to touch the little white box, Xan shooed the bot towards May. It reluctantly spun around and offered May the box.

"Can you find a lighter?" she asked. The bot seemed to have already anticipated her request and produced a pocket lighter for her. She smiled, patting it on what she assumed might've been its head.

"Alrighty then, let's get out of here," Xan chirped. The cooing was steadily growing louder. "I've no clue what that sound is, and I don't particularly want to find out."

With a nod of consent, May jammed herself back into the tube. Upon their return to the living room, May reclined on the couch and carefully pried a stick from the box. Time had stuck the papers together a bit, but the smell was unmistakable, if a little stale.

She savored the ritual of taking the cylinder between her lips, convincing the rusted pocket lighter to take a flame, gently breathing the flame into the herbs, and watching the embers devour the tip as she filled herself with smoke.

May took a slow drag, lost in her ecstasy. "So much better."

Behind her, doubled over the back of the couch, Xan heaved a dramatic cough. "By the thumbs of O'Zeno, you *breathe* that stuff?" he wheezed.

She stamped out the cigarette on the coffee table. "Are you alright?"

"I'm fine," he assured her. Sudden concentration contorted his face. "But I think I've forgotten my sister's ex-girlfriend's brother's name." He looked around, searching for it in the smokey air. "Yep, it's gone alright."

"You have a sister?"

"What? No," he laughed hoarsely, "'course not, don't be silly."

May nodded slowly. While she couldn't have said that Xan was ever *on* his rocker, she definitely and unequivocally knew now that he was certainly *off* it.

May stood. She walked a dejected walk to the pack of cigarettes on the table, gave them a dejected sigh, and, with utmost dejection, she said, "Guess now's a good time to quit."

"Oh, well a little," he coughed again, pushing a puff of grey smoke from his lungs, "poison never killed anytuhnt."

"It's okay, I just need to get it out of my system." She flopped onto the couch and rubbed her head.

"I know what'll cheer you up. Hang on, we're going to the movies!"

He leapt to the control panel of the *Audacity* and set a series of coordinates he had keenly memorized.

## ELEVEN
# THE THING FROM PLANET EARTH

The drive-in was a semi-failed business located on a semi-failed docking hub on Lesser Greater Titania. Engaging water colored plans of what the hub should've been still hung, dusty and askew, from the main lobby walls.

As a docking hub, it was fairly useless. The occasional small ship would settle there to fuel up, but quickly be on their way once they saw the sorry state of the station. The nightly movies accounted for the hub's biggest source of income.

A white sheet, ripped in places by space detritus and held aloft by four unmanned buoys, and a projector that had fallen out of a wormhole constituted the theatre. There was a rumor that the projector was haunted. Invariably, right at the climax of whatever movie was playing, the projector would stop and spend two minutes fast-forwarding through the entirety of *It Happened One Night* in silence before continuing on as if nothing had happened at all. It was an annoying glitch to most, but a free bonus movie to the idealistic.

For Xan, the two quick minutes of *It Happened One Night*, were absolute bliss.

61

The *Audacity* landed on the hub platform and Xan tossed a few crystals onto the teledisc where they promptly ceased to be.

The crystal is the most widely accepted form of payment in the universe. This makes Earth fairly rich in comparison to most planets, which is a shame because they wouldn't discover this until most of Earth's natural quartz mines had been squirreled away for pennies in the pockets of hippies, who would someday all be extremely wealthy by intergalactic standards.

May remained sprawled across the couch, her eyes glazed over like a pair of doughnut holes. Sighing, Xan climbed down from the control panel and into the living room to crouch beside her. "Hey, mun. Do you want to watch a movie? It's a buy one get one free sort of deal!" He beamed. She shrugged. "Alright then." He picked her up to no protest.

From the port-hole by the table, they had a perfect view of the screen, and he propped her up in a hover-chair. Her eyes locked onto the screen convincingly, but her mind still replayed the sight of Kathy vanishing and the destruction of everything she'd ever known. It was a little more than an alien movie could break through—even a movie as enrapturing as *The Thing from Planet Earth*.

Xan, of course, knew it was a wildly inaccurate portrayal of humans, but he couldn't help but glance at May during the scene where the human mauled the main character's sister.

"You wouldn't happen to have a taste for flesh or anything would you, May? 'Cause if you do tell me now. I won't be mad, I promise. I just want to know."

May shrugged, half listening. "Haven't tried it."

Xan swallowed audibly at her answer which didn't put him at ease in the slightest.

After hours of needless violence, the sound cut out and *It Happened One Night* sped across the screen like a cheetah on coke.

"Ah now, see, *this* is my favorite part! I've found that things are so much more enjoyable when you don't have to pay for them. I mean, I paid for the other movie but this one's a free bonus movie," he mused as he watched Clark Gable zoom about.

"Why did you wait for me?" May asked quietly.

"Hmm?" Xan was entranced by Claudette's taxi hailing.

"Why didn't you leave me on Earth?" she clarified.

Thoughts, thought Xan, were clearly going through May's mind. "You wouldn't have had much fun down there as it was. Yvonne's gone a bit mad, I think."

"Sure, but why did you rescue me? Twice." She looked at him now—really looked at him. This was reality. This was her life, and it seemed like she would be spending the foreseeable future with this pale blue creature on a ship some incomprehensible amount of lightyears from where she was born.

She felt a panic coming on. It was times like these, her body screaming for air and her chest tight, that she really needed to slowly fill her lungs with dense, toxic smoke. "What am I going to do?" she wheezed.

"Woah." He leaned back dangerously far in the hover chair. "First of all, you don't have to do anything, you can just kinda be, you know? Works pretty well for me, anyway. And secondly, I didn't really rescue you. I just happened to be in a position to help you not die. Twice. It's not that big a deal."

"I could've died," May said. She looked around for something—anything familiar or comforting. When she found nothing at all familiar or comforting, she started to hyperventilate.

"Hey, wait." Xan looked around too, as if he could help her find whatever she had lost. Failing, he held out a gloved hand. "Here, hold my hand. It's an old Tuhntian tradition but-"

She grasped his hand tightly; the solidity of it helped her re-orient herself.

"Distract me," she said.

"Right, uh, sure. What do you get when you mix a house plant and a rhinoceros?"

"I don't know, what?"

"Oh, zuut, I was hoping you would know. Um. Tell me about Earth—what do you do for kicks?"

"Not that."

"Yeah, of course, sorry."

On screen, the bedsheet between Claudette and Clark fell and the horror flick started up again, a terrified alien scream wrenching their attention back to the film.

"Uh, how about that?" He pointed to the screen where a rabid, naked human absconded with a limp green arm between its teeth. "If you change your mind about cannibalism, give me fair warning, alright? I saved your life after all. I deserve a head start, I think."

May almost smiled at the absurdity of it, squeezed his hand and dropped it. "You've got it." She could push the horrible things back, she decided. Alien media was much more interesting than an existential crisis.

The credits rolled, and Xan turned to her again. "What now? Taeloo XII has some of the best ice cream and the worst novelty sunglasses in the universe. Truglian 9 is fun but a little risque. Oh! How do you feel about hats?"

"Hats?"

## TWELVE
# STRAWBERRY-FLAVORED LIP TINT

The yellow light beamed Kathy directly from Earth into a grey jail cell aboard the *Peacemaker*.

"Hey!" she called through the bars to the lanky purple alien standing guard over her cell block. He approached her with all the confidence of a newborn giraffe.

"Yes ma'am, how may I help you?"

Kathy was a bit taken aback. "I, uh...I would like to speak to someone in charge. I want to know where I am and why you've brought me here, and I think I deserve to know."

The alien nodded reassuringly. "Not to worry, ma'am, you will be returned to your city and assigned your Personal Handbook for Life on Earth in just under an hour. May I offer you a refreshment? Juice of the lemon? The helpful gator, perhaps?"

He turned and plucked a plastic cup half filled with blue Gatorade from a table covered in snacks and drinks.

"No! It could be poison for all I know."

"As you wish." He set down the drink and returned to his post. A large gun of some sort was slung over his shoulder, but Kathy somehow doubted it was deadly. If they wanted her dead, they would have done that already.

The cell they'd brought her to was not roomy, but not cramped. It was a perfectly decent holding cell with a private restroom and a few clean white benches jutting out from the clean white walls. Cleaner, thought Kathy, than her own restaurant's benches from the look of them. On the benches across from her, a simple-looking couple tried to comfort their sniffling toddler.

She let herself succumb to the clean white bench and sat down, resting her head against the wall. She wondered where May was. She wondered if the couple across from her would be of any use but doubted it. They had their hands full and Kathy wasn't great with kids.

She was on her own.

Just as she'd been on her own to cover May's shifts when she had disappeared. She wanted to be mad, but after all that had happened, she assumed May had a reasonable excuse. Alien invasions did make it a trifle harder to come in to work after all.

The work got easier, though, as the reports of alien abductions grew. Eventually it became too much of a problem for the government to cover up. Alien abductions were a thing that happened. They became just another threat of city-life, like someone breaking into your car or stealing your knock-off Gucci bag with your favorite strawberry-flavored lip tint.

Kathy licked her dry, uncolored lips. She missed her favorite strawberry-flavored lip tint. She supposed the aliens had taken that, too. All drugstore makeup was probably theirs now. Would aliens use drugstore brand makeup? Probably, thought Kathy. Everyone did, after all. Even if they claimed they didn't.

People lied. And people got abducted. That was life.

"Attention humans of Sector B518, prepare to be returned."

Returned? Kathy had not been expecting to be returned. Which was a bit dense of her seeing as they had told her point-blank that she would be. Kathy was a smart woman, but she was extremely mistrustful.

Besides, she didn't necessarily want to be returned.

Everything was gone. No job, no car, no strawberry-flavored lip tint because all the damn aliens were using it on their chapped purple lips.

She stood on a sidewalk before an intersection she'd seen a million times but did not recognize. The city was uncannily familiar without being comfortingly so. Should she move? Were they expecting her to do something now?

A whirring metal ball the size of her head and weighed down by a thick canvas bag descended from the clear sky and addressed her. "You have been assigned to Sector B518." The floating sphere's voice simultaneously sounded like her Great Aunt Missy and her high school softball coach, Mr. Kevin. "Here is your manual. Please follow all instructions carefully to avoid punishment." The sphere produced a long, thin claw and grabbed a binder from the canvas bag that hung over its body.

Kathy gingerly took it. The cover read, "Human 740282042: Food Service."

"Damn," she said.

The sphere made a sound that almost read as a "tsk" of shame and zapped her with a tingling electric shock. "Punishment 459 Executed. No swearing. You will be monitored until you are functioning properly. Please consult your manual." It beeped pleasantly.

Kathy stared at it.

"Please consult your manual." It floated a little closer to her now.

Kathy opened the binder and began to read. The orb, satisfied, floated further away.

The table of contents itself was massive. This book seemed to cover everything from workplace manners to hygiene practices in great detail. Each instruction had a designated punishment for disobedience. She read her daily schedule. It was nearing the work hours. She glanced at the sphere, and it buzzed a warning.

She went to work.

## THIRTEEN
# FANCY HATS

"Hats!"

"Sorry?" May asked.

Xan catapulted from his chair and raced to the intershoot. "We need hats! You'll see." He disappeared down the tube.

The *Audacity* still loitered in the movie parking lot, despite loud warnings to shove off after the film had ended. May hoped no one cared enough to actually make them leave.

Moments later, Xan reappeared balancing seven or eight intricate conglomerations of feathers and lace on his arms. Atop his head now perched a spectacularly crafted black leather tri-corn hat resplendent with fluffy white feathers and brocade trim.

He dropped the pile of gaudy hats before May and picked the first one off the pile. "This one's excellent, a proper old-fashioned A'Viltrian statement hat." He plopped the white-feathered thing on her head. Its large, asymmetrical brim dipped down below her eyes.

"What's this for?"

"Do you like it?"

"I suppose." She wiggled it around on her head until she could see again.

"Terrific! Alright, hang on." He reached for a button on the control panel and typed something into the auto-pilot. The rocket shuttered and spun, tossing them to the floor. May laughed as she was thrown from her seat onto the soft shag carpet, the mass of feathers and lace toppling into her.

"Where are we going?" She crawled back into her chair and reconfigured the hat as the ship evened out its course.

"Have you ever been to a Vagran Rocket Derby?" he asked, re-applying his own magnificent hat.

She raised a humored eyebrow at him.

"Well, have you?" he pressed, leaning towards her.

"I think it's safe to guess that I haven't."

"Oh, right. Yep, sorry, that was obvious." He waved away the question with his hand. "They're huge events. Millions of people show up to these things—some aren't even officially recognized as people, but they show up anyway. It's about the only thing that keeps planets out of constant war with each other. There are pre-shows, food, arcades, gambling, and of course the hats. No better excuse to wear a gorgeous hat." He flicked at a feather that threatened to dip below his eyes and kicked his feet onto the console.

The hover chair tilted back dangerously under him, but May supposed it couldn't tip over seeing as it had no legs.

She was wrong.

The unbalanced chair spun out from underneath him, depositing him on the floor once again. After a moment's confusion, he shrugged. "Safer down here anyway." He made himself at home on the carpet.

Stars blurred by on the view screen in front of her. She saw a vague reflection of herself wearing an enormous hat in the dark screen.

Everything felt surreal. No matter how hard she tried, she couldn't get her brain to understand what was happening to her. Nevertheless, it was, so she accepted it. If she wasted time worrying about it, if she wasted time thinking about Earth or trying to convince herself it was all a dream, she wouldn't be prepared for whatever horrible thing happened to her next.

The alien curled on the floor beside her didn't seem dangerous but if *he* didn't kill her, the lack of real food *would*. She shook her head to dislodge the thought. The corn could keep her going for a while if she didn't expend much energy. After that? Well, she'd get to it when she got to it.

The view changed. A rainbow of lights beeped past in a steady even stream, almost like streetlights. The rocket slowed and she could see what they passing more clearly, silvery buildings the tops of which stretched into the clouds and the bottoms of which disappeared into a thick fog, compact hover cars with bulbous windows and decorative fins, bridges stretching between the buildings over which tall and well-dressed purple beings scurried.

"Are we in a city?"

"Yep!" He bounced up now, leaning over the console eagerly. "This is the biggest transportation hub on Vagran. You've got to park on the planet and take the shuttle to the stadium."

May never enjoyed public transportation on Earth and doubted very much that she would enjoy public transportation on Vagran, but public transportation be damned, she was excited, and Xan could tell. He offered her a crooked grin.

"Never been to another planet before?" he asked.

May shrugged. "Oh, loads of times. Grocery runs, mostly. Doctor's appointments."

Xan's grin tripped, stumbled for a moment, then caught itself. "Really?"

"Joking," she assured him with a smile as weak as herbal tea.

"Ha! Oh, right. Yeah. Ha...grocery runs," he mused, turning back to the window to watch the city.

The autopilot brought them to a docking field, righted the ship, and parked it—albeit with a touch of a wobble. This maneuver and the accompanying shift in the ship's center of artificial gravity would have made May's head spin if it wasn't spinning already from culture shock.

"Alright, come on! I've already bought our tickets." He tapped the BEAPER on his wrist with his nose and ran to the teledisc.

"What is that?" May asked as she joined him on the platform.

"This?" He unclipped the wristband and handed it to her.

"It's a BEAPER. I think it stands for Benevolent Electronic Assistant Personal Resource, but the acronym may be lost in translation." He laughed lightly, scratching behind his ear where a translation chip had been implanted several hundred orbits ago.

May studied the cuff which was woven metal all around and looked like it could repel bullets, were it asked nicely. It could, in fact, repel bullets but only on a wrist more skilled than Xan's. A smattering of small buttons sat flush at the top beneath a strip of light. Xan pressed one button and a holographic screen popped from the strip of lights like bread from a toaster.

"Teleport?" it asked in bold blue letters that hovered in the air. More settings and information crowded in small letters below it, but Xan ignored these and swiped the letters upwards, atomizing the word. The scenery changed around May and this time she barely noticed being torn atom from atom and recomposed elsewhere. Perhaps she could get used to the teledisc after all.

Eyes wide, May held the BEAPER out to Xan, having more interesting things to observe now. They were in a tube of metal, much like a subway. Or at least May thought so; she had never been on a subway but knew from movies what they ought to look like. She nearly could have believed they were back on Earth, traveling in a subway along with cosplayers from a nearby sci-fi convention.

A pinkish slime snored on the ceiling of the tube they were in, dripping steadily on the bald heads of three very large pig-like things reading what appeared to be holographic newspapers on the benches across from them.

"Now I know this is all new to you," Xan whispered to her, "but don't stare at those guys. They'll gut you in a milliblip if they notice." May glued her eyes to the floor.

"These Ladies, however, *want* to be looked at." He waved to three of the most stunning women May had ever seen, their hair glistening with starlight, their clothing multi-layered and structural, their skin a velvety dark burgundy and their faces set with several large, doe-like black eyes. More eyes than any one face should rightfully play host to.

"What are they?" May whispered.

"Those are Ladies. They're training to be Queens. Or, more likely, will end up killing each other horribly to replace their Queen. Might even kill their Queen. It's a nasty business, really. I once saw one rip another's throat out with her teeth on an elevator. Made for an awkward ride. Tough to have a casual conversation about the weather with someone who's picking throat out of their teeth with a toothpick. Wink at them, they like that." He winked, and the Ladies giggled politely in reply.

"Queens of what?"

Xan shrugged. "Hard to tell, maybe Titania. Could be from Estrichi, but they don't look like the punctual type." He laughed at his own joke; May did not. "Because—the time thing." He was mildly disappointed that his brilliant joke had fallen on uncultured ears. "Estrichi is...oh, never mind. We're here!"

The tube screeched to a halt, and the slime that clung to the ceiling slid sickeningly to the floor. "Pardon," it squelched as it oozed out past them and slipped through the seal in the door which flung open a moment later to reveal an enormous complex awash with beings.

The pig-creatures were beginning to smell. May hurried out of the doors in front of Xan, slipping on the trail of slime that the pink thing had left. She caught herself on the edge of the subway door. Xan offered her a steadying arm, but she didn't take it, preferring instead to wipe the slime from her feet on the door jamb and step around the puddle.

"Non-slip boots." Xan contorted to show May the

textured bottom of one of his heavy, black boots. "Immensely practical. Fashionable, too. Important."

"I haven't had a chance to change. Or anything to change into." She picked a thin swatch of latex from her ripped white suit, worried that she would be stuck with it forever.

"Zuut! I was so excited about the hats, I forgot you needed something to wear, too. I'm going to have to go back to work."

Somewhere in the back of her head a banner unfurled to display the word "freeloader" in bold block letters. Her first instinct was to phone her bank and find out if they could convert her savings into whatever currency they used out here, which, for many reasons, not least of which being that there is no known conversion rate from USD to ICS, was not possible.

"Don't worry about it," she said, finally. "I'll get a job."

The repertoire of strange looks Xan could give her was bottomless. This one conveyed something between pity and humor and was decidedly her least favorite. He didn't reply.

"I have skills and experience," she said. "If nothing else, I'm obviously well suited to food service."

"I like your gumption, May!" He patted her back, and she felt a little better. "But no one will hire a human."

She felt a little worse. "What do people have against humans?"

Prejudice was no stranger to her. Even in space she couldn't escape it.

"Oh, nothing, they've just never met one. I mean there are rumors, of course. Nasty rumors—I'd rather not get into it. You saw the film. Humans are a largely untested species."

"You don't believe the rumors, do you?"

"Psh!" He laughed, swatting at the air. "Naw, of course not! But I know a lot more about humans than most. Though I had rather assumed you all came in shades of grey or black so the brown's a bit of a surprise."

"Listen." She stopped, grabbing his arm so he wouldn't walk ahead of her. "I'm not a freeloader and I will find a job."

"Okay, alright. Sore spot?" he asked.

Releasing him, she nodded and turned her attention back to the rows of shops, all of which looked like potential employers to her.

Was this life? Even in outer space? She needed clothing and food to live, needed money to get those things, needed to work to get money. Yes, that seemed to be the sum of it. Life.

Why, she thought, could she not have been picked up by some futuristic spaceship with a food replicator?

They moved through the dark and crowded terminals of the stadium with relative ease, weaving through throngs of beings who stood staring at the giant screens or yelling something into their wrist. At last there was a break in the throngs and a dappling of bright light where the store fronts gave way to a brightly lit arena. May hadn't been to a sporting event since she was in color guard a decade ago, and even then, she had been there for work, not pleasure. She didn't think she particularly liked sports.

These thoughts plagued her as they searched out an empty patch of bleacher to sit on. She took a deep breath and immediately regretted it as the foul stench of what she had to assume was alien sweat and something not entirely unlike hotdog water offended the back of her throat.

The noise, the colors, the *smells* threatened to overwhelm her senses. Better than giving herself even a second to think about Earth. Finally, they sat, sandwiched between a thin leaf-colored person on May's side, and a statuesque woman who not only had the bearing of a statue but also appeared to actually be carved from marble on Xan's. The crowd hushed, the lights dimmed, and the smells graciously receded.

A holographic image of star-studded blackness formed in the center of the arena, blocking May's view of the crowd opposite them.

Xan shimmied in his seat, the woman beside him giving him deliberate sidelong glance. "You're going to like this," he told May.

An eerie metal face appeared as a screen overlay at the upper left corner of the everything-ness, and May felt the whisper of a round of applause that never really got going. "Welcome to the 789th Orbital Vagran Space Races." The metal face moved almost too well, more lifelike than life itself, its voice as nebulous as the remnants of an exploded star.

Beside the face, another in-set screen emerged to display footage of a needley silver rocket. The camera panned up its length as if it were a scantily clad lady in an old, over-sexualized film, its swooping fins four shapely legs, its sensually curved hull scintillating with points of light, its sleek nose pointing snobbishly upward.

May realized her mouth was open and closed it.

Three more equally gorgeous rockets were featured this way.

She sat forward on her seat and watched as the in-sets melted away and four color-coded digital markers appeared to the left of the screen, pointing out the locations of the ships which were far too small to be seen from this distance.

Music floated into May's head, seemingly with no point of origin; it bloomed from the center of her being. It was soft, orchestral, suspenseful. In a flurry of strings, the music accelerated, and the digital markers began to move with the rockets that appeared as tiny, colorful specks in the distance. In-sets to the corner of the screen showed a close-up as the rockets blurred past a camera, the robot announced each light-year marker the rockets passed. The music reached a crescendo as if something were about to happen and the specks, which had been growing steadily, suddenly grew much faster.

The entire active time of a typical rocket race is about as long as it takes to order and receive a latte at your local coffee shop on a Tuesday afternoon. A massive cloud of glittery confetti bloomed above the audience and the music trailed off into nothingness.

The silver rocket appeared once more on the screen, now docked on a patch of lush blue grass, its sharp fins sunk deep into the soil. The camera zoomed in on three figures beside it and the audience cheered the winners with a deafening roar of enthusiasm. After the relative peace of the race itself, the sound was piercing and uncomfortable.

The gears in May's head spun as she watched the winners accept their earnings. Pursing her lips, she glanced at Xan who was idly trying to make friends with the stone-faced woman beside him. He had a rocket ship. She wondered...

# FOURTEEN
## SUSPICIOUS

Back aboard the *Audacity*, Xan brushed the inside of his coat pocket with his fingertip, a few granules of crystal dusting his gloved finger. He sighed and the granules floated away on his breath. He sighed heavier.

There are two constants that are absolutely universal. Nearly every developed society that has ever existed and ever will exist discovers the need for these two things right from the start. The first is, of course, thumbs. The second is money. Though multiple physical incarnations of multiple deities have done their darndest to convince societies that money and the accumulation thereof is not the meaning of life, none have been successful.

Because of this, Xan needed a job. And also because of this and the neurosis that accompanies the fear of not having money, May desperately *wanted* a job.

May watched the alien sigh at the dust.

"That's the last of it?"

Xan nodded. "That's the last of it," he confirmed. "Well, guess I'm off to work." He plugged a few numbers into the *Audacity*'s read-out and rested a finger on The Button Which Typically Made The Ship Go.

79

He looked as if someone had sneezed in his soup. Then as if it were the only soup left in the world. Then as if he would accept and eat the soup, but he wouldn't be happy about it.

He pressed the button.

They traveled in silence, which was highly unusual. May sat beside him in the co-pilot's seat and tried not to stare in astonishment at how utterly unhappy he had somehow made his cartoonish face. While work to her was a blessed comfort, a boon in an expensive and uncaring world, it was one of few activities that could throw Xan into a bit of a brood.

The ship settled at last on a faded square of concrete. On the view screen the sky shone an uneasy yellow, the red sun boiling away above them, a maze of stucco and wood panel buildings stretching to one side, a series of what looked like cars on the other. Below, a smattering of people slumped between the cars and the buildings. Faded brown letters stuck out from the stucco walls of the foremost building, ominously spelling out the words "The Agency" in serif caps.

May wondered if the font had serifs in whatever alien language it was actually written in, or if the translation chip was taking liberties with the graphic design. The translation chip thought it a bit rude that May assumed it had done anything but recreate the font with striking precision.

"Is this where you work?" she asked.

Xan shrugged noncommittally. "Eh, more or less. Occasionally."

"Would they hire me? I need a job and you've got an in already."

Xan's eyes widened, but May couldn't quite tell what emotion flitted behind them.

"*Why* can't you?" He sprung from his chair and catapulted onto the teledisc. "Oh, lots of reason. It's not great work for a human. I mean a human has never done it, probably can't. Also it's boring, and it's dangerous, and you could get lost! Or maimed! Anyway, you're too short and not blue enough. Oh, and gloves. You need your own gloves. Bye!" He vanished in a tornado of words that left confusion, rather than debris, in its wake.

May thought this was all very sudden and perhaps a bit contrived, almost as if some great unknown force needed him to leave her alone in the *Audacity* for a decent amount of time and didn't bother with thinking up a better excuse. And so, she was left alone on the ship.

Except she wasn't alone. In the absence of Xan's near constant chatter, she could hear every thought that macheted its way through the thick rainforest of her subconscious. She did not care for these thoughts.

The image of Kathy fizzling away under the yellow glow broke through the vines first and wrested its way into her conscious mind. Had that happened to her mother? Oh, God. Her mother was right. Her mother was right about everything. *May* was the kook who didn't see the obvious warning signs of an alien invasion.

Her chest felt tight and she needed a cigarette. It wouldn't help the tightness, but at least then she'd have a tangible reason for the constriction. She dove into the couch cushions, digging out the box that she had stuffed away and prying a stick from the warped cardboard. The lighter still lay on the table and she thumbed it on, lighting the tip of a stick.

She inhaled deeply and remembered the bum. The bum was right. The *bum* was right. She inhaled again and remembered the Gremlin that had hit her. She'd been hit by a car, but it left no mark. Had she even been hit? She inhaled again and remembered August and IX; if they weren't ripped to shreds, they were impossibly far away and—she coughed.

She'd forgotten to exhale.

Her legs were shaking, so she drew them up underneath her and made herself small on the lumpy orange couch. There was no guessing how long Xan would be out, but she hoped she had time for a decent breakdown before he returned. At last, she buried her face in a flattened brocade pillow and cried.

# FIFTEEN

# REALLY, REALLY THICK

August was raking through yet another pile of plastic straws when his BEAPER dinged. He was being reassigned to a new territory.

He had been combing the same section of space for two inches worth of beard hair growth. Estrichi time proved difficult for him to master and he found measuring his beard length to be much simpler. IX (whose name he still could not remember) seemed to think it was three Earth years, but he doubted it had been that long. Perhaps beards grew slower in space.

After August and IX repaired the Gremlin and christened him *Robert*, they quickly realized they would need a source of income if they were to survive. It wasn't difficult to become a junker. All you needed was a ship and a willingness to dig through garbage every day. This made it the perfect, if only, career choice for August.

He had become something of a scientist. Every new item required him to apply his half-remembered version of the scientific method. First, upon unearthing an unfamiliar object, he would pose the question, "What the hell is this?" Then, depending on whether or not IX was within earshot to enlighten him, he would form a hypothesis.

These hypotheses usually centered on cursed objects or fertility talismans and were typically fairly far off the mark. Still, he would whip out his ancient InstaLabeler, label the object with his assumptions, and set it aside for later exploration.

Once, August almost got a laugh out of IX by misidentifying a crumbled yoghurt cup as a ceremonial death chalice. Almost, but not quite. She was as stoney as the petrified biscuits he found in abundance near Astffadoo 2.

IX kept the *Robert* from breaking down. Or, more accurately, repaired it when it inevitably did break down. August looked for scrap metal. Sometimes plastics. Occasionally he would get very lucky and find bits of moldy rugs. But now, finally, he had paid his dues and was off to a premier landfill. This was the good trash, the kind of trash that made other trash feel like garbage. This was rich people trash.

"Where to?" August asked the BEAPER on his wrist, which he typically and incorrectly called a watch. The alien didn't talk much, so he had taken to speaking with inanimate objects. Fortunately, this particular object would listen, unlike that ornery shovel.

His assignment scrolled across the face of the watch. "1613 Centauri VII." He pulled his fancy eye patch from his pocket and slapped it on; he wanted to make a good impression.

"We're moving out!" he said to the purple alien who lived with him. There was no reply.

She was in her room again, August noted with annoyance. Sometimes when she went into that little room she had slapped onto the side of the *Robert*, she would stay there for weeks. Her absence was tough on August; he was a social creature and needed something to talk at.

Once, after a particularly long stint alone, he cornered her and wouldn't let her leave without an answer as to what she did in there. She had told him she was "downloading" and he gave her a confused look. She had told him she was "meditating" and he gave her a confused look. Finally, frustrated at the apparent language barrier, she told him she took very long naps. He accepted that.

Technically, he could pilot the *Robert* on his own, but he abhorred flying. He very noisily began the system checks necessary before taking the Gremlin into space, hoping that his clanging around would alert her to his intention to relocate.

Finally, she emerged.

"What took you so long? I was starting to forget what you looked like!" August said playfully. He attached and unlocked the steering wheel, but he purposely did it backwards so she would shoo him away and take over.

IX sat in the pilot seat and August relaxed beside her on the passenger's side. "August, have you noticed that I am blind?" she said, knowing full well that he hadn't. She also knew that he didn't know her name, but she had wanted to see how long he could keep up his charade. She ignited the engine and jiggled the gear shift.

August tried to hide his shock, then realized she couldn't see it anyway. Sure, he had noticed that her eyes were as white as the inside of a delicious, crunchy, sweet apple, but he figured it would've come up by now if she couldn't see with them.

"But how do you-"

"How do I function? How do you function with just one eye? You adjust; I learned to account for it. I have had nearly two thousand Earth years to do so."

It was nice of her to use Earth years around him. Still, it always creeped him out when she talked about being immortal. Or nearly immortal, as she would hastily correct. It was spooky to know she was a few thousand years his senior. Spooky quickly became annoying when he discovered that his skin had begun to wrinkle around his eyes, and she could not relate.

"So, you're blind. That's cool. I guess that explains why you're always asking me to read things for you. I just figured you got a kick out of my mispronunciations." He laughed; despite her mysteriousness, he had to admit he enjoyed her company. It would be a terribly lonely and frightening Universe out there on his own.

"No, I do not care for your mispronunciations. I have decided to leave you now. Yvonne is out there, and I believe I have figured out how to help her." She brought the *Robert* into orbit and August felt the familiar wash of space sickness. While he wanted to return to Earth someday, he wasn't prepared to make the long journey through space, and he doubted he ever would be.

"Oh...who—who's Yvonne again?" he stammered, trying to decide if keeping his eye closed or open made space travel less horrid. Neither did.

"Your captor for six Earth months."

"*That* Yvonne, right, of course. And—and why do you have to stop her? I thought you liked being a junker." He smiled wryly at her. She had never once given him the slightest hint of an indication that she was enjoying herself.

"Enough questions, August. At our next stop I will purchase a ship with my share of our earnings, and we will go our separate ways. May you find what you seek," she quoted a popular junker farewell at him.

August swallowed. He couldn't keep the hurt out of his face but at least he could keep it out of his voice. "May you find what you seek."

# SIXTEEN

# LASERS?

May had fallen asleep on the couch and woke with her face pressed to a damp pillow. Whether it was damp from tears or spittle, she couldn't tell and didn't care to know. At some point she'd tapped the lit cigarette out on top of its box and, once she regained her senses, had the sense to feel ashamed of herself.

Crying? And smoking? This was not how an adult dealt with their issues. Well, perhaps it was, but it was not how *she* dealt with her issues, she thought, grabbing the box along with the spent cigarette. It had to go.

She looked around. There had to be some sort of disposal system aboard the ship, but she couldn't guess where. She set the box back down for now.

Something on the couch caught her eye. The old spaceship manual flopped over the arm of the couch like a dead fish. An intriguing dead fish, though. If she could stand to read it, it might tell her where the disposal was.

She picked up the heavy paperback tome and started from the beginning, working her way through the untranslatable words with context clues, and whispering notes to herself like she had seen savants do in movies.

May read for hours, dog-earring pages she wanted to go back to, memorizing words the chip couldn't translate to ask Xan about later, forcing back the forest of depressing realizations about what she'd lost by filling her brain with more information than it could reasonably process in one go. If nothing else, she learned how to re-align the three external fins of the ship.

She read as if the words were building a fence around the edge of a cliff in her soul that overlooked a churning grey ocean of depression. Would she ever see an ocean again? Were oceans just an Earth thing?

Finally, she set the manual down and grabbed the cigarettes again. With steely determination, she crushed the box in her hand and marched to the console. A large red button on the control panel opened the airlock hatch in the wall beneath it. She threw the cigarettes into the hatch, closed it, and watched the last pack of cigarettes she'd ever see drop out of the ship and onto the concrete below.

The airlock wasn't meant to be used when the ship was parked. She felt a bit bad about littering.

She had killed a lot of time. Perhaps an entire Earth day, even, and Xan had still not returned. The ship was eerily quiet without him around, and panic threatened with a flutter in her chest. She was alone on an alien planet and she'd just littered which was probably illegal like it was back on Earth. *No.* She caught the pendulum of her wayward thoughts before it could dive into another swing. There were things to do.

The squeaky intershoot door would be a quick fix. And why not, to show her appreciation for the strange alien being who had taken her in?

In the living room, she found a seam in the plastic paneling that matched up with the tool storage room in the *Audacity*'s schematics. With an experimental tap at the seam, the door slid open to reveal a room filled with glistening tools on rows of untouched shelves. May walked in, beaming as if she'd just discovered sunken treasure and not a disused utility closet.

May got a wild look in her eye as she tried to match up

the appropriate tools for the door fix. Tucked away in a glass jar on a high shelf, she found a dense sponge-like creature. She twisted off the top and it lazily rose out of its home, stretched like taffy, crawled onto her hand, and climbed up her arm using millions of minuscule suckers. It had no apparent eyes, but one end had ostia holes that were expressive enough for May to get the impression that it was quite pleased indeed to be out of its glass prison and perched on her shoulder.

According to the manual, it was an Osculum and functioned as an all-purpose tool for cramped areas that no human or alien fingers could reach. She liked the Osculum, and it appeared to like her. Well, it appeared to like her hair which it had suctioned onto and was rhythmically pulling on. She carefully removed her matted hair from its mouth. The creature nestled into the crook of her neck and vibrated. Listening closely to it, she could hear a gentle purring.

"Don't go back to sleep," she admonished it.

She grabbed a bottle of oil, a metal tool for leverage, and a spindly brush.

The door was stuck now in the open position, vibrating as if desperately trying to break free of some mysterious force willing it to stay ajar. May peered into the shaft of the elevator-like tube. The Osculum tipped forward and she felt its tiny suckers start to release, ready to work after ages in storage. She spread the thick black oil onto the hairs of the brush and offered it to the Osculum. It crawled onto the brush and levitated with it, bobbing up and down.

She jammed the metal tool between the door and its sheath and pried it apart, allowing enough space for the Osculum to float through with the brush. The creature carried the oil to a gear that was jammed in the back. May smiled. This was easy enough, she thought.

She flicked through the manual as the Osculum did its job only to be stopped by a horrific squeal. The door sprung to life, flinging the metal tool against the wall and threatening to squish the Osculum between the gears. May jammed her body into the entryway, keeping the door open as far as she could.

"Are you okay, Osy?" A soft purr came from the back of the door. She sighed in relief, but the door was free to move now and there was no way for the sponge to crawl back out with the leverage tool halfway across the room.

She probably should have consulted it about shutting off the power, but hindsight wouldn't save the mission now. The only tool she could possibly reach was the manual. She stretched her leg out and caught the book with her toe (it's my sad duty to report that May had unusually flexible toes). After some finessing, she grabbed the book with her hand, jammed it into the door to keep it open, and sprinted to the metal tool which was lying on the other side of the room. The manual buckled under the pressure; she had seconds before it would give in to the force of the door.

She speared the tool in as deep as it would go between the door and its sheath and twisted it, opening the gap again. The Osculum slipped out from the re-opened crack. As soon as it was free, she released the door and let it whoosh back into place, the bent manual spilling onto the carpet.

The sponge looked at her, or at least she assumed it was looking, then it looked to the door, then back at her. With a trill of joy, it suctioned itself onto her cheek and made a kissing noise. She laughed as the sponge tickled her face.

"Okay, Osy, you're welcome!" She peeled the sponge from her face and set it down.

After feeling like a husk of a person—a feeling which was redoubled on account of her exclusive diet of canned corn—for the past few days, she finally had something of a purpose again: to transform the *Audacity* into a properly functioning ship.

By the time Xan arrived back, almost a week later, the ship was nearly unrecognizable and May lounged on the couch, eating canned corn with a spork.

"Oh, you're back. That took longer than I expected."

"Yeah, well, me too, starshine." His orange hair fell in ragged locks over his eyes and he pushed it back as best he could.

"Xan, what *is* your job?" May sat up, setting the corn on the table. She had taken the initiative to look up "The Agency" on the ship's computer, but she didn't want him to know she'd been snooping.

He draped like a wet noodle over the back of the couch. "You really want to know, don't you?"

"It's why I asked," May encouraged him.

"Alright, then. I'm a freelancer."

"Well, that explains a lot."

"Does it? Excellent!" He vaulted over the couch back and sat down properly for once.

"No, I mean, what sort of freelancer?"

A noise like gears grinding came from deep in his chest. "Anything, really. Just a good old hired hand. Hired body. You know..."

"Xan, are you a sex worker?" May finally asked.

"Pah! Me? Ha, funny you should mention that." He laughed nervously. "Kinda. You cleaned!" he said, changing the subject with the speed of an auctioneer.

"I did. But Xan, seriously. There has to be a better way to make money."

"Oh, it's not so bad! I mean, it's work. Work's a drag anyway you spin it. Though, ironically, the drag work's usually the best." He kicked his feet up on the table and stretched, his arms coming to rest over the back of the couch. "But it's good gem and with a body like this, it'd be a crime not to share," he surveyed his stringy body. "I suppose," he amended, poking curiously at his soft belly.

"Uh-huh," she followed his gaze. He had a body like a cat. Stretched to full length he was extremely thin, but when he got into one of his many unusual curled up positions, any fat he did have clustered around his middle. As far as she knew, she didn't have a "type" she was particularly attracted to. If she did, however, he wasn't exactly it.

Now he sat up, trying to get the conversation back on track. "You cleaned!" he repeated happily. She let him change the subject this time.

"I also fixed the door, recalibrated the sensors, downloaded the latest software update, changed the oil, returned the chrome siding that fell off, found a real mirror in the basement, cleaned the gunk out of the nozzle, and found the shower. Which you should've told me about earlier, by the way. Oh, and I unpacked and installed the lasers."

"Lasers?"

"This ship came with six Ultra-Ray-Super-Destroyers. I figured they would be of more use to you if they weren't packed away in a box."

Osy chirruped from her shoulder. "Oh, and I made a friend. Its name is Osy."

Xan nodded. "Lovely," he said as he removed his boots.

Human eyes are curious things. Due to a lack of cones, and—scientists will someday find—a lack of imagination, there are many things that are outside of the human sight spectrum. When faced with one of these things—be it a color, a shape, or a logical contradiction in the promises of a politician—the human mind gets very, very uncomfortable and does anything short of crawling out the ear canal to avoid perceiving the thing.

Tuhntian feet are outside of the human sight register. They are such an unusual shape that humans simply cannot bear to look at them without some normal-foot shaped covering such as boots. May now looked at Xan's feet and very much wished she hadn't.

"Oh, my God, put those back on." She shut her eyes tight.

"What?"

"Put your boots back on, please! Please," she begged.

Xan nodded. "Okay," he said carefully. "They're back on."

May relaxed and opened her eyes. Much better.

"Thanks," she picked up her corn again and slowly picked at the kernels clinging to the inside of the can as she spoke. "So, this is a racing rocket, isn't it?"

"That she is!" he said, patting the couch proudly.

"Have you ever raced her?"

The couch shook with Xan's guffaw; May waited. "Oh, you weren't kidding?" The aftershock of the laugh peppered his voice. "Uh, no. No, I have not. Why?"

"It looks like an easy way to make money, and you've already got the rocket."

"Do I?" He nervously pulled at his collar.

"I think I can race her. We could make good money that way." It was a long-shot, but it was the best idea she'd had.

"Alright well, first of all: no. And second of all: absolutely not. Thirdly, I would like you to consider a resounding negatory, and for my fourth point..." He concentrated for a moment. "Sorry, haven't got a fourth point. But the former three still stand."

"So, that's a no?"

Xan smiled and tapped his temple. "Ah, you're a quick one! Really, though. It's dangerous and horrible and we *will* die. Not even exaggerating. I'll be dead and you'll be dead, and the *Audacity* will be little more than a beautiful orange smudge on the side of an asteroid."

Somehow, May very much doubted that was true. But she was tired again, having expended energy her strict diet of canned corn was not eager to replace.

She would let it go for now.

# SEVENTEEN

# TASTES LIKE MISDIRECTION

May had been sleeping a lot. A dangerous cocktail of depression, lack of a proper daylight cycle, and nutritional deficiency was to blame. It was impossible to tell how many days she had been stranded in space, but she'd slept at least six times since she was abducted so she guessed a week.

The intershoot made a sucking sound, heralding Xan's appearance.

"Last one!" He tossed a can of corn onto the couch beside her and she curled her lip at it. Corn, she had come to believe, was not food. She needed a steak and a cigarette and maybe two or three leaves. Not a cold can of corn. She curled into herself, trying to squeeze away the headache that she'd had for at least a day now.

Xan didn't seem to notice or care, as if food wasn't vital to his survival. When she thought about it, she realized she'd never seen him eat real food, just a variety of crunchy snacks in untranslatable bags. The question plagued her, as so many did, but she was too weak to ask. Eventually he'd bring it up, she figured. Hopefully, before she died of starvation.

If this was truly the last can, it was a death knell. She had combed through the basement with a flashlight looking for a steak but quickly moved on to looking for anything she recognized as food. The rock-hard Hostess Zebra Cake she had found behind a stack of cinderblocks did not qualify.

Frustrated, she realized she once again needed his help. "What do you eat?" She lolled her aching head back on the couch and tried to focus on him—the problem being that there appeared to be three of him and she didn't know which to look at.

"Me? Anything! Whatever pops into the basement. Hasn't killed me yet." He smiled broadly at her. The smile stuck to his face but faded from his eyes. "What's wrong?"

"I can't keep eating corn," May explained.

"Ah, well, nothing to worry about then. There isn't any left."

"I need to eat something." She gave up trying to look at anything and closed her eyes.

"Well, sure, eventually! You can't be hungry already though, right? I mean, you've eaten all the corn. There was a lot of corn."

She felt his unusually long nose touch her face and jumped back with a start. "What?"

"You fell asleep." He was still extremely close.

"No, I didn't."

He hummed an unconvinced hum and squinted at her. "You were snoring."

"Ah," she sat forward, holding her head in her hands and staring wide-eyed at the shag carpet. "I really need to eat," she said, more to herself as she tried to work out what to do about that. She heard the can pop open beside her and Xan thrust the open cylinder of golden kernels into her field of vision.

"Then eat! Look, I don't know how often humans are meant to eat but I've got a plethora of crystals now thanks to my suavery. We can hop on the IFI and see what's around. There's bound to be something you can stomach out there."

"IFI?" She took the corn from him and forced herself to

swallow some.

"Invisible Floating Intelligence. No idea what it is or where it comes from but it's hooked up to the ship and it-"

"Oh, right." She remembered reading about it in the manual; she'd even used it to research The Agency. "It's like the internet with fewer cats."

"Sure. Just like that." He patted her arm obligingly; he didn't have the heart to tell her there were entire religions built around the cats of the IFI.

The corn, though devoid of any real nutrients, was beginning to rouse her.

"You don't eat much, do you?" she said once she'd finished half of the horrible can.

"Me? Relatively not, I suppose, compared to you. I eat mainly to quell the boredom. You don't seem to enjoy it quite as much."

"I've got to eat to survive. More than corn."

His eyes got so large and round May could see the white around his irises. "You're kidding?"

"Unfortunately no."

"May June July, why didn't you tell me? Goddess! Are all humans this bad at communicating? I mean, zuut, Lucy eats all the time in the show, but I figured it was just a sort of social nicety, not something you legitimately had to do." He flung himself over the back of the couch and plugged something into the console. The ship sputtered beneath them but didn't move.

"Parking brake," she called to him over her shoulder.

"Right," he said. The ship sped off but May barely noticed before she drifted back into rich, chocolatey sleep as thick as custard. She dreamt of cigarettes rolled with leafy greens.

This time when she awoke, a small garden's worth of food had appeared on the couch. The air smelled of soil and starchy vegetables. On the other side of the coffee table, Xan sat cross-legged and munched on something from a silvery bag.

"Nutrients!" He stretched his arms out to the sides, gesturing to the bounty. A few crisps flew out of the bag, and he gave them an offended look before snatching them from the carpet to pop in his mouth. "How'd I do? Think you'll live?"

"Depends," May held up something that looked like a malformed carrot—at least it was orange.

It might kill her. There was a high likelihood she would die if she ate the carrot-like vegetable. She thought about that for a second. The carrot might kill her. Then again, there was a one-hundred percent chance she would die if she didn't eat something, and Xan watched her intently, waiting for her to try it.

If she died, it would probably upset him. She didn't want to upset him. She put the carrot between her teeth, bit off a chunk of it, and chewed. Xan leaned in, waiting for a verdict as if he were watching a cooking competition reality show rather than a masticating malnourished mammal.

"Oh," May said.

"What?" Xan rose to his knees.

"Huh," she said.

"What?" Xan leaned heavily on the coffee table between them.

May shrugged. "It tastes like a carrot."

"Because it is a carrot," he confirmed.

She nodded, then laughed. "Yeah. It's a carrot."

"I am aware that it's a carrot," Xan said.

She laughed harder and took another bite. It tasted so good. She hated carrots. This carrot, though...*this* carrot had saved her life, and she loved it. Tears of relief perched on her bottom eyelashes.

"What do I owe you?" she asked just as she used to when Kathy brought her a latte from the coffeehouse across the street.

"Aw, hey, it's just gem." Xan shrugged, tipping his head back and emptying the last crumbs of whatever he'd been eating into his mouth.

"I want to pay you back. For this and the tickets." The banner which read "freeloader" had made a nice little nest in the cockles of her brain where it taunted her regularly. For the time being, the crunch of the carrot drowned it out, but she knew it would be back.

"Really, don't worry about it," he insisted.

May squinted at him. "Alright, what's your angle?"

In May's experience, men weren't inclined to be particularly nice to her unless they wanted something from her. Even when they wanted something from her, they often weren't inclined to be particularly nice. Now, with her faculties once again functioning properly, she began to question his motives.

"Uh," Xan looked down at himself, cross-legged on the floor, "forty-five, maybe fifty?"

Colloquial terminology, it seemed, didn't translate terribly well.

"I mean," May set the carrot down now, "why are you helping me? What do you want?"

"Ah. Ulterior motives. What makes you think I want anything from you?"

"Well, you're a man so—"

"Ah, see, that's where you're wrong! I'm a Tuhntian."

"Sure, but a *male* Tuhntian."

Xan shook his head. "Ehh." He lifted his hands as if weighing his word choice. "Closest human approximate, I suppose. Anyway, what's that got to do with anything?"

"Male humans aren't just nice to women for the sake of being nice."

"Oh, come now, that can't be true!" He cleared a space and sat on the coffee table. "Fred's nice to Lucy. Sometimes. Huh." His smile slowly sank. "Well, the point remains. I'm not a male human."

May had begun to realize that beating around the bush would only get her a bush with a nice little moat surrounding it. "Are you trying to get into my pants?"

"Good goddess, no. Why would I want to be there?"

"Sex." The bush had been beaten. The bush was dead.

"Aw, mun. Look, you're very sweet but I charge quite a lot for that sort of thing. I'm sure we could work out some kind of friends and family discount but honestly, in the past thousand orbits or so, everyone I've met has wanted that. I thought maybe we could, you know," he paused, trying to gauge her reaction, seemingly not wanting to offend her, "not?"

May laughed, sat back a little farther in the couch. "Good to know you're not looking to get a piece of this."

"Of what?"

"The carrot." She finished the vegetable. "Really, though, you must have a reason for keeping me around."

"You honestly don't believe that I just might enjoy the companionship? Fine, then." He looked at her seriously now. "Okay, so humans have a concept of karma right? Is that translating?"

May nodded.

"Right, so karma. You do something good you get something good. Do something unspeakably horrible and unspeakable horrors tend to follow you. Makes sense, right? Balancing the scales of the Universe and whatnot. I've got a bit of scale balancing to do, as it were, so don't you dare go messing with that alright? It's a gift. Not often I get a chance to do something nice for someone else adrift in the vast nothingness of the unfeeling cosmos. So I'm taking the opportunity and you're not going to stop me."

"What unspeakably horrible thing did you do?" May chose another vegetable from the pile that looked and, to her mild surprise, tasted like a beet. "If I'm going to be used as a cosmic bargaining chip, I'd like to know what the stakes are."

Xan's gloved hands covered his face, rubbed it as if to reset the conversation, then landed in his lap again. "It's not important," he said simply.

"It's not important, or you don't want to talk about it?"

"Going to go with both on that one. Definitely both. Don't worry, I didn't, uh...didn't kill anyone. How's the beet?"

"Tastes like misdirection."

"Oh. Uh, that's not what it's supposed to taste like."

"It's good, Xan, the beet tastes good. Thank you."

Xan smiled wildly now, the light returning to his eyes at last. "You're welcome!"

EIGHTEEN

# SOOTHE YOUR VENDETTA

Having regained her strength and experimented with a few less obvious vegetables from the selection Xan had brought her, May was in much better spirits.

There was more tweaking to do to the ship if she wanted to convince Xan to race. The ship seemed to be optimized for evasive maneuvers rather than speed. Long strings of information that loitered in the depths of the ship's computer struck her as odd, words like "confidential" and "restricted access" peppering the ship's backlogs.

"Xan," May spun the hover chair round to face him. "What was the original purpose of this ship?"

He froze, blinked, then rebooted. "Popcorn," he said before bolting down the intershoot.

That, thought May, was not the purpose. She gave up for the time being and flung herself across the couch, accidentally banging her head on a hard bit in the arm. From between the cushions, she yanked out a flattened brocade pillow to cushion her skull.

Her tense, aching muscles began to relax, the wrinkle in her forehead clocked out for the evening, and she felt her consciousness sinking into the couch like a wayward sailor with weights tied to his legs.

Something dropped atop her from above; she gave it a half-hearted groan and peeked at the disturbance. Xan perched awkwardly on her legs, trying to make space for himself while holding aloft a sizable bowl of what May presumed was something like popcorn.

"Popcorn?" Xan offered her the bowl. He finally threaded his legs under hers in a way that was at least moderately comfortable for both parties.

Grabbing a popped kernel, she studied it for a moment. It certainly looked like popcorn. She licked up the small, fluffy piece and chewed it suspiciously. It was dense and sweet until an unexpected punch of unmitigated umami materialized out of nowhere to attack her tongue.

She tried not to make a face. "All yours."

Xan reached the toe of his boot out and pressed the power button on the obscenely old earth TV. The screen exploded to life with an audible pop and something very strange filled the screen.

"What the hell is that?"

He quickly turned a dial on the side of the box that changed the channel until it was nothing but static. "Eh-huh, well, when two beings love each other very much..." he began.

"Alright, I get it."

"I might be able to pick up some signal from Earth out here. It'd be really old, though," he warned.

May laughed, "Oh, no—I've had that all my life. Show me something alien!"

Xan squeezed one eye shut in concentration. "Alright, well, alien to *you*," he specified, "would be some fairly boring sorta stuff. You know, typical game shows, talk shows, experimental fruit based sensory analysis shows. Garbage if you ask me. Now Earth TV—that's art!"

May didn't care about the format of the show, she wanted to see something new. "Please?"

Xan shrugged his shoulders and stretched his leg out again, turning the dial until something came into focus. "Ah, see this... this is what I mean." He shook his head.

May's brow furrowed as her brain tried desperately to

make some kind of sense out of what it was seeing.

"The average fully grown male ch'stranda has three noses, a dubious tail, and a vendetta," said a pleasingly lit white sphere.

The scene cut to a blurry image of something like a pale long-bodied cat chasing its own tail in a purple field.

"Its desire for entertainment is so great," said the voice of the white ball, "it frequently pays vast amounts of money to-" the voice cut out and a red and green flashing screen tried to sear some sort of image into May's retina. She thought she heard distant screaming. "In search of this great fortune. Sooth your vendetta watch"—the same flashing screen and distant scream assaulted May's senses.

She waved her hand in front of her as if waving away what she'd seen. "Okay, you're right this is awful."

With a click of his tongue, Xan shut the TV off and stuffed a handful of popcorn in his mouth. "Would I lie?"

"Maybe," she readjusted herself to face him. "You know not everyone who enters the space races dies, right?"

"Yeugh, not this again. Alright, yes, that's a bit of an exaggeration. But only a bit!"

"I need some way to earn a living. I've been studying the ship and I think we could race her."

"May, I don't know if you've noticed or not but I'm not exactly struggling to pay rent here. It's fine! As long as we've got enough gem to keep you fed there's nothing to worry about." He rested his hands on her shoulders. "Relax!"

May was not relaxing. Without a purpose, without a job, what was she? Just a human lost in space being kept as an alien's pet. Briefly, she wondered if there was a support group for this sort of thing on the IFI. Somehow, she doubted it.

"I don't want to impose on you. If you don't want to race, that's fine. You can just drop me off somewhere and I'll figure myself out." It wouldn't be impossible, she thought, to survive out there. Maybe he was exaggerating about how hard it would be for her to find work as a human, someone was bound to give her a chance if she asked around enough.

He dropped his hands from her shoulders, slumping a little now, with the distinctly deflated look of roadkill.

"If I agreed to race, would you stay?" His jaw moved as if he were physically chewing over the idea. In actuality, he was trying to dislodge a popcorn kernel from between his teeth with his tongue.

"Uh." May suddenly felt like an ungrateful semi-truck. "For a while, if that's what you want."

"And then?"

"I don't know, I haven't really thought about it." She had—a lot. "I could settle somewhere Earth-like and try to make a life for myself. Maybe if the racing works out, I could afford my own ship with my share of the winnings."

"Ugh alright then."

"Alright?"

"Yes, alright. You can race. But," he held her face in his hands now and locked into her line of sight so intensely she felt he could see right through her skull and, for all she knew of him, he might have, "the *Audacity* is my life. She's literally all I have in the universe. If anything happens to her, it better kill me, alright?"

"Um, alright."

"I'm hard to kill, May! So, if you're going to mess up, go big."

"Uhh." He was squishing her cheeks a little now, making it difficult to reply.

"Good." He smiled again, freeing her face and her gaze at the same time. "Have you ever flown a rocket before?"

"You keep forgetting we don't have space travel on Earth. But I studied the manual, and it doesn't look difficult."

He shrugged. "It's not, shockingly."

"How did you learn to fly it?"

"Oh, I've tremendous grace under pressure. And this." Xan fished something on a thin gold chain from his coat.

"What is that?" May asked. It looked like a lump of grey clay with glowing Borax crystals embedded in one side.

"Just your average run-of-the-mill chunk of the first star ever created," he said, an edge of pride in his voice.

May laughed. "Sure. What is it really?"

"I'm serious! Yvonne gave it to me back when we were together, before she left me and joined the military. It's supposed to be a good luck charm. No idea how it works, but it does." He laughed and tucked it away. "Never run out of fuel, always in the right place at the right time, physics-defying TV signal—that sort of thing."

"Yvonne. Not the same Yvonne who abducted me, right? Tell me that's just a common name out here."

He flashed her an apologetic smile. "The very same. I've honestly no idea why she did that to you, though. She was nice back then. Well, I say nice. She was a decent person back then. I say a decent person...you know, let's just settle with she was different when I was with her."

May's lips twisted to the side, unconvinced that she was entirely safe with someone who used to date her abductor and unconvinced that the gently pulsating rock he'd showed her was lucky.

"Different meaning she didn't abduct people, destroy planets, and extract teeth?" May asked, tapping her cheek where the hole in her gum still bothered her.

"Uh, well yes, yes, and no." He smiled widely but not happily and pointed to the space between his first and third upper molars. Or, at least what May thought might be molars. He had quite a few more teeth than the average human—minus one. "She was an exploratory biologist before the war. Old habits," he shrugged.

"She sounds delightful," May joked.

"Huh, yeah. Really top of the line. I mean, she is top of the line she's insanely brilliant. Just uh, not an expert in hospitality. Obviously."

May had to agree. "I'm sorry."

"Why? It's not like you made her do it!" He leaned in conspiratorially, squinting at her. "You didn't make her do it, did you?"

"No, it's just what humans say when we feel bad about something that happened. Even if it's beyond our control."

"Huh. Well then, I'm sorry, too. But enough about Yvonne and her various affronts to decency. If you're going to be a racer, you need to look the part, and rocket racers don't wear shredded white latex suits. They wear whole white latex suits!" He picked a fleck of rotting latex off of her shoulder. "Your suit's a mess."

It was. At this point, it barely covered any part of her. Standing, she picked off what was left of it until she stood in her undergarments. With the shreds of a suit balled in her fist, she walked to the control panel and pressed the red button on the console—or rather, tried to press the red button. Xan pounced on her, throwing her to the carpet.

"Not that one!" he yelled as he rolled off of her. "Zuut! You nearly killed us." He was breathing much faster than he needed to.

It seemed the more time he spent with May, the more he pretended to breathe, like a bad habit he had picked up.

"Relax, Xan, it's the garbage shoot." She stood and pressed the button. The panel under the controls opened and she tossed the remains of her white suit into it. The panel closed and the latex rags puffed out into space.

She tilted her head at Xan who was splayed across the floor. "Please tell me you knew that," she said.

Xan blinked, incredulous. "It's a giant red button. Usually giant red buttons are the ones you don't press until you're ready to die."

May flipped through the manual and showed him an illustration of the button in question with an arrow pointing to it that labeled it "Refuse."

"Oh, hmm."

"What have you been doing with all your trash?" she asked.

"I just throw it into the basement wormhole. It takes it somewhere else; I don't have to think about it anymore."

It is not by coincidence that the US Government has a secret task force based out of Area 51 whose purpose is to collect and study clippings of Day-Glo orange hair which have appeared on Earth at seemingly random intervals and in seemingly random locations for thousands of years.

# NINETEEN
# THE STUFF

May shivered. The suit she'd been wearing up until recently, shredded as it was, had been excellent insulation. Her bra and panties were not. She stood a little closer to the view screen, soaking up its warmth.

"Are you going to be warm enough in that?" Xan asked, watching her shiver beside the screen.

"I didn't realize it was so cold in here."

"Ah, yeah, those standard issue suits really keep the heat in! If you're warm blooded, at least. Are you warm blooded? Oh goddess, I hadn't even thought of that."

May nodded. "Technically."

"Well, let's not have you standing around shivering. Go find something to wear in the basement—I need to order a gallon of latex."

"Do I really have to wear a latex suit to race?" The little white number she'd been stuffed into had left red marks around her thighs and armpits as it chaffed against her. The more it tore away, the more comfortable she'd been the last couple of days.

"Why, don't you want to? I'll get the good stuff, not that flimsy plastic wrap they had you in on the *Peacemaker*."

"Is there a difference?"

"Oh, is there!" His legs folded up beneath him on the hover chair and he used his teeth to rip off a glove so he could count properly on his fingers. "You've got your standard issue trok—thin and cheap, fond of working its way into crevices you didn't know you had. Then there's the mid-grade fibrous latex that forms a wonky sort of weave when it dries. What you want," he pinched part of his suit and pulled it until it snapped back with a satisfying thwok, "is the Fusion Lay-Flex™. Unless, of course, you're an ascetic. In which case you want the scrap blend."

May shook her head. "Definitely not an ascetic. How much does it cost? Before you say anything, I insist on paying you back."

"Ugh, boring. We can discuss terms when we're dead which, seeing as we're entering the space races, shouldn't be too long now. Get something to wear in the meantime. I'm going to hop on the IFI and tele-express order the stuff!"

"The stuff?" May laughed.

"The stuff! Just go," he shooed her away.

The basement wasn't exactly somewhere May wanted to be caught in her underthings. It was dark and cold, and May felt more vulnerable in just her bra and underwear, as if the thin layer of white latex would have been enough to protect her from whatever was lurking in the shadows.

Illuminated by the gentle glow of the intershoot, she could see about three feet in front of her, but she knew the basement was at the widest part of the ship and stretched well past her line of sight. Somewhere there was a light, but she couldn't find it.

She whistled into the blackness. The whistle was returned with a rustling sound as something drifted toward her. The Fidobot, she hoped.

"Hello, um," she addressed whatever had stopped in

front of her. It was just out of her range of sight in the darkness. "Can you find me a shirt?" she asked it.

More rustling as it began its quest. In the meantime, May leaned against the intershoot to absorb as much warmth as she could from the mechanics whirring away inside it. After far too long, a grey t-shirt landed in a pile at her feet. That was strange, she thought. Last time, the Fidobot had handed the pack of cigarettes to her. Perhaps it didn't like her as much as it liked Xan. She didn't blame it.

The shirt smelled musty, but clean. On the front a faded logo proclaimed, "That is, is it not, Yurkunfle."

She shook her head, unsure if the translation chip was having difficulties or if the shirt honestly didn't make sense. Still, it was warm. Slipping it over her head, she thanked the Fidobot and re-entered the intershoot.

"I don't think the Fidobot likes me," she told Xan when she reappeared in the living room. He was at the control panel, bent over his BEAPER and typing something.

"Whatcha mean?"

"Well, it just sort of tossed this at me."

"Oh. Did you whistle?" He turned his gaze on her, eyes wide.

"Yes."

He curled his lips in, shaking his head. "He hates whistling. Degrading." Xan quieted for a moment, his eyes flicking over the words emblazoned across her chest. "Ha! That's hilarious! I can't believe that was down there."

"I don't get it. What's funny about it?"

"Yurkunfle! It's...it's yurkunfle. It's funny, there's nothing to get."

May gave a half-smile. "I'm glad you think so. When will the latex be delivered?"

As she spoke, two jugs of white liquid appeared on the teledisc.

"Oh," she said.

"Perfect timing feature on any orders within eighty light-years of a storage hub. The second you start to wonder where your package is, it's delivered. Useful but spooky."

A slip of paper appeared in the air above the jugs and

drifted down. May caught it. "It says, 'You're spooky' with the 'you' underlined. That's unsettling."

"Eh, the price of convenience is privacy, I suppose."

Another note appeared.

"'The price of convenience is three-hundred-sixty-seven ISC,'" May read.

Xan stood, tossed a few crystals into the air above the jugs of latex, and watched them blip out of existence.

"Well, let's get these into the vat and print you a suit." He hefted a jug in each hand and slung them into the intershoot.

The Medibay rose to meet them. May had been here before to use the shower. The only shower, May had noted, onboard.

Typical Class 20 Racing Rockets are built to house a team of five. Five private quarters with five private beds and five private showers. The *Audacity* was no exception—it had been built with room for five to live comfortably.

So it was odd that, when May had gone to look for these quarters and perhaps claim a room of her own, she hadn't found a single bedroom. Eventually, she figured out that where the bedrooms should have been was directly above the basement wormhole. All those showers—all those comfortable private beds—had been sucked halfway across the universe.

Beyond the Medibay was the wardrobe. The wardrobe was not, as one might imagine, stocked with ready-made clothing, but rather housed a machine that printed whatever was needed out of Fusion Lay-Flex™.

The machine consisted of three parts, each ghastlier than the last. The first part was a large iron vat that siphoned into a thick tube which ran around the second part—a person-sized chamber—and plugged into the third part which looked suspiciously coffin-like with thick metal studs that sealed it closed.

Xan poured the latex into a vat and pulled a

Frankensteinesque lever on its side. The person-sized chamber glowed red, and a monitor sizzled to life beside it. He stared at her expectantly.

"What?" she asked.

"On in," he motioned towards the blood-red chamber as if it were the entrance to the state fair.

May stepped a toe into the capsule, but Xan stopped her.

"Woah, hey there. You don't want that shirt to be permanently bonded to your skin, do you? Because it will be if you wear it in there. Saw it happen once. Still have nightmares about it."

"Ah," May said. She would need to take everything off then. "Could you turn around?" she asked, heat rising to her cheeks.

Xan's eyebrows tipped like poorly balanced scales. "Turn around?"

"Yes. I'd like some privacy."

"Ohhh. Oh. Is that a human thing? That must be a human thing. The Panseen are awful weird about getting naked, too. Alright, tell me when it's safe to lay eyes on you again." He laughed but obliged and turned to face the back wall.

May took off her new shirt, slunk out of her underwear, unhooked her bra, and stepped into the chamber. She let the light envelope her, turning her dark skin bright red. Outside, Xan backed up until he could see the screen but not her and tapped something on it. Nothing happened. Again, he pressed his finger to the screen.

"What the-" He bent closer to the screen. "Oh. Not a touch screen, huh." He pressed a metal button on the edge of the screen instead. The red light of the chamber cut out and an intensely blue light took its place. The machine made a horrific cacophony of bangs, rattles, and murmurs as it drained the vat of latex into the metal coffin beside May.

"Right! That should do it," Xan addressed the vat of latex as May stepped from the chamber. "Go ahead and open the mold." He grabbed something from the darkened back of a shelf on the wall beside the machine and held it out behind himself. "You're going to want to use this before you put it on."

May took the bottle. The packaging was satiny purple and the proclaimed "Personal Lubricant" in hedonistic cursive. It was the first of many times she would begrudge her translation chip. She squeezed the liquid onto her fingers and spread it over her body until she shone like a professional bodybuilder.

With well lubricated fingers, it was difficult to lift the lid of the mold.

"Need help?" Xan heard her struggling with the lid.

"Nope." At last she slipped her fingers under the lid and pushed it up, revealing a shiny holographic suit that shimmered in an array of dancing colors. She peeled it back from the mold and stepped in through the neck which stretched wide to accommodate her before snapping back in place. It felt like faux silk, but somehow better. Was this what real silk felt like? She couldn't say for sure, but it was likely.

"I'm decent," she informed Xan who was impatiently playing with settings on the machine.

"Didn't need as much latex as I figured," he said happily, shutting down the machine. "Oh yeah, look at you!" He gestured broadly to her. "Right. Now, that's a suit you can race in."

May found her own arm difficult to look at now as the holographic shimmer of her suit played wild tricks on her eyes.

"Yes, but is it shiny enough?" May asked, watching the suit as it picked up and multiplied light waves with rabbit-like gusto.

Xan grinned. "Oh, it could always be shinier. That's for another day, though. Now, hair."

"Hair?" May ran her fingers through her kinky brown locks. Or, rather, May stuck her fingers into her kinky brown locks and got them hopelessly entangled there for a moment. "Just give me a wide-tooth comb and five hours."

Xan dove into a darkened shelf on the wall. May heard him pushing around various bottles of what she hoped was not lube until he crawled back out, brandishing a box of hair dye.

"Purple?" He shook the box encouragingly.

"Oh, no, that's not necessary."

"Well, sure it isn't necessary, but neither is eating and you do a zuxing lot of—hold on. Hold on. Can humans even see color? Zuut! I never thought about that. I bet this is just dark grey to you. Oh, mun, that's so sad."

May grinned at him. "Absolutely no clue what purple is. Color? Is that a weird alien food or something?"

His comically shocked face relaxed. "Joking, aren't you?"

She nodded. "Purple hair it is. Let me comb it out, first. This is going to take a while so we might as well end this chapter."

"Agreed."

# TWENTY

# SEXUAL VENOM

The New Earth was a thing of beauty. Pride grew in Listay's chest as juicy and sweet as a llerke as she watched from her Control Tower. If she weren't dehydrated from neglecting to take care of herself for the past half season, she would've shed a tear of joy.

Perfect city planning was not hard, thought Listay. It was really a shame that humans had it so backwards. Roads don't need to curve. Roads that curve are useless. Why would anyone, thought Listay, build a curving road when a straight one fit around square buildings so neatly?

Listay was lost in her pondering of the shear frivolity she'd seen when first studying Earth. Fruit scented lip-tints, especially, vexed her. Why not simply moisturize your lips and then eat a fruit? Humans, she had found, required a lot of nutrients, and it made little sense to simulate the smell of food when they needed to consume it anyway.

It was unimportant, Listay admonished herself. The fruit-scented lip-tint had been incinerated and, as far as she was aware, not a tube of it existed anywhere on Earth.

One of the benefits of being overlord of a perfect society was that there was no need of her. Her BEAPER never hailed her with emergencies because all eventualities were accounted for. The system she'd invented was infallible. Once every rotation, a single Rhean soldier reported to her.

If any questions her manuals didn't answer arose (unlikely), she would be told. If dissent brewed amongst her officers (unheard of), she would be told. If anyone had a complaint to file (unseemly), she would be told. The reports were short.

Her life was nearly perfect. Nearly. There were but two things she longed for that her efficiency wouldn't bring to her no matter how she wished it would: Yvonne, and a proper, fresh llerke from a real farm, not the replicated llerkes the *Peacemaker* provided.

For just a moment, she allowed herself to daydream of a cool but sunny planet, her armor swapped for gloves, knee pads, and a straw hat, Yvonne sipping llerke juice on the porch in a soft floral dress that miraculously didn't clash with her silvery hair; a mass of beautifully unpredictable llerke vines and branches clustered in uneven rows as far as she could see.

There was something peaceful about the chaos of nature, something so opposed to filing and sorting that it completely shut down that part of her overworked brain and actually allowed her to relax.

And that was Yvonne, too. Listay sensed the wilderness inside her, and it was tantalizing.

"Report, ma'am."

A thick Rhean soldier stood at rapt attention in her doorway, awaiting permission to continue speaking. "Go on, Wali," she said, ready for the usual "Nothing to report, ma'am."

"There's a message for you from the *Peacemaker*."

Her heartbeat fluttered up to a disagreeable fifty-seven beats per beoop. She tapped her BEAPER, which then emanated Yvonne's striking visage.

"Thank you, Wali. Have a nice day." Listay waved him away.

Wali scampered dramatically out of her office. The soldiers were deathly afraid of her, though she'd never given them reason to be. On the contrary, she felt she'd always been rather pleasant to them. It was puzzling, but she had a hunch that Yvonne was propagating the terror.

Chaos arranged Yvonne's face into something neutral, emotionless.

Listay had done her job well. Too well. It was sickening. No one could suck all the fun out of an alien invasion like Listay. Patience, though, was key. The longer the facade of order was allowed to permeate the populace, the more desperate for the freedom of chaos they would become.

"General," Yvonne barked. "I would prefer to have a direct line of contact to you. I've been waiting all day to talk to you."

"Yes." If Listay had had the water to spare, she would have begun sweating at that. "Of course, Mistress Yvonne. Must have been a glitch in the system."

Yvonne hummed. "Mmmm, keep lying to me," she said with deliciously sexual venom.

Listay swallowed nothing.

"I'm becoming restless," Yvonne sighed at her. "Tell me, are there any roguish bands of dissenting humans? Any growing rebellious organizations I might endeavor to squash?"

It was Yvonne's turn to lie. Rebellious organizations were exactly what she hoped for. She would let the humans do the work of collecting a congregation for her, banding together in secret to oppose the strict rule of order and committing little acts of chaos in desperate attempts at having some control in their lives. Then, like an ocean in the middle of the desert, Yvonne would pour herself out to her ready-made followers to be worshiped once again as the goddess she was.

"Not that I'm aware of, ma'am. I will do a more thorough

report on all disobedience and look for patterns of rebellion. Shall I have suspects executed?"

Zuut, thought Chaos. Perhaps the humans weren't quite as resilient as she had hoped. She combed through Yvonne's ravaged memories once more, looking for anything that might be of use to her. Ah, of course. A little luck on her side might just tip the scales in her favor.

Chaos teased her host body's simmering consciousness with the idea. Her chest constricted, her body shook, Yvonne still refused to give up. She'd lost IX, protecting Xan was her last hold-out.

A weak chant of "don't you zuxing dare" tried to drown Chaos' thoughts until she relented and turned her attention back to Listay.

Chaos made Yvonne's mouth pout. "If you kill them, where's the fun for me? Send me names, and I'll deal with them personally."

By "deal with them," Yvonne meant, "appear in their dreams as a heavenly messenger of glorious chaotic freedom and feast on their adoration." Naturally.

"Yes, ma'am, of course." Listay said briskly. Then, less briskly and perhaps as a result of the creeping delirium lack of sleep, food, and water had gifted her, she asked, "Is there anything else I can help you with?"

Yvonne smiled at her coyly. "Come tend your garden."

## TWENTY-ONE
# A TERRIBLE, FIERY CRASH

"Enough with the hair," May said at last. Her previously dark, thick curls were now purple. Very, very purple. She wasn't sure exactly how he'd done it, but her hair was now also free of tangles and shaped with the skill of a seasoned topiarist. Alien technology, she was sure, had played some kind of role in the transformation, along with absolutely outstanding patience, tenacity, and finger dexterity on Xan's part.

Hair was rather serious business to him.

"Quite right." He gave her hair a final comb through and vaulted over the back of the couch to sit beside her, smiling an accomplished smile which morphed into something of a grimace. "I suppose you'll be wanting to actually fly the ship now."

She shrugged. "You could race her."

"Ha! Hilarious. Really and truly very funny."

"Do you know how to fly her off of autopilot?"

"Well, sure! Haven't I told you about how I came to own the *Audacity*?"

May sat up a little now, turning to him with the interest of a cat who heard a can opener. "No, how?"

"Well, it's quite a story. Picture it: Trilly on Tuhnt, 7200 —it's the thick of the War of Reversed Polarization."

"I have no idea what you just said and can't picture any of that," May informed him.

He seemed to snap out of it. What *it* was, exactly, May couldn't put her finger on, but for a moment he was in it and now he was out of it.

"Right. Well, what I mean to say is that yes, I have actually flown the *Audacity* on manual before. But I don't like to make a habit out of it."

"Wait, go back. Tuhnt? Is that where you're from? Can we visit?"

"Yes, and why not?" He knew why not. He changed the subject. "Let's get this over with. I'll show you how the autopilot works, first." He rolled over the arm of the couch and climbed into the co-pilot's chair which hovered by the control panel.

May stood now, making a mental note to never interrupt an anecdote of his again, and rolled into the pilot's chair. Not allowing a moment to think about what she was about to do, she kicked off the parking brake and pushed The Button that Typically Made The Ship Go.

Nothing happened.

Something should have happened.

She surveyed the dials on the control panel, one in particular catching her attention. It glowed red and flashed in silent desperation. "We're out of fuel."

"Ah, yeah that happens. Better make some coffee."

"No, thanks."

"Oh, not for you. Sorry, that was unclear. It's for the ship." He hopped over to the simple coffee machine which was nested into the wall.

"Coffee?"

"Yep," Xan fiddled with the machine. "Cheaper than rocket fuel, at least. A *lot* cheaper."

"That's not possible. You know that isn't possible. Rockets take hundreds of thousands of gallons of fuel." May watched in horror as a tar-like sludge crawled from the nozzle and into the carafe.

Xan scooped up the carafe and took a swig of the

steaming, thick liquid, running his tongue over his teeth to clean them.

"Luck charm." He patted the bump under his coat. "*Audy's* run on nothing but coffee as long as I've had her! Don't think about it too much." He twisted a cap off the control panel and began pouring the sludge into the ship.

"Fair, but have you considered," May said, watching him dubiously, "that she might run better on rocket fuel?"

Xan nodded. "I don't doubt it. But have *you* considered that it would cost an Anat's con to fill the tank? It's really best that you just accept the incredibly dodgy science behind it and move on. Besides, she likes it!"

The background hum of the *Audacity's* engines vibrated louder as the coffee hit the tank in the base of the ship, purring like an eighty-ton house cat in a field of catnip. The fuel dial calmed down, fading into an uneasy orange-yellow. Fully fueled, the light would be a brilliant green, but Xan had only ever seen it that color once and he hadn't, at the time, had the capacity to appreciate it.

"That should get us a few good practice runs," Xan said, sliding the carafe back under the nozzle. He watched May with renewed energy now, the caffeine having returned the wild glint to his eyes.

May swallowed.

She put her finger on The Button Which Typically Made The Ship Go.

She did not make the ship go.

Even on autopilot, May thought, with the tweaks she'd made to the rocket, hitting an asteroid or particularly large bit of space junk would crush them like an aluminum can under a car tire.

Xan, tired of holding his head up to watch her expectantly, rested his chin on the control panel, and looked between her and the button on which her finger perched. "Oh, go on." Using his nose, he pressed her finger down on the button, and the ship flung itself into the pin-pricked blackness.

The stars only blurred for a second until the ship was moving too fast for them to see even starlight. Autopilot shouldn't have done that. May cut off the engine and reversed the thrusters to bring them to a stop; this she accomplished with a second press of The Button Which Typically Made The Ship Go which also typically made it stop.

"Woah," May breathed, her eyes still glued to the screen. "That was really fast."

Xan glared at the view screen. "Too fast if you ask me. She's never done that in autopilot. Either that coffee was stronger than I thought or..." Xan flashed her a terrified look. "Goddess, May, you didn't. Tell me you didn't do it."

May shrugged. "Didn't what?"

She knew.

And she had.

"Don't make me say it. Don't do the thing and then make me say it."

"I did lots of things," she said coyly.

"Oh, my goddess. You did, didn't you?" His long, gloved fingers pried off a panel of plastic trim just under the console and scooped out a bundle of cut wires. "By the thumbs of O'Zeno, you're a madwoman."

"It was one of the recommended modifications!" she defended herself.

"Sure, if we were running an illegial hinterplanet race with a death wish!"

"We're guaranteed to win without it."

"May! Without the Collision Cushion, we're *guaranteed* to perish in a terrible, fiery crash. Besides, it's illegal to race without the Collision Cushion installed. Careers have been ruined over it. Mostly because the pilots perish in terrible fiery crashes but occasionally, they survive long enough to be punished severely first."

"That bad?" May rested her head in her hand and her elbow on the control panel.

Xan blinked meaningfully. "Yes, that bad. No one's ever gotten away with it."

"But if they had, you wouldn't know."

His mouth opened and closed for a second as retorts formed and dissolved in his brain. "Well, sure, but still. Still. No way. Fix it, or I'll...I'll take back the nice things I said about your hair."

"You wouldn't dare," she teased, coaxing Osy out from behind her neck.

"Oh, but I would!"

May slipped the Collision Cushion circuit out of her suit pocket and handed the thin silver square to the Osculum which took it, but not without what could be regarded as a sassy sort of eyebrow-raised look. The creature drifted into the open control panel and, with an odd proficiency for a sponge, re-connected the chip and twisted the raw wires back where they belonged.

When the sponge was finished, it floated lazily back beneath May's hair, and Xan popped the trim panel back into place. "Alright, now try it," he said.

This time, when May pressed The Button Which Typically Made The Ship Go, the stars streaked by at a more reasonable speed. Which was still, of course, unutterably fast.

This time, when she stopped the ship, it was more out of boredom than terror.

This time, Xan rewarded her with a half-hearted and poorly performed sort of thumbs up-smile combo.

"Great, so you can push a button. Good to know. Unfortunately, autopilot isn't really encouraged in racing. Would be a rather boring time if it was, I imagine. Switch her over to manual, and oh...goddess, I'm going to regret this, but we've got to find some obstacles to work around."

"Like an asteroid field?"

"Like an asteroid field," he confirmed begrudgingly, pulling up a navigation inset on the view screen. "Specifically, like this asteroid field."

He pressed his finger into a patch of irregularly shaped dots on the screen which, when pressed, sent the ship's autopilot a string of complex coordinates that Xan only understood in the way that a lab rat understands that pressing a lever deposits a pellet of Purina rat chow. The autopilot took them there, streaking past stars until it reached the agreed upon destination: smack in the middle of a plume of asteroids.

It was a miracle, or perhaps just a bit of good luck, that they hadn't hit one.

The ship held steady, and May watched as the slowly drifting hunks of rock and metal danced around them. There was no clear and obvious path through.

May sighed, remembering that Xan had made her promise to, if she could not avoid damaging the ship, kill him extremely dead. While she felt that he was perhaps being a little overdramatic, she had to respect that this was *his* ship. She tried to psych herself up for the possibility of screwing up really, really badly.

"You're going to want this." Xan fished the good luck charm from under his coat and handed it to her. She studied the gently pulsating glow of the crystals for a moment before taking it and pulling the gold chain over her head. May didn't necessarily believe in good luck, but she also believed that not believing in good luck would mean she had bad luck, so she did her best.

There are certain things science can't explain about the Universe, and every time science *tries* to explain these things, they spitefully cease to be. The concept of luck is one such thing. Another is that strange noise that every car over a certain age makes but never while anyone other than the owner is driving it.

"Just try not to scratch her, please," Xan said as May tucked the star under her suit. "This particular shade of orange paint was outlawed ages ago for causing spontaneous photic retinopathy and the only can of it I've ever seen for sale cost more than this ship is worth."

"I'll do my best," May said as she consulted the manual, flicking a series of recommended switches, turning a series of recommended knobs, pressing a series of recommended buttons, and praying a series of recommended prayers. "Time me?"

She glanced at him. He did nothing.

"Are you going to time me or...?"

"Oh! You mean now? Time you starting now?" He fiddled with his BEAPER. "Okay."

"Did you start the timer?"

"You told me to!"

"No, when..." She sighed. "When I go. Start the timer when I start the ship."

"But you said-"

"Yep, I know what I said. Just...restart the timer and when you're ready to start it say 'go,' okay?"

"Alright. Go!"

She did.

## TWENTY-TWO
# RUDE MOONS

1613 Centauri VII is not the kind of planet people plan to settle down on. The only draw of the single settlement on VII is its proximity to several of the finest landfills in the galaxy. It is because of this proximity to decent landfills that August decided to stay on 1613 Centauri VII indefinitely.

Mostly retired junkers and their partners lived there, but occasionally active junkers or tourists would pass through. Some of them would stay for an orbit or two. If they stayed any longer, they ended up staying for good. Not because the settlement was nice, mind you, but because it was a cesspool for the particular strain of laziness that killed wanderlust.

Seven, as the locals called it, was a horribly plain planet. Where there wasn't thin, wispy blue grass there were thin, wispy blue trees. Where there wasn't either of those there were buildings cobbled together with scraps of metal and plastics that junkers had brought to the planet over the years. The sun was smallish and hot; to August it seemed like a never-ending summer.

There were three moons, but August didn't care for any

of them. They all had suspicious grimaces as if they were upset that their little blue planet had been colonized by strangers and trash. The moons judged him, but the people were friendly, all too busy to stay for long and cause trouble or too old and worn out to care about causing trouble. There was a small brigade of Peacekeepers, but they had grown lax from lack of action.

Now, August kept track of the passage of time on a wall in the Robert. The days here seemed a little short, so he figured he was a bit behind Earth time. He had given up on Estrichi time long ago. As far as he could tell, he had been on Seven for six Earth years or about 2,190 shaves of his beard, which was growing much faster on this planet. It had to be a space thing, August thought.

It was a long time to stay anywhere for him. His mother had been in the military, and after the age of thirteen he'd been pin-ponged across the world. In fact, Seven had started to feel more like home to him than any place he'd ever lived. He was reminded of something the alien woman had said years ago: "You adjust."

The alien woman had been on his mind a lot recently. He wondered if she had found what she sought; he wondered if he had. One early morning in the fourth month of his sixth year on 1613 Centauri VII, by his reckoning, August awoke with a word etched in his mind.

"IX?" he said. What was an IX? And why couldn't he stop replaying it in his head like a catchy song? It had to mean something to him.

He tried to push it to the back of his mind and went about his day. He had heard that there was a delightful young traveling barber in town and he desperately needed a trim. His blond hair had grown wild and was streaked with white where there used to be brown. He was pretty sure he was only about thirty-five now, but life as a junker was stressful.

August walked through the market. Every day there were more unusual faces and wares. He had seen the strangest and most beautiful the galaxy had to offer, and in his early days, he had tried to seduce them all.

He became less and less picky as time wore on, then he

became less and less interested. Eventually, he quit trying all together. He hadn't looked another being in the eyes and felt a sense of familiarity in a long time. It should have bothered him, but it didn't anymore. He was content just to be. To take the shuttle to nearby planets and pick out some shiny things to sell or barter with and come home to rest in the *Robert*.

Today, though, something very unusual happened: he met another human.

"Hey there, handsome," a smooth, deep voice called to him and it shot through like a dart to a dartboard. They were speaking German. He hadn't heard real, true, proper German in over a decade.

Via his translation chip, he could understand most any language as long as the words had some sort of German counterpart. But he could tell from the accent, the smoothness, the ease with which he heard it. Someone had spoken German to him. Beautiful, sweet, silky German. While there was nothing about the language that was *actually* silky, to August it sounded like whipped cream.

He spun and saw a slight, androgynous person leaning on an empty counter. They slinked up to him. "Do you remember apples?" the person whispered, just loud enough for him to hear.

August nodded enthusiastically. "Yeah, of course!" When he was very young, he had lived on his grandfather's apple farm in Potsdam. Nothing could stroke the sleeping cat of nostalgia more than an apple.

The person reached into their pocket and produced a gorgeous, gleaming red delicious. August's mouth watered in a way he had forgotten it could. "What have you got to trade for it?"

"Anything." August nearly grabbed it with his teeth and ran off, he was so taken with lust.

"Anything at all?" They whispered in his ear.

"Uh-huh, whatever you want, take it."

"The contract is seal-" they were cut short by a plasma beam between the eyes. It didn't seem to bother them much.

"You zuxing trok! Can't ya' see I was making a deal here?"

August didn't know what language the person was speaking now, but they had switched out of the silky German.

"No. You were taking advantage of a human. Away with you." He heard an oddly familiar voice behind him, the attractive German and the even more attractive apple dissolved into a yellow toadish-snake and slithered away.

August was very, very confused.

"Apple?" he said forlornly, his brain trying to catch up with what had just happened. He swallowed. He wouldn't be needing all that lubricant.

A tall, periwinkle-skinned Rhean touched his shoulder. "August, that was an Anat. There is no apple."

The moment she touched him he put two and two together. "IX! IX! It's you!" He was even more excited to see her than he had been about the apple. He wrapped his arms around her in the first hug he'd given in months and, oddly, the first hug he'd ever given her.

IX was a little taken aback, mostly that he now knew her name.

"I've missed you so much, where have you been? Why did you leave? What happened to you?"

IX laughed lightly. "I was on a fool's errand. Come, I will fix your hair and tell you all about it."

"My hair?" he asked.

"I have been cutting hair for a living the past few years. I find it to be an enjoyable medium of creative expression," she said.

"Uh..." August tried to think of a delicate way to ask how exactly she cut hair. Fortunately, IX was ready with an explanation.

"I don't need to see your hair to know it has grown past your shoulder blades," she said. "My sense of touch works perfectly well."

"By all means, then. To the *Robert*!" he said.

Back on board the *Robert*, IX sat him down at his table—
*their* table again—and set to work. "August, I have not
been transparent with you." She pulled at a knot at the
nape of his neck; she could feel she had her work cut out
for her.

"Shoot." He kicked his feet up on the table in a way that
he thought looked cool yet interested. In actuality, it just
made IX have to bend over even more.

"Seven Earth Years ago I received a psychic message
from Yvonne-"

"Hold on, seven? Oh man, I was off by a whole year!" he
interrupted her.

"Yes, seven. It seemed Yvonne was ready to-"

"Wait, sorry, psychic? So, like, in your head?" he
interrupted yet again.

IX breathed deeply and tried not to rip the tangle from
his hair. "Yes, August. I got a message from Yvonne. She
and I—or, rather, a younger version of myself-"

"Huh?"

"August, we lost twenty Earth years in that wormhole,"
she explained. "Right now, a younger you is still on Earth
doing whatever it is humans do with their time."

"I see."

"It seemed like it would be the perfect opportunity to
help Yvonne," she said, whipping out a pair of shears to
do away with the knot entirely.

"Help her with what?" August could sense he was
starting to annoy her, but he really, honestly wanted to
know what she had been doing and he was getting
hopelessly lost. He felt a good chunk of hair disappear
and worried he had asked too many questions.

"I'll start at the beginning. Close your eyes."

He obeyed. Her pale purple fingers caressed his
temples, and he saw images behind his eyes as clear as
watching a film. She began combing through his hair as
the image cleared and he saw her, minus her crisp blue
military suit. Minus anything but some oddly shaped and
colorful foliage, actually.

"Woah, are you sure you want me to see this?" he

checked.

"You are familiar with Rhean anatomy by now, August," she replied.

He nodded. He was.

In the vision, IX was lying in a field of soft grass beside another Rhean. IX herself had clear grey irises rather than the milky white he'd always known her with. It all looked a little staged.

"It is staged in a way, August. These are my memories. Even a Rhean's memory, though detailed, can be imperfect."

Ah, she could hear his thoughts. Wait—was this an all the time thing?

"Yes," she said.

Oh, he thought, that explained a few things. Can all Rheans hear thoughts? he wondered.

"No, it is not easy. Now hush. A long time ago, Yvonne and I were in love. We met at a rebel bar at the start of the War of Reversed Polarization between Rhea and Tuhnt. She was talking about inventing a super anti-weapon that could scramble the circuits in a standard commission plasma zapper from four light-years away. I told her I could make one that could do it from twenty."

The scene changed to show a bar, a heady smoke in the air, Yvonne chatting with a gaggle of intent listeners, IX interrupting. They were all clothed this time, August noted a little sadly.

"Yvonne had just ended a relationship with a Tuhntian. Usually there are stages to grief, but Yvonne never seemed to move on past anger at 'that Poslouian-slug-grass-eating-coward' as she eloquently described him. She still loved him, though. I remember how she would scroll through endless lists of Tuhntian casualties during the worst of the war. She told me she was hoping to see his name. She was lying."

Again, the scene changed. Now the pair were in a dingy laboratory slaving over machines. He swore he could smell the molten metal and heavy chemicals in the air as he watched the memory of them working together.

"We saw a great deal of success, but our greatest

success was Yvonne's undoing. We commandeered the *Peacemaker*, the largest ship in the Tuhntian arsenal. It was unique in that it was powered by a star drive."

He watched as Yvonne took to the bridge of the ship, IX standing proudly beside her. Then, suddenly, the memory of Yvonne got an unmentionably strange look in her eyes. He heard her voice, echoed and distorted by time as if it had been recorded on vinyl and was being played back decades later.

"We can end this now," Yvonne said. The memory of IX's face contorted.

"How?" IX's voice came from behind him as she re-lived the memory.

The memory of Yvonne smiled cruelly, and she placed her palm on the control panel of the *Peacemaker*. A beam of light washed out the memory, turning everything white, then fading into black. August opened his eyes. IX had stopped working on his hair.

He spun around to look at the Rhean. "What happened?"

Silver streaked IX's face, but her voice was steady. "I do not remember, but I suspect that Yvonne destroyed Tuhnt and everyone on it. She committed genocide."

August was too invested now to care about his half-trimmed hair. "But Yvonne wanted to save both planets! I thought you wanted peace."

"My Yve did want peace. I spent years studying her, trying to figure out why she had changed, what had happened. The only conclusion I could come to was that something on board the *Peacemaker* had driven her insane. There was something evil in the star that the engineers siphoned into the Stardrive."

She began to comb his hair again, almost absently. He turned around to allow her to finish.

"Seven Earth years ago, I left because I thought I had finally figured out how to help her. All I needed to do was find her. But, alas, I searched the universe to no avail. We traveled so much back then. Or, I suppose, back now. The only other option I foresee is to meet her at Earth exactly when we left. The date is still stuck on the *Robert*'s dashboard, correct?"

"Can't make it budge!" he said happily.

"Excellent. Now all we can do is wait," she said, carefully trimming his beard.

"Hold on, how did you find me if you couldn't find Yvonne?"

"You stayed right where I left you, August. It was not difficult."

"Oh, right. Where's the ship you bought?"

"I sold it when I saw the *Robert*."

"You sold a nearly new ship because we have this piece of junk?"

"It is cozier here," she said. August had to agree.

## TWENTY-THREE
# SKEDADDLING

"How many more times do we have to plough through this asteroid field before you're reasonably convinced that you're a competent pilot?" Xan spun impatiently in the hover chair. The first run had left him terrified, the second catatonic, the fifteenth run had left him passingly anxious, but by the twenty-first he was bored.

"You're right. It's time to find a different asteroid field. I think I've memorized this one."

"Or we just find the nearest race and go for it! Our fate is inevitable, no sense keeping it waiting."

"And what fate is that? Death?"

"Well, yeah. Why keep Death waiting around, right? I'm sure She's a busy Lady." He started another pot of the sludge he called coffee.

"Xan, are you depressed?"

"What?" He tapped the coffee maker impatiently.

"Are you depressed?" May repeated.

The coffee creeped from the spout. "No idea what you're saying, mun." He tapped his temple. "Translation chip must be wonky. Coffee?"

"No, I mean-"

"Not a coffee drinker, are you?" He tipped the pot into his mouth and chugged all twelve cups of the heinously thick black liquid.

"Not really," May lied. She loved coffee, but that did not look like coffee. The harsh twang of chemicals meant it didn't smell like it, either.

Xan licked the black film of coffee from his teeth and grinned at her. "Onward towards certain doom!"

Certain doomed looked a lot like Detroit. The nearest races, according to the IFI, were held on the Planet That the Sanitation Department Forgot—Platamousse Annex.

Warning signs littered the parking bay, drowning in piles of garbage. Some signs were so overcome with trash that only the top line of their message was visible, like an upturned mouth gasping for air above the surf. "DANGER," they wheezed.

The less encumbered signs spoke to the risks of breathing the air there for longer than five minutes. Newer signs, their posts only partially drowned in refuse, guaranteed death at two minutes. Still newer neon signs proclaimed, "Do not exit your vehicles under any circumstances. Disobedience will result in instant death."

"This planet seems nice. Why didn't you take me here first?" May asked as she set the *Audacity* down on the starting platform with surprising grace.

"Oh well, once you've been to Platamousse Annex you've seen it all. I was trying to save the best for last." Xan laughed nervously. "And by the looks of it, this place will definitely be the last."

The view of outside flickered off, replaced by the face of an android whose skin shone like liquid mercury. It was difficult to pin a gender to their face which was heavily sculpted and square around the jaw with delicate eyes and plump metal cheeks and lips. The android's voice, even, could not be said to be masculine nor feminine— only sharp and unfriendly.

"Entrance fee is five hundred crystals," they said. A sneer tweaked the thick metal lips. "Teledisc coordinates G:73,38,70. ICS only. I-owe-yous will result in immediate incineration."

May bit her lip and glanced at Xan. His palm was full of crystals which he carefully counted out. He handed her two small, clear shards.

"Is this five hundred crystals?" May asked.

Xan snorted. "No, mun. That's what's left. It's ten." He wrapped his fingers around the pile of crystals in his hand. "Didn't realize dying would be quite so expensive, but hey, you can't take it with you." He shrugged and tossed the crystals onto the teledisc where they sizzled away.

The screen cleared and May could see around them again. Beside them six very new, very shiny rocket ships stood like a firing line. Though May was amongst their ranks, she felt that she was in the crosshairs.

"How old is the *Audacity*?" May asked quietly.

Xan winked an eye in concentration as he did the math. "Must be about two thousand."

"Two thousand what?"

"Orbits."

"Isn't that like a year?" May had been trying to learn Estrichi time, but the conversions were imperfect.

Xan shrugged. "Sure, if you like."

Two thousand years. She was competing in a two-thousand-year-old rocket ship. "We're screwed, aren't we?" she whispered.

"You say that as if you're just realizing this. I have literally been telling you that we are going to die for the past couple of rotations."

"I thought you were being dramatic."

"May. *May*, look at me." He swiped his hands out to the sides for effect. "Do I look the type to overdramatize my estimations of catastrophe?"

May squinted at him. "Yes."

"Well, perhaps you misjudged me."

"Perhaps," May agreed outwardly.

It was too late. The *Audacity* shook as clamps cinched it

to the spot. She'd read on the IFI that, in cheaper races, clamps were used rather than digital sensors to ensure pilots wouldn't take off early. The clamps would not open again until the race began.

"Welcome participants, I am your infallible Overseer," the metal face said from the screen. The sneer had been replaced with something slightly more pleasant. "Today's race is sponsored by Pluff's Buffing. 'If Pluff Can't Buff It, It Can't Be Buffed.' First prize is two thousand gem, everyone else can zux off. Feel free to hurl yourselves at obstacles but please do avoid running into the cameras; I grow weary of ordering replacements. The race begins at my whistle and ends when the final rocket clears the towers of Platamousse Proper."

May prepared to press the button that typically made the ship go and hoped that this time it would.

A tea-kettle of a whistle sounded from the android and six shiny new rockets sped from the platform. A lifetime passed in the span of a nanosecond as May jammed her finger into the button. The ship strained and shook as if some ghastly giant had looped a finger in one of its fin vents. The finger released, and May at last felt the force push her back into the hover chair as she chased after her disappearing competition.

Half of her brain shouted at her that she was at a disadvantage, that the clamps hadn't fully unhinged and that she deserved a re-do. The other half of her brain was busy keeping the rest of her alive.

The competitor's rockets fell away. It took May a quarter of a second too long to figure out why. Something skidded off the hull of the *Audacity* and—as she spun the ship sharply away—she watched a horde of comets plunge themselves into the nothingness above her.

Watching the comets was a terrible mistake. A sound only a foley artist could appreciate reverberated through the *Audacity* as May scraped the hull of a massive, decommissioned starship. She pulled away from it, allowing herself an ill-chosen ninth of a second to stare at the ghost ship.

In that ninth of a second, three infant star-whales

blessed the rocket with curious nibbles.

Once she was out of their reach, May looked at Xan. He seemed curiously relaxed, as if he were considering funerary floral arrangements and important details for his eulogy.

Looking at Xan was, naturally, another terrible mistake. The upper fin of the *Audacity* caught on what appeared to be an enormous plaster donut with pink frosting and sprinkles. The ship ricocheted away from it.

It took May exactly one sixth of a second to re-stabalize the ship and a further tenth of a second to figure out where she was in relation to the finish line. Shockingly close. Maybe, just maybe, the luck charm had done its job after all.

She flung the rocket through the towers of Platamousse Proper and pulled the *Audacity* in beside six shiny new rockets.

"By the thumbs of O'Zeno! We made it!" Xan vaulted into her, lifting her off the hover chair and into a spine-snapping hug.

"Xan, we lost. We lost horribly," May gasped, pushing him away to little effect.

"Sure, but we're alive and we've got ten crystals to celebrate on! Let's get down to the planet, wave to our adoring fans, then peruse the bars. Platamousse Annex is a trok-hole, but I've heard many a story about the wild before, during, and after-parties on Platamousse Proper. Since there's always a race, there's always at least one of each type of party in progress!"

A sudden hush thickened the air when they arrived on the planet. Echos of the jubilee that had preceded them still reverberated around the massive viewing arena.

The surface was lushly greened with, May found upon closer inspection, plastic flora. From a distance it all looked very Earth-like, down to the bright and fluffily clouded sky, though it was a bit too green for May's comfort. She was surrounded by verdant fields on which rows of multi-colored rockets were parked like glistening flowers, and massive floral archways that stretched so far into the sky they became masses of blurred colors at their peak.

"Right so, no adoring fans."

Someone in the stands weaponized a drink cup in their direction, cueing a chorus of untranslatable curses and translatable, but inappropriate, name calling.

Xan flinched, but the cup landed a good five feet away. "Okay, well, skedaddling." He reached for May's hand and pulled her in the direction of the bleachers, straight for an opening beneath them.

When the crowd began chucking offerings of half-eaten food at them, they broke into a run.

The main lobby was vast, and they disappeared into the sea of beings like two grains of particularly uninteresting sand. The tall walls of the lobby were black-green marble, fitted with golden gilt doorways and decor. Green statues of creatures May could only hope were mythical inhabited alcoves along the walls. May ushered Xan into one of them, affording them a bit of privacy from the masses.

"What was that about?" She brushed a dusting of crumbs from her purpled hair.

Xan shrugged, wiping something pink from his shoulder. "Oh, several things, likely. Probably blinded a few people with the *Audacity*. Lost terribly. You're a human. I'm a...well, let's just say there are some people who'd very much rather I weren't alive. Come to think of it," he looked at her as if his entire life where flashing before his eyes and she wished for a moment she could see it too because he sure as hell wasn't sharing, "probably shouldn't have done that."

"It's too late, now. And we're out five hundred crystals." May rested her forehead against the dew-claw of something horrible. The marble felt nice on her hot face as she tried to think of a solution.

Xan leaned against the pedestal, taste-testing the various sauces that dotted his suit.

"Mm, this one's good." He offered her a finger coated in

red. She opened a single eye to survey him warily. He nudged his finger closer.

"I'll pass," she said, closing her eyes again and sighing into the marble creature.

There was one way to make back their money. She was fairly certain it would work, too. It relied on a bit of luck but that wasn't in short supply if Xan was to be believed. It sure felt like it was. Then again, they hadn't died.

Maybe that was the best the charm could do in such an outlandish situation.

"Okay," she turned around, resting the back of her head against the statue now. "I think I know which rocket is going to lose the next race. Is there a gambling scene here?"

"Ohoho, *is* there?" Xan said with great bravado as he finished wicking away the detritus of their misdoing. He said nothing further.

May blinked at him. "Is there?"

"Yes. Yeah, there is. Follow me."

"So, Oh Omnipotent One, how do you know who's going to lose? Don't tell me you neglected to mention that you're a time traveler, because that would be extremely impolite of you."

"Not a time traveler. The fin clamps stuck. I couldn't get her off the ground when I was supposed to. That's why we lost."

Xan pretended to be surprised. "Oh, was that it? Not that we were in an old militarized Class 20 Ship with a pilot who didn't know forbinated from unforbinated a season ago."

"Still don't know. Militarized?"

Xan puffed at her. "Alright, I'll give you that we were at a disadvantage. But what are you planning on wagering, huh? Thought of that?"

She stopped. She hadn't.

"Shoot," she whispered. "I could bluff?" she asked him.

"Not likely. You've got to surrender your wager."

May ran her fingers through her rolled bangs, pulling them back just to have them spring forward again due to the tenacity of the alien hair product.

"Is there anything valuable in the basement?"

"You know, you would think, you really would, that a localized miniature wormhole would be a little more discerning about the kinds of miscellany it sucks up, but no. Zuxing thing just spits out rubber bands and plastic twist ties which are fun, don't get me wrong, but a Tuhntian can't live on rubber bands alone."

"So, that's a no."

"Yes. That's a no. Hey, mun," he draped an arm over her shoulders, "we've got ten crystals left. We might as well spend it on a decent drink at a nice bar, cut our losses, and shimmy on out of here in style. It was worth a shot but *Audy's* just not meant for racing."

She looked at him miserably. Thoughts that wouldn't be of any help to her raised the machete again and started thwacking their way through her mental rain forest. Now though, and even worse, the thoughts were of self-pity and the biting mosquito of failure.

"Damnit, Xan. I'm sorry. That was dumb."

"What? No. No." He patted her shoulder, winced, then said, "Okay, well yeah it was kinda but not entirely! It was sort of a good idea. I mean, she was built as a racing rocket, after all. And you are zuxing good at flying her—or better than I am at least. You're just a human-"

"Just a human?" she cut him off.

"I mean—well, what I mean is a human's never raced before so..."

She began to look like a candle left on a car dashboard in the middle of a summer heat wave in Florida.

"Ah, zuut. Don't look at me like that, starshine." He bit his lip as if punishing himself for what he was about to say. "You're sure you know who's going to lose the next race? Swear on your Queen?"

"Don't know what that means, but yeah. Yes, I'm sure."

"Ehhhh-you-can-wager-me-I-guess," his voice was strained and husky.

"Huh?"

"I said...you can wager me. I guess." He looked mighty displeased.

"What are you talking about? I can't wager you. You're not a commodity."

"Oh, believe me you can and I am. You better not lose though. If you lose-"

"You're dead, right?"

"Uh..."

"Everything's death with you." They began to walk again.

"N-no. I wasn't going to say that. I was going to say if you lose you owe me a drink." He laughed nervously.

"Uh-huh. Don't worry, I won't lose," she said as she worried she would lose.

## TWENTY-FOUR
# HALLUCINOGENIC APHRODISIACAL NOODLE BAR

Back on Earth, May hadn't had the time, energy, or incorrigible peers needed to engage in night life. Even if she had had those things, she lacked the desire to do anything but sleep at night.

She imagined what a rave must be like. Neon lights, she knew, were a necessity. Loud music was probably up there on the list of "Things to Do" when planning a rave. She supposed alcohol must be a facet, and likely some sort of illicit or at least dubious substances with vague names like "Jazz" and "Kablam" would be passed around and smoked or snorted or licked—she wasn't sure how exactly people were ingesting their drugs nowadays. She imagined people sweat a lot during such an event and that sweat would probably get on her.

This party, she surmised, was something like a rave. Or at least something like what someone who'd never been to a rave thought a rave might be.

There were, however, a great deal more noodles than your typical rave could boast.

Scantily clad, if indeed clad at all, individuals lounged about the perimeter of the bar and fed each other noodles from red plastic cups. The noodles were not, as one might imagine, anything special. They looked like rice noodles because they were. As it turns out, humans are the only sentient beings in the Universe who can digest gluten. And, even then, it's not an easy feat. Rice noodles are inter-galactically popular.

These noodles, like the noodle that tempted Adam and Eve to eat from the Tree of Knowledge, had a dastardly secret.

Xan loudly sucked air in between his clenched teeth at the sight of them. "Alrighty so whatever you do, do not-"

A creature that wasn't so much a human as she was an upright gazelle draped a long rice noodle over Xan's nose and gave him a slow blink so intense her long eyelashes waved like a flag. He stiffened, his eyes crossing as they looked at the offending string of gluten-free pasta.

"Don't eat the noodles," he whispered to May, plucking the noodle from his nose and returning it to her with a forced smile. The gazelle thing snorted her indignation, grabbed the noodle from him, and spun away to look for better pickings.

"Aw, you hurt her feelings," May teased. "What's wrong with the noodles?"

"Oh, nothing, I'm sure they're great! It's just-" Another noodle lassoed his nose. Looking down, May saw a short, greenish, mustachioed being holding the other end of the noodle.

Xan cringed in a way that might be read as a smile to someone with a degenerative eye disease and slipped his nose from the noose of the noodle.

"They're hallucinogenic and-" He paused as a beautiful purple woman slung a noodle over May's shoulder. "Aphrodisiacal." Xan finished as he plucked the noodle from her shoulder and returned it to the rebuked Rhean with an apologetic shake of his head.

May tried not to laugh as more noodles propositioned them. "This is where the gambling happens, then?"

"Yep. In the Noodle Bar. You're not going to have any

issues wagering me here," he said, now draped with so many noodles they reminded May of tinsel on a Christmas tree. He looked tired.

She nodded and a noodle slid from her hair.

They shimmied through the throngs until they reached the bar, leaving behind them a trail of momentarily broken hearts.

The bar was circular and the multi-limbed, over-eyed, red-skinned woman who worked it slung cups of noodles to voracious customers as if she were a machine built for that express purpose. "Oy! We've got a wager to put up. Where do we-"

"Eat," said the woman, slinging a red cup in their direction.

"Oh, alright." He tipped the cup back and swallowed the nest of noodles whole.

"Woah! So, you can eat them, but I can't?" May asked.

"Please, May, give me a little credit. With a job like mine you get that knocked out of you pretty fast. I would prefer it, however," he looked at her warily, "if you stopped metamorphosing into a sexy avant-garde lamp."

"I'll try." She sighed, shaking her lamp shade at him, tassels flying.

"Where can we go to put up a wager for the next race?" he asked the bartender.

"What've ya' got to wager?" She paused her noodle slinging to the dismay of the creatures surrounding the bar and leaned into him conspiratorially.

He smiled broadly and winked.

The bartender squinted at him. "What?"

"Me," he said, offense peppering his voice. "I'm the wager."

"You?" She eyed him for a moment. "Eh, whatever. Third door to the right. Tell 'em Dontel sent ya'." She looked him over once more. "Naw, tell 'em Maritov sent ya'." Again, the noodles were slung.

"That'll do!" He straightened up and slipped away into the hoi polloi, parting the sea of sweaty alien bodies just enough for May to slip through relatively untouched. Once they were in the hallway, he shook his head to dislodge the noodles he'd amassed. A cavernous sigh escaped him as he stood before the door, blocking May from reaching the shockingly banal metal handle.

"What's wrong?"

"Oh, nothing. Just preparing. You're sure you'll win?"

"Yes! The clamps were faulty. Whatever rocket starts from our position is going to lose," she whispered, not wanting to be overheard.

"What if they fix the clamps? What if the clamps were caught on some part of the *Audacity*? What if no one starts from that position next time?"

May put a finger to his mouth to shush him, then dangled the good luck charm around her neck with her other hand.

"That's what this is for, right?"

"It's not infallible! I mean, past a certain point you cross well out of the constraints of luck and into absolute improbability."

"It's highly probable that I'm right about this."

Xan grit his teeth, looking miserable.

"What's the worst that could happen?" May asked.

"Death?" Xan blinked at the doorknob. "Yeah, death, I guess. Not so bad, I suppose. If that's the worst. Might as well. Alright, well, good luck." He turned the knob. He wished he hadn't.

On the other side of the door, a scene entirely unlike the noodle bar in every important way and in many unimportant ways assaulted their senses.

Firstly, their sense of smell. The noodle bar smelled a touch like sweat and Chinese food, sure, but this was downright evil. May smelled the sweat of beings who didn't give a slorpfignut if anyone found them attractive or not and, in fact, rather enjoyed turning people off.

Sight was nearly entirely out of the picture at this point. A light fog glowed greenly in the air and accounted for the only luminescence in the windowless room. The things they *could* see, they very much wished they didn't have to. The fog's green light touched on a pile of crystals glinting from a raised platform to their right, and that was where the pleasant imagery ended. Rows of scowling faces turned up to the fog as if they were preparing to give it a good what-for any moment now.

One of these faces, one of the taller and meaner of these faces, turned to the open door and fixed May with a devilish glint. The body attached to that face swam forward, wiggling like a snake lifting itself off the ground.

May was unsure if the creature's skin was green, or if the light just made it seem that way. It was unpleasant though; of that she was certain. His cold finger trailed under her chin and she felt Xan's hand on her shoulder. Whether he was hoping to protect her from this thing or trying to steady himself, she couldn't tell.

The face was pock-marked and the kind of evil old-young that makes one wonder if it really is possible to stay young by bathing in the blood of virgins. "This the wager?" his voice echoed oddly in May's translation chip, as if there was more than one person in there.

"Uh, no." Xan grasped both her shoulders now and slowly pulled her back.

She was glad he'd said something because her throat was tighter than a waist trainer's corset.

"Tada!" he said. "It's me. I'm the wager. Soak it in, fellas. You could be the proud owner of your very own limited edition Tuhntian. We're in short supply nowadays what with the..." He glanced over his shoulder at May with wide eyes. "Oh, you know. Maritov sent us back," he finished, practicing a semi-convincing smile on her that he then turned to the pock-marked man.

A muttering came from the room as the up-turned faces turned downwards and discussed this. "Add him to the pot!" a voice shouted above the buzz.

"Aye."

"Aye."

"Aye," said several other voices that bounced off the walls.

The pock-marked creature looked put-off for only a

moment before focusing again on May who was well in Xan's shadow now.

"Acceptable wager. What be the prediction?"

May had rather hoped she'd get to look at the rockets first. At least she remembered her starting position.

"The rocket in slot three to lose?" she proposed.

"Vague," sneered the pock-marked man. "Oy," he shot over his shoulder at the crowd. "Who's on three?"

"Ol' Joeybillums in *Comet Crusher*," a single helpful voice replied.

"*Comet Crusher* to lose for the blue twink," the pock-marked man announced then shoved Xan, with surprising strength, towards the pile of crystals.

"I'm going to win, okay?" May shouted after him.

"Oh, not a doubt, mun. Not a doubt," he shot over his shoulder doubtfully.

"Someone's gonna have a little blue pet tonight!" the pock-marked man announced to the crowd. "Kornackuk, think the husband'd mind?"

A densely muscled yellow-green man that wouldn't have been out of place on the cover of a Harlequin romance novel, aside from the massive tusks, winked at Xan. "Yurten will be well pleased with my winnings," he confirmed.

Xan shrugged at May. "Could be worse," he said with surprising nonchalance as he was placed on the platform with the crystals.

"That blue ass is mine," rung from the back. A rough skinned and sharp man stood on a speaker. The softly glowing fog above them imploded with a kaleidoscope of color and reformed into a holoscreen, giving him the complexion of a living disco ball.

"May!" A semi-transparent force-field of blueish light popped into existence around Xan and the thousands of crystals. He banged on it with his fist, but, as it was made of nearly invisible light, the action resulted in him looking like a garish and rather loud mime. "May, I do not want to go with that man!"

"I didn't realize you were this popular," May said, weaving through the crowd to get closer to him. Offense ghosted across his features but settled on an expression of begrudging accord.

Sweaty alien bodies pressed into May from all sides. A drink clattered to the floor and something that smelled like alcohol flecked her calves. She stared up at the holoscreen which displayed an establishing shot of the trash-planet the race started on. The ships lined up, a black-and-white checkered number settling into spot three. That was it. *Comet Crusher.*

The air sparked with tension. May swore she felt her hair standing on end from all the electricity in the atmosphere.

"Ey, you!" shouted the pock-marked man. "Cut it out."

May peeled her eyes away from the screen to see Xan clawing experimentally at the force-field, searching for a weak spot. He relented and draped himself forlornly over the crystal pile. The electricity in the air dissipated.

The mood shifted and May turned her attention once again to the holoscreen. The race had begun but she'd missed the first eighth of a second and, as such, couldn't see if the clamps had stuck or not. *Comet Crusher* was, however, decidedly not in the lead.

Time stood still, as if paused, while she watched the race. Or—no it didn't. Chattering alcoholics swirled around her at normal speed. The race, though, seemed to be moving in slow motion. Or perhaps not at all.

"Sorry fellas, bad signal."

The holographic molecules burning above her began to move again. A sharp pain in the back of her jaw told her she was clenching her teeth well beyond their recommended bite force.

A winner lit up the screen with fanfare....and it was not *Comet Crusher*. Someone to her left whooped as a second rocket passed the towers. It, too, was not *Comet Crusher*. A third, a fourth. *Comet Crusher* was still out there, still trying.

May had never wanted someone else to fail so much in her entire life. She felt a little shitty about that, but desperate times.

A rocket called *Mister Manicotti* made a valiant effort for last place, but in the end, the infant star whales tripped *Comet Crusher* up just enough to allow the pale-yellow *Manicotti* to make fifth place by half a nose.

*Comet Crusher* had lost, but May had won. She felt she should smile, cheer, perhaps. Was that what people did when good things happened to them? She tried on a smile; it felt nice. It felt really nice. She'd won!

A sharp scream of frustration came from the man on the speaker. "Grab the zuxing Tunhtian!"

The nice moment, the smile, the inclination to cheer fled.

May's shoulders sagged with exhaustion for a second, but Xan's newly freed body slammed into her, an arm noodling around her waist as he pulled her through the curling mass of gamblers.

## TWENTY-FIVE
# GREAT.

This was now the second time, in as many weeks, that May found herself running for her life. It was not at all like she'd imagined it would be, running for her life. She imagined blood pounding in her ears and the cold chill of pursuit at her back, the pounding of feet behind her growing ever closer. Like she'd read in books. That would've been far preferable because at least that would've been familiar.

Instead, she experienced her legs moving in a rhythm she did not set, her chest aching for a cigarette—or no, wait—that was oxygen it craved, and a trail of alien obscenities slowly becoming quieter as Xan's long legs ferried him far ahead of her.

The obscenities became louder as he impatiently waited for her to catch up, then quieter again as he inevitably sprinted ahead of her, until finally he grabbed her hand in his own to force himself to stay by her side. Or rather, to pull her along like a limp banana peel.

They emerged at last in the green, darkly marbled main entrance hall. May looked for the horrifying creature that had shielded them from the onslaught of weaponized concessions.

Light from the surface of the planet poured in through a massive doorway.

"Are we," May wheezed, "close enough?"

Xan pecked at the BEAPER on his wrist with his nose. "Theoretically!" he shouted back to her and they fizzled away.

The sudden shift from being in such a dark, green location to being bombarded with the bright orange of the *Audacity*'s neon living room made May wince. Xan leapt up the stairs to the control panel and brought his fist down on The Button That Typically Made The Ship Go.

"Well, that was absolutely horrifying." He pulled on his coat to straighten it and reshaped his pompadour with his fingers. "I know I've got a certain charm, but zuut that guy was ravenous! Did you see his eyes? Like a mushroom before a ch'stranda I was to him. Odd skin color, though. I know it was dark in there but he almost looked-"

May squeaked in surprise as she was shoved off the teledisc by a pile of crystals that had not been there a nanosecond ago.

"Aha!" Xan jumped from the control panel and grabbed a handful of crystals.

"Christ, that's a lot of crystals," May said, thinking that perhaps this was the end of her career as a racer. She was almost disappointed by that.

"Orbits worth! Blitheon, I've never seen this much gem at once."

The massive, shimmering, glittering hill of life-sustaining minerals disappeared. Just blipped right out of there. The only proof that the crystals had existed at all was in the smattering of shards on the carpet surrounding the teledisc and what Xan had collected in his hands.

"What?" asked May.

"Ahh, zuxing pirates!" Xan growled. "Loitering around, hacking telediscs, being generally reprehensible. May, I hope I'm not being a bad influence on you, and I feel I've been cursing quite a lot more than normal lately, but by

Quanzar's laser-sythe what the zuxing trok? Excuse my Rhean."

"It's fine. That fucking sucked," she agreed.

He gave her a confused little smile, seeming to forget that almost a million crystals had been swiped from them before they'd even had a chance to celebrate. "Was that an Earth profanity?" He shoved a handful of crystals into the pocket in his coat and offered the other handful to her.

"What clued you in?"

"You ever notice how you can tell when someone is cursing even if you have no idea what they're saying? Something about the energy of a word, I don't know. And you can say anything, anything at all, and make it sound like an obscenity, too."

May sat on the arm of the couch, closed her eyes, let herself fall back into the squeaking and ill-padded cushions.

"Something completely innocuous. Spanner, for example. You can say spanner in such a way, with just the right inflection, that it sounds for all the world like something your third great aunt would *hit* you with a spanner for saying."

Words flowed over May like lukewarm unlimited free refill coffee. Half the words got through to her. She heard "spanner" and wondered briefly if there was one on board because that would probably be of some use to her at some point.

She heard "great" and latched onto it for a moment. Everything was not great. Or everything *was* great, but in a sarcastic sense. Or perhaps everything was *actually* great. Great also meant big. Everything was big. It was a lot. It was her, in an orange metal tin, surrounded by a great, big everything.

She shuddered. Everything was a lot of things.

Great, she thought. Just great.

She wanted a cigarette painfully. Putting anything in her mouth at this point would probably help or at least distract her enough to not care. Xan was still rambling about curse words.

"...now the really interesting thing about cursing is that

—"

"Xan? Would you mind making me a cup of coffee?"

"Oh! *Now* you want coffee. I thought you didn't like coffee."

"Desperate," she said simply. Her eyes were still closed but the bright orange of the ceiling and the walls in the ship bled through her eyelids.

She felt the couch shift below her and cracked an eyelid just enough to see Xan digging around in the cushions for something. He plucked out a strangely angled bottle sloshing with cobalt blue liquid.

"This is a lot stronger than coffee, if that's what you're looking for." He winked at her, swirling the liquid in the unmarked bottle.

"Alien moonshine?" May asked. "I'd love some." She'd never had the desire to do it herself, but Kathy frequently brought a water bottle filled with moonshine to work. She never asked who made it, where, or how, but invariably on hard nights Kathy would wordlessly pass her the bottle.

Xan smiled, set the bottle down, and ricocheted off the couch to the weird little coffee nook behind the control panel. From a cabinet beneath the coffee maker, he produced two ceramic mugs. May couldn't imagine an alien potter making mugs like those. They looked like they'd been stolen from a diner in the forties.

"Stole these from a diner in the forties." Xan laughed, handing her a chipped mug and pouring out a scant ounce of the beverage.

May sniffed it; it smelled strong. "You've been to Earth before?"

"What? No. No, I think the diner was on Pan in orbit 7243. That was bad orbit. Come to think of it, they all were. Let's drink!"

He poured himself a mug-full and set the bottle down on the carpet beside the couch.

Nothing she'd eaten had disagreed with her yet. The corn came close, and that was the only Earth food she'd had since her abduction. It was reasonable to assume this blue liquid wouldn't kill her outright at least, so she tipped it back just far enough that she could stick her tongue in it.

She recoiled, glad she hadn't actually taken it into her mouth.

"What is this?"

"Marsupian wine, the finest Tuhnt has to offer. The only Tuhnt has to offer. Had to offer. It's good right? Not amazing, grant you, nothing extraordinary, but it's good. Does the job." He drank a little more and settled into the couch, eyes closed as he savored the drink that looked, smelled, and tasted like blue Listerine.

After the day—no, week—no, life—she'd been having, she was up for drinking Listerine.

She took a sip.

She would never trust the tip of her tongue again.

Had May been a trained sommelier, she might have awed at the freshness of the bouquet, the notes of vanillin and creme de cassis, the full-bodied palate, the cascade of current and black-pepper, and the whisper of violet just at the finish. She was not, however, a trained sommelier, and as such she felt the wine was good. Very good, in fact.

She felt a little ashamed for thinking it was alien moonshine.

She hummed softly, joining Xan in the recesses of the old couch as she indulged. Beneath her, the *Audacity* purred, happy to be carrying them far away from Platamousse.

"More?" Before she could answer, Xan tipped his mug, pouring half of what he had left into hers.

"I couldn't possibly," she said with faux bravado just before taking another sip.

So, she'd failed.

She'd screwed up the race and lost everything she'd won back via a random act of meanness. It was really quite terrible but somehow, whether by virtue of marsupian wine or having a friend to share in the burden of misfortune, she felt alright.

Content, even. Was this what contentment felt like?

"Where's the next race?" she asked, her contentment spiraling into confidence.

"Ha! You might want to slow down on the wine, mun." Xan sped up, downing the last of his mug and looking for all the world like she was about to give the rest of hers to him.

She curled over her mug protectively. "Don't you dare. I'm of sound mind, and I think we should race again. If the clamps hadn't stuck, we would've won."

Xan squinted a disbelieving eye at her. "You're being facetious again, right? Because we most certainly would not have won."

"I might not have lost, at least."

"Alright, okay, fine. Maybe we can find a pre-beginner back alley race."

"Good."

"Great," Xan said on a sigh.

## TWENTY-SIX
# KATHY WITH A "K"

Human 740282042 was a happy blonde. She was happy because she thought that her dreams were reality and vice versa. In her dreams, she worshiped a beautiful silver-haired goddess who brought her to the most exquisite places in the Universe. In her dreams her body was immaterial, her spirit undulated with the whole of everything like a grain of sand in the Sahara. Human 740282042 liked her dreams.

Human 740282042 got zapped.

"Hey! I wasn't doing anything wr"—*zzzzaap!*

She huffed, realizing her mistake. She was plating up sustenance and she had accidentally dropped a bit of lentil soup on the tray. She wiped it and set the tray down on the conveyor belt that would convey it out of the kitchen and into the waiting hands of a hungry human.

There would be no conversation about the niceties of the menu, no exchange of money, no complaints. The "no complaints" part was nice, at least. Human 740282042 did not miss getting yelled at but being zapped by a floating metal ball seemed a poor trade-off.

"Cathy," the conveyor belt whispered to her.

She woke up a little and blinked.

"Cathy!" Conveyor belts were meant to convey food trays, not whispers.

"That's not my name," said Human 740282042.

"Yes it is. Cathy, listen to me, I have important news."

"It's Kathy with a 'K.'" She wasn't sure why she'd said that. She hadn't said her real name in days—weeks? She got a warning zap and remembered why.

"Wh—how can you tell?" the belt conveyed.

"I can tell." Another warning zap.

"Alright, Kathy, listen to me. You've had the dreams about her, haven't you? The Tinsel Haired Goddess."

Dreams? No...that was real life. This was the dream.

"Sleep upside down tonight and she will appear to us all. It is time."

"Upside down? Like, with my feet on my pillow upside down or hanging from the ceiling like a bat? You've got to be more specific with your cryptic messages." *Zzaap!*

The conveyor belt was done talking.

"Like a bat?" she asked desperately. *Zap!* She hoped she didn't have to sleep like a bat.

Kathy peered out into the cafeteria through the small slit that carried trays through. She saw a man walk away, his polo shirt looked like it had been twisted into a very tight rat-tail and never properly ironed out.

# TWENTY-SEVEN

# HONEY IN THE GYROSCOPES

Listay had a sticky situation on her hands. Or, more accurately, she had a sticky substance on her hands and a sticky situation to deal with as a result of this sticky substance.

The substance was honey, and the situation was that her human-watching spheres were inexplicably and inexhaustibly attracted to it. She pulled apart the inner casing of a particularly hedonistic sphere which had seemingly plunged into a vat of the stuff. The golden bee secretion coated the thing inside and out, gumming up its systems perhaps permanently. It was less effort and cheaper to make new spheres when they got into honey.

There was something wrong with the food service humans, of that she was sure. When she'd begun compiling Yvonne's list of dissenters, she'd been distressed to find that nearly every human on the list worked in food service. It then followed that something the food service workers had access to was inspiring their rebellion.

And then the honeyed spheres began rolling in. That was it. The honey.

Somehow, perhaps by some ineffable rule of robotics that not even their most advanced Rhean scientist could've accounted for, the spheres loved honey. Couldn't get enough of it. They couldn't smell it, couldn't taste it, and yet they craved it like pigs crave mud in which to sprawl.

Hundreds of spheres had been collected, dripping and useless. A quick review of their final moments of unhindered video typically revealed a line cook or a sous chef tempting the sphere close with a fingerful of honey, clicking and cooing at it as if it were a stray dog rather than a piece of highly sophisticated alien tech. They would then rip off their shirts, twist them into a rattail, and whack the spheres out of the air while they were distracted.

Listay hated sticky things. She could hardly stand to look at the poor sphere, which was gunking up her desk, vibrating in honeyed ecstasy, its circuits permanently saccharine.

She touched her fingers together, cringing at the slight tackiness as she pulled them apart. She needed a shower and a serious talk with her programming unit. Consecutively, not simultaneously.

Perhaps Yvonne would know what to do.

Chaos loved sticky things. Especially when things that ought not be sticky were. The robotic spheres Listay had employed to aid in enslaving the human race were not meant to be sticky and so Chaos had, in her infinite and god-like wisdom, given them just enough sentience to love one thing and love it with an unyielding passion: honey.

And the food service humans were the perfect candidates. The industry ran under its own moral code, organized in a way that made Chaos curl her toes, underground networks and connections abounded in the food service community. And the cooks really were the best at rebellion. They weren't quick to strike and fizzle out like other rebellions had been; they understood the importance of letting things simmer.

Listay had been hailing her for quite some time, about the honey thing, no doubt. Let her squirm a little, thought Chaos. Let her get her fingers sticky.

Chaos had some prophetic dreams to appear in.

## TWENTY-EIGHT
# RASKOV THE BEAUTIFUL

Something wretched woke May. A piercing, squealing sound like a whistle being blown by a semi-truck, so loud she could feel it in her teeth, shuddered through the ship then stilled, leaving an aching silence.

"Well, that was wretched. Wonder what could've-" Xan was interrupted by the whistle blowing semi-truck.

May peeled her cheek from his latex-clad shoulder and rubbed her face. The empty mug fell from her lap and onto the carpet, giving a soft thunk that was all together much more pleasant than whatever wretched thing was happening to the ship.

"It sounds like something's scraping against the hull," she said. The sound stopped.

This disturbed Xan. If something were scraping against the hull, it would have to be fairly large. If something were scraping against the hull, it would likely be doing it again. If something were scraping against the hull, it would certainly be damaging the paint.

Few things could persuade Xan to leap into action. The thought of losing even a fleck of precious Obtrusive Orange was one of them. Followed closely, of course, by a poor TV signal.

They climbed, with some trepidation, to the control panel, May taking to the pilot's chair and Xan leaning close into the view screen. On the view screen, the cool inky blackness of space was interrupted by a cooler, inkier blackness. Squinting, May could just work out that the cooler, inkier blackness was vaguely phallic in shape and sidling up to the *Audacity* for another go at rubbing against it.

May had never enjoyed being rubbed against by things that were vaguely phallic in shape and prepared to make a speedy retreat.

Before another blow could be dealt, however, an inset in the viewscreen manifested a face from which May immediately recoiled. Not because it was in any way unpleasant—much the opposite. This face was attractive, and this face knew it.

A ruggedly cut and tanned face with a perfectly imperfect goatee and a tasteful swoop of shiny black hair smiled at them in a practiced way.

"Can I help you?" May's customer service instinct slammed into her brain and made her greet him with a mix of apathy and resignation that somehow screamed polite servitude.

In her peripheral, she saw Xan's hand cover The Button That Typically Made The Ship Go. She shooed his hand away; she wanted to see what subcategory of ass they were dealing with first.

"Yeah, starlips, I think you can."

Right, that one.

"Ugh, what is this guy? A two in heat?" Xan mumbled.

"What?" May asked.

"Never mind. Don't help him."

"What do you want?" May addressed the face again, politeness slipping quickly down the drain like the detritus of an overly fatty meal.

"Calm down, babe," said the face in a way that he must have known would have the opposite effect. "I want to make you a real racer, yeah? What's your name, babe?"

"Xan," said Xan.

The face crinkled a little. "I was talking to the hot chick, bro."

"What, am I not the-" May nudged him hard and shook her head.

"It's May," she said.

"What a name! Haven't heard a name like that in a while. Call me Raskov the Beautiful."

"No, thank you." May moved to shut off the communication line.

"Wait! Wait. I saw you race on Platamousse and I want to sponsor you. Just give it one race, babe; in the right circle you'll be unstoppable! First prize is ten thou, second prize is five. Won't cost ya' a gem, neither. Just want to see another human succeed."

May's finger paused along with her brain as a single word got lodged there.

"You're a human?"

"What, don't I look it, babe?"

Mays lip curled; he did. She hadn't seen a complexion like that since she lost August. The thought that he was probably dead itched at the back of her brain. She ignored it.

"You'll front the entrance fee?" May asked, but before Raskov could answer, Xan paused the communication line.

"Right, so," Xan looked at her seriously, "he's clearly trying to scam us. Let's jet."

"Maybe." May sat in the pilot's chair and thought for a moment. "He might just genuinely want to—" May cut herself off with a laugh. "No, you're right. I don't trust him as far as I could race him." She turned the communication line back on.

"I'm sorry, I'm going to have to decline. Have a nice day," she said, not sure it even was day. She tried to tap The Button That Typically Made The Ship Go but the *Audacity* groaned like a petulant child and refused to move.

"Babe. It wasn't an invitation. Now are you going to let me warp you or will I have to tow you all the way to the Pipes?"

May switched off the communication line again and put the ship in manual. "Men," she muttered under her breath like a curse. "No offense," she offered half-heartedly to Xan.

"None taken. Not a man," he reminded her.

She shrugged. "Guess not. Think we can shake him?"

"Nope."

"Thanks for the vote of confidence." She pressed her foot into the accelerator and steered away from the dark ship. The *Audacity* inched away from Raskov the Beautiful. Inches, unfortunately, mean little in relation to the vast everythingness of open space.

Raskov's face appeared again and May tried to turn it off.

"He hacked the com line," she sighed.

"Of course, babe! You didn't make it hard. Aha! That's what she said, am I right? I'm right."

In a desperate attempt to dislodge his words, May smacked her forehead against the control panel.

"Hold on, she didn't say that," Xan tried to defend her—not knowing exactly who "she" was.

May patted his knee. "Don't overthink it."

"Looks like I'll be towing you to the Pipes! Tha's alright, babe. It'll be good to have some time to talk. Not many humans out here. Not many compatible species, either if ya' catch my drift." He laughed as if he'd said something absolutely hilarious. May's eyebrow twitched; she didn't think it could do that.

"Sorry, I'm not compatible either," May intoned.

"Wha?"

"Like a Barbie doll down there."

"Huh?"

"I don't want to fuck you," she said at last.

"You just met me; how do you know?"

"Psychic," May answered.

"You're weird."

"Uh-huh."

"I like weird chicks." Raskov licked his lips. "Always wild in the sack."

Xan slunk under the control panel and gestured for

May to join him.

"This guy's a zoup-nog. If we unlock the hyperdrive, we'll at least get there faster. He'll have to let us go to race, we can just high-tail it in the other direction when he does!"

"Oh, I'm not worried about that," said Raskov. "Also, I can hear you and I'm not a zoup-nog. I'm actually very intelligent. High IQ. Not that a stupid alien would know what an IQ is."

"Zuut." Xan's teeth ground together.

"At least if we let him use the hyperdrive maybe he'll shut up." May shrugged and unlocked the hyperdrive latch. "Alright." She stood up again. "I will race, but know I'm doing it because I want to."

"Uh-huh, sure thing starlips. Warping away!"

"You do realize it's a hyperspace hop, right? This isn't *Star Trek*." May didn't know how a hyperdrive worked exactly but she *did* know it wasn't the same as warping. The manual had led her to believe that no one really knew how a hyperdrive worked and that those who studied the intricacies of it tended to go insane.

"Nerd."

"Oh, my God," May looked heavenward—or, rather, looked in the direction opposite to gravity since there was nowhere she could look at this point which wasn't, strictly speaking, heavenward—and shook her head in amazement.

They had followed her. Somehow, they had followed her.

"Ugh, religious nerd. It's not sexy, you know." The spacescape before them winked into darkness, then a sickly yellow glow illuminated an enormous vault door.

"Where are we?" asked Xan.

"The Pipes, bro. Duh."

"He's going to need to stop calling me bro," Xan informed May seriously. She wondered what Xan would do if he didn't and decided she didn't want to know.

The Pipes, to use the colloquial term, are a system of derelict pipes running between the desert planet of Astffadoo and its wettest moon, Chummy. The ancient Panseen who colonized Astffadoo felt that the most elegant solution to Astffadoo's complete lack of water was to build a pipeline from Chummy to Astffadoo. This plan was so foolhardy, so idiotic, that to this day an infrastructural faux pas is still inter-galactically known as an "Astffa*don't*".

Though Chummy dried up from embarrassment long ago, the pipe system remains, incomplete and structurally unsound, jutting off of Chummy like a malformed limb. It's only value lies in that it's wide enough to safely hide an illegal five-rocket race from the authorities, and that it curves and branches off in enough places to make that race extremely interesting for the parched onlookers who wait on the planet below, watching via cameras installed along the length of the Pipes.

It was here that Raskov brought the *Audacity*, to the derelict main water tank on Chummy. On Platamousse, May had been intimidated by how sleek and new the rockets lined up beside her were. Now, she was intimidated mostly by the general air of intimidation these rockets exuded.

These ships, in sharp contrast to the professional racers, had gaudy gold trim, additional fins that May knew where not integral to the handling of the ship, and hulls painted to such a high gloss that the dim lights had trouble getting a grip on them.

"A'ight, babe, race starts in ten."

"Ten what?" May asked.

"Oh, for the love of—just ten," said Raskov.

"Fine. What are our destination coordinates?"

"Woah there, starkiller, you're gonna have to figure that out yourself. Just follow the green lights, babe. You're gonna be great. I'll be waiting for ya' at the finish line! Oh, and smile for the cameras, babe."

"No."

A polite "thank you" tried to crawl its way up May's throat but fortunately she was able to squash it this time.

He ignored her, and she was grateful.

"Esteemed racers," said Raskov. "You know the drill. Run the Pipes, follow the green lights, and if you're gonna wipe out try t' keep the smoldering wreckage outta the way of the pros, yeah? Landing pad's all lit up like Christmas or some shit so ya' can't miss it down here. As we say back on Earth: Ready, set, go!"

The shut-off valve before them began to grind open, its massive disc of a door moving only slightly faster than a geriatric knee-replacement patient on the mend.

A crescent of green light escaped from around the edge now, steadily waxing. Engines revved in a way May didn't think rocket engines could.

May bit her bottom lip, watching the sliver of green light carefully grow. At some point, she would have to go for it. The *Audacity* might even have an advantage here because she wasn't outfitted with a million decorative bits that could be sliced off in a tight squeeze.

Xan looked from her to the sliver and back. "You're not planning on ramming the ship through the opening before anyone else can get a chance to get ahead, are you? Because it looks like you are. It very much looks like that's what you're planning to do."

"On the nose." May smiled, threw the ship into manual drive, and threaded her around the shut-off valve.

TWENTY-NINE
# THE PIPES

"Did we make it?" Xan asked, eyes closed tight as he braced against the control panel, his fingers splayed and curling into it as if he were trying to hold the ship together himself.

"It would appear so," May said as she pressed the ship onwards into the pipes which were lit by rows of bright green LEDs on either side. "Can you check the rear view? Is anyone else out yet?"

Xan called an inset into the lower left corner of the view screen. It showed the opposite side of the shut-off valve. A gaudy purple ship scraped through, sparks jumping from its hull as it pushed into the pipes.

"One's out. Nope—two. Not looking great back there, though. I think that one lost a fin. Wait, we didn't lose anything did we?"

"Don't think so," May said.

He decided to check anyway, pulling up the maintenance log in place of the rear-view.

"Nothing new to report. Nothing old, either. Not much at least. Aw, you got rid of the parking wobble? Loved the wobble, gave her character."

"You've got enough character for the both of you," May said, gaining speed.

He couldn't argue.

The pipe that stretched before them was brightly lit by the green lights, broad, and suspiciously obstacle-free for as far as she could see.

May thought this was strange and said so. Saying so was, of course, a bad idea. It went something like this:

"This seems too easy," May said.

"Shouldn't have said that."

"Why not?"

The pipe which had looked, from a distance, like it went on forever, suddenly twisted to the left.

May pulled the ship around, scraped it against the metal wall, wiping out a row of perfectly good green lights, dropped the ship down to avoid a metal panel that drooped from the ceiling of the pipe, narrowly missed the purple rocket which overtook her, and cursed.

Xan had the look of a startled house cat, his fingertips disappearing into the abused foam armrest of the chair. "That's why not. Gurtrine's Mandate—it's a function of irony."

"What?"

"Well, the story goes that Colonel Gurtrine the Third Great Colonel of-"

"Tell me later." May hated to cut him off mid anecdote but the purple rocket was now the size and color of a fast-moving grape, and they were no longer in the lead.

Four points of white light grew in the distance before them where the single, wide pipe she'd been enjoying branched into four smaller pipes. None were green-lit.

"Just follow the green lights *babe*," May mimicked Raskov angrily under her breath. "Any ideas?"

"Uh, follow that ship?" Xan pointed to the fast grape. The fast grape, unable to choose a pipe to continue down, smashed itself on the joint between the two leftmost pipes. The ship lit up like cherries jubilee, then dripped sadly to the rusted pipe floor.

May slapped her hand to her mouth; her eyes couldn't physically get any wider. "Shit, Xan!"

"Alright, I'm not giving any more racing advice. You're on your own, mun." He buried his face in his hands.

As if appeased by the flaming grape's sacrifice, the second pipe from the left flickered green, giving May just enough time to angle the ship through it.

"That was dark," May said as they entered another long stretch of green pipe, smaller now.

"Uhuh."

"Like, really dark," she insisted, trying to process what she'd just seen.

"Yep."

"Ugh," May shook her head to dislodge the sight of the exploding rocket and pressed on. She flipped on the rear-view herself this time, Xan too busy curling into the co-pilot's chair.

Three flecks of reddish light pursued her. She was far in the lead again now that—well, now.

The pipe she was in grew steadily danker, and swaths of metal sheeting were missing from the siding. If she'd wanted, she could have forced the ship through one of those openings and left Raskov the Beautiful and his blood-hungry course far behind.

She was winning, though. And the prize was ten thousand crystals. Or, at least, that's what she assumed "ten thou" meant. For all she knew, it could have been ten thousand horrible pickup lines.

Still. Winning felt really good, and even the flaming ball of ship that she'd overtaken couldn't dry up the flood of adrenaline.

She kept going. Maybe Raskov wasn't lying, and she'd get her ten thousand. Maybe he was, and she'd get to punch him. Either way, she won.

Ahead, the pipe fell away entirely, revealing the planet she had to assume was their destination. It glowed redly, the curvature of its surface just visible and steadily disappearing as they approached.

Behind them—not much. Something small and yellow, a fleck of green, a dot of blue.

"Xan, we're going to win!" May bounced in her seat and pressed the ship onwards towards victory.

He peeked over his gloved fingers, relaxed, and unfurled. "It would seem so. It would certainly, definitely, seem that way. Don't know how much 'we' was involved, though."

Suddenly, horribly, the ship went dark.

No brilliant view screen, no twinkling panel lights, no ambient orange glow.

It was silent, too.

And cold.

And the oxygen was thinning.

"Zuut," whispered Xan from somewhere beside her.

May's mind ping-ponged with wild abandon between what she knew, what she thought she knew, and what she wished she knew.

She knew inertia dictated that the ship would continue to travel toward the planet. She knew that the ship would crash nose-first into the planet if she didn't get the thrusters back. She thought she knew what had happened—they had run out of fuel. She wished she knew just exactly how much time she had to brew another pot of coffee.

The answer was exactly not enough.

Most Tuhntians have impressive night vision. Xan, however, had spent entirely too long gazing lovingly at the *Audacity*'s eye-searing hull, enraptured by the beauty of the Obtrusive Orange paint, mesmerized by her smoothly arching curves. This had caused him some degree of photic retinopathy.

His vision was, consequently, shit.

Xan trundled to the coffeemaker and began brewing a cup anyway, fumbling in the dark over the well-memorized ritual of pouring a healthy filter-full of grounds, sliding it into the machine, and turning it on.

With no electricity to feed it, the machine did not turn on.

May's fingers ran hurriedly along the underside of the panel searching for a switch she knew existed but had never actually taken the time to look for: the emergency back-up generator.

"Xan! Where's the back-up generator switch?" May

shouted at him. If anyone knew where it was it would be —May groaned—it would be her. Ship manuals didn't exactly strike Xan as brilliant literature.

Regardless, she felt him dive under the control panel to begin flicking every switch he could find.

Incidentally, in a heated round of Street Fighter, Xan's button mashing skills would far out-pace May's terrific reflexes and outstanding hand-eye-coordination. Xan would win every time, much to May's chagrin.

The lights flickered, the coffee maker gurgled, the engine gave a satisfied hum.

"Ah! That was it!"

"What did you hit?" May asked as she prepared the ship for re-entry.

"Uh," Xan popped out from under the panel, his finger pressed tightly to a switch. "I think it was this one. Could've been one of the other ones, though." He pulled up the maintenance log to see how much damage he'd done. "Wobble's back," he smirked at her.

May shook her head, but laughed. Bellow on the planet of Astffadoo squatted a landing pad strung round with cheap string lights and painted with obscene symbols in neon green spray paint. That was definitely her destination.

The landing was wobbly but successful.

# NEWTON'S CRADLE

The dream campaign had been a massive success. Appearing in dreams was fun, anyway, Chaos mused as Yvonne's body lounged in her throne—or, more accurately, her office chair. Humans were vulnerable asleep, and it was so easy to just slip in and move things around.

And the dreams were working.

Chaos had certainly felt more like herself and less like Yvonne as of late. She hadn't thought of IX in almost an entire rotation—*damn it*, she thought. Thinking about not thinking about IX had ruined her streak.

The pink feathered stylus she'd been fiddling with disappeared.

She'd been losing more office supplies that way lately, too. It seemed she was once again capable of actually damning things. She would need to be more careful about that.

Now she entertained herself, as many demigods do, by creating and uncreating life.

Eons had passed, perhaps more, since she had the capacity to create life at will. Now, it was rudimentary life, but it was nothing to sneeze at. All life, even rudimentary life dislikes being sneezed at.

Her first test had been to bestow life upon the Newton's Cradle on her desk. She gave it the ability to procreate and cackled gleefully as each ping of the metal spheres created another sphere until the cradle quadrupled in size.

Next, she tried to give it free will, unbound by the laws of physics. She sent the left-most sphere flying and, rather than pinging against the next sphere, it floated away, broke free of its strings, and bounced around her office walls happily, appreciating the illusion of freedom.

Finally, she gave the cradle a conscience. She pulled back the left-most sphere, let it go, watched it ram into its neighbor who, rather than transferring the momentum to the right-most ball as it ought to have, hiccuped with silent sobs.

It was a marvelous microcosm of the human condition.

She encouraged the Newton's Cradle to turn to dust and it agreed to the proposition.

Tomorrow at 12:43 AM Earth time, her followers would congregate at the base of the Control Tower to watch as Listay, their cruel dictator, was dethroned. Chaos had set the date and time to her liking. She would, of course, be ever so slightly late. Or perhaps early, she hadn't decided. Whatever felt most chaotic at the time.

Chaos made Yvonne's mouth—no, it was her mouth now—smile slowly. Her plan was working. Slower then she'd hoped, but still.

She wondered just how far she could take this body now.

Would Yvonne be able to fight back at all?

There was a way to test this, kill some time, and gain a bit of an advantage over Earth. All it would take was a special order at *The Agency* and a little luck.

She considered her plan. Yvonne didn't stop her this time.

# THIRTY-ONE

# MANCHESTER BATTALION

May had never in her life been cheered by a crowd. She thought, at first, that the noise emanating from the dusty green beings clustered under the tin roofed open air porch was a battle cry and that perhaps she should hurry back to the ship and escape before they set upon her.

They kept a respectful distance, though. Their whoops and hollers, their straw-hat throwing, their cat-calls and loud whistles carried on the dry, dense air. She looked to Xan who shrugged, smiled, and waved. May scanned the audience for a human face. Raskov had to be among them, his long black ship rising obscenely from the ground behind the crowd.

"What the fucking hell was that?" pierced the cheers. There he was.

The audience parted like the Red Sea, if Moses had been 5'7", muscled, and wearing nothing but an arrangement of leather straps studded and held together with bits of metal.

Moses also likely didn't curse. But he might have.

The man who was not Moses strode purposefully toward them. May had half a mind to get back on the ship, but the other half wanted her crystals. She'd won, she deserved them. She wasn't about to get cheated yet again.

"That was winning. Where are our crystals?" she demanded as he approached.

She felt Xan lift his wrist to bring them back on board the ship, but she put a hand out to stop him. He made a very small, very worried, sound at her.

"We aren't leaving without them," May insisted as Raskov continued towards them. He didn't have any weapons and May knew this because if he had, he would've pulled them by now.

"The hell you are. How did you get through the electromagnetic field? No one's ever gotten past that. Did you know about it? Are you with the fuzz?"

He was so close now, May could smell the leather of his outfit, the old cigarette smoke in his goatee, and some kind of alcohol on the spittle that flew at her. Had she liked him even a little bit, she would've settled for a pack of cigarettes in place of payment. She did not, however, like him, and wouldn't let him off that easy.

"It was hard, but we did it. And *that's* what she said. Isn't it, May?" Xan beamed with pride.

May stifled a laugh. "You get one," she told Xan, "one 'that's what she said' joke. I hope you're happy with your choice."

She forgot Raskov was there for a moment. Raskov did not forget he was there.

"Hey, you don't ignore me," he pointed at her menacingly, then backed off a little, his hands up. "Right, babe, I'll tell you what. I can't pony up the cash right now, but I'm hankering for an intimate connection with a foxy gal. If ya' ditch this pathetic gay-ass blue bitch and come with me, I'll give you the whole Universe." He spread his arms out, and May took that as an invitation.

She lunged at him with her entire body, her right fist hankering for an intimate connection with his jaw. Xan snaked his arms around her shoulders and tried to hold her back, but she could see nothing but Raskov's smug, evil face and she could hear nothing but her heart which had switched places with her brain, apparently.

"Alright, we're leaving. Forget the gem," Xan said, raising his BEAPER again to teleport them back to the *Audacity*.

"Damn, bro, control your bitch," Raskov told Xan.

He should not have told Xan that.

"Get him, May!" Xan released her and barreled into Raskov, knocking him to the ground where Xan, by virtue of surprise and a few hundred extra pounds of dense Tuhntian bone, was able to hold him down for May to get a good shot at him.

May jammed her knee into Raskov's gut, pulled her fist back, and threw it into Raskov's startled face. Or, rather, she tried to throw it into Raskov's startled face.

His face was gone.

His whole body was gone, actually.

May's fist contacted the brick-wall that was Xan's sternum.

"Do not move," something metallic shouted at them. They didn't.

May froze, kneeling in a soft pile of grey dust with her fist to Xan's chest. It must've looked rather odd, she thought. Where did Raskov go? she thought. I wonder what this soft pile of grey dust is, she thought, then realized that her second thought probably explained the last.

"On your feet. Do not attempt to flee."

They obeyed, finally confident that looking around wouldn't get them killed on the spot.

Two massive androids who looked unsettlingly like chrome clones of the Michelin Man without the cartoonish grin—without, it must be said, a face at all—sprinted towards them across the red earth. One produced a kind of miniature hand-held shop-vac and began to clean up the remains of what must've been Raskov with the professional nonchalance of a well-paid nanny cleaning up spilled Cheerios.

May's mouth was dry, her heart and her brain switched back but only just.

"The criminal has been eliminated. Justice is served," said the chrome nanny Michelin Man, packing away the shop-vac.

"You will submit to a database scan," the other Michelin Man told May, standing in front of her. She couldn't help but notice the logo printed in enamel across its chest which read "Cosmic Constable". She thought perhaps her translation chip was acting up and tried to see the word "Police" which was more familiar to her, but the chip insisted that the logo read: "Cosmic Constable" arched over a tiny spiral of stars with "Manchester Battalion" smiling beneath it.

It's a curious defect of military issue, lower grade Rhean translation chips that under extreme duress the dialect differentiator tends to go wonky.

May stared at the insignia and tried to not think as the robot held its palm up to her face. The palm glowed blue, scanned her face, then retreated.

"Cleared to abscond," it told her. She wondered if she should thank it, but the words didn't come out. Probably for the best, she thought, as it rolled off to address the green onlookers.

The robot that had cleaned up Raskov scanned Xan's face in the same way but did not say "Cleared to abscond" as Xan so desperately wished it would.

"Suspect. You are under arrest."

"Oh! Terrible cock up luv, I've just remembered I forgot to turn the telly off! Blimey mess that'd be, just have to pop back to the ship for a tick. Run!" Xan bolted to the sound of gun fire, reached for May's hand, and teleported them up to the *Audacity,* slamming into the button that typically made the ship go, then reached under the console to pull the ship into hyperdrive.

The ship jumped through hyperspace.

May had never experienced a jump before. It was disorienting, but since she was already extremely disoriented by what had happened, it actually circled back around and helped her get her head on straight again. She sat cross-legged on the thick orange shag, staring at a little cow-licked bit of orange fiber but not actually seeing it. Her fuzzy peripheral vision saw Xan walk shakily down the stairs and drop to the floor beside her.

He slung his gloves across the floor—May might've been seeing things but she could've sworn an arc of gold glitter flew out of the gloves as he did so—and slapped his hands across his face.

After a while of blurry-eyed silence, she finally brought her sight back into focus. The forearm of Xan's suit was shredded and dripping with something thick and silvery.

"Well, that was interesting!" he said, drawing his hands down his face. "Let's agree to never speak of that again, alright? Alright, terrific." He rolled up to sitting across from her and gave her a wince-shaped smile.

"What happened?" she asked, a bit dully.

"Uh, we won and Raskov got was what coming to him. Or so it would seem. We're a few light years away from all that now. That's what happened."

May shook her head. That didn't sound like what happened, but she supposed it must've been. She got to her knees shakily and used the couch arm to help her stand. "Are you hurt?" she asked tiredly, gesturing to the thick silverly gunk that dripped steadily from his arm.

"Me? No, why do you ask?"

She pointed again.

He looked. "Oh that? Always been like that. Don't worry about it. Let's um...let's see what sector of the galaxy we're in, eh? Could be some good television around here."

"Why did they want to arrest you?" May asked coldly.

"Oh, uh..." his BEAPER began beeping. "Hmm, that's odd. Hasn't done that in ages." He was silent for a moment, reading. "Huh. It's the Agency. Special order, double pay, easy job!" He smiled at the BEAPER, then at her.

"Someone wants to pay me—specifically me—seven hundred crystals to screw in a light bulb! Wait, is that screw *in* a light bulb or *screw* in a light bulb?" he muttered to himself, reading over the message again. "Oh, okay. Yeah, they just want me to fix a light. Groovy."

Xan engaged the hyperdrive, and before May could comprehend what exactly was going on, they were back on the planet Forn, parked in the Agency lot.

"Back in a bloop!" he said, and fizzled away on the teledisc.

# THIRTY-TWO

# VODKA FOR THE MACHINES

August and IX were celebrating. Or rather, August was celebrating, and IX was working to bring an ancient android they had found on Preliumtarn back to life. The poor thing was miserably decrepit, but IX was determined to fix him. Cutting hair had grown tedious rather quickly and her interest in the fine sciences of robotics and engineering had returned.

"Come on, IX," August whined, leaning against her work table and shifting it just enough that she missed the connection she was attempting to solder by an eighth of a millimeter which would, if unfixed, cause innumerable problems down the line. She removed the goggles she had scraped together—a rudimentary version of the goggles she'd invented for herself back on the *Peacemaker* which allowed her to see what she was doing—and turned her milky eyes towards August.

"'Come on' is not a complete sentence, August. What would you like me to come on to?"

He grinned at her. "Not me, that's for sure!"

"August," she scolded. He thought he heard a hint of playfulness in her voice, though he might have been projecting.

"Let's do something fun! It's been fifteen orbits to the rotation since we went through the wormhole. We should have a party or something to celebrate. You've been working on that thing for twenty blips straight!"

"You mean twenty beoops. A blip is very short, August."

"I just hate parties," came a barely audible, low groan from the android that hadn't otherwise shown a single sign of life since they brought it on board.

"What was that?" August asked.

"Oh. I suppose it has been on this whole time," IX said curiously.

She wiped the grease from her hands onto her grey work-coat, removed it, and slung it over the android as if it were a bird she was putting to sleep for the evening.

"I know little of human celebratory customs. Would you like to imbibe alcoholic drinks together for a few beoops and then pass out so I may continue working on this? Perhaps we could bake a cake and bury a small infant in the dough for luck. I am not sure where we will get an infant in this sector, but we can certainly try."

August's eyes grew wide. "IX, it's supposed to be a plastic baby, not a real one. Do...do you think we bake and eat children on Earth?"

"I assumed it was customary," she said.

"No! Okay, let's go with the first one. What've we got in the old stash, eh?" he asked.

"Old is the operative word. Do you recall the night that you-" she began.

"Oh, uh-huh, good times," he cut her off.

"And you asked me never to let your lips touch a drop of alcohol again? I am, however, willing to forego our agreement for a short period if it is important to you."

"Let's just bake a cake. Child-free, if you don't mind."

IX nodded. "And gluten-free," she added as they crawled into the hatch-way that led to the extension IX had built as a kitchen for August.

August sighed. "I accidentally poisoned you once and you won't let it go."

"I nearly died, August. Would you 'let it go' if I had

poisoned you?"

August dropped into the kitchen, skipping the last few rungs of the ladder and regretting it as his knees complained up at him. "No, probably not, no. Gluten-free and child-free, I promise. Could you grab the stuff that reminds me of butter from the basement, please? My knees are aching."

"I could replace them, if you wish."

August shook his head. "Every time you say that it sounds more like a threat than an offer." He opened one of the cabinets in the cramped kitchen and began collecting things that would more or less make something cake-like.

Suddenly, a rabid star-whale rammed its great head through the hull of the *Robert*, took one menacing look at August who snatched a butcher knife to fend it off, bared its sharp, ugly teeth, and clamped its jaw around August's hand, rending it from his forearm with a sickening pop and floating away into the emptiness of space, never to be seen again.

Or, at least, that's what August would tell anyone who asked.

It just wasn't appropriate for a prominent junker to admit that he had lost a hand in a baking accident.

IX returned to the kitchen, a stick of something like butter in her hand. "I have located the lubricant stick." Something was wrong. The kitchen didn't usually smell this metallic, and August wasn't usually this quiet. "August?"

"Knife, blood-" *Thwump*.

"August, are you injured?" she asked, pulling her goggles on so she could get a better idea of what was causing his distress. "Oh, I see. That looks quite bad, would you like help?" she asked, his response was a weak groan. "I will be back in a moment. Don't die, please."

Hazily, August thought she must be really worried about him. She never used contractions unless she was worried.

IX climbed quickly back to her work station, gathering an armful of tools. From under her coat, she saw the left

189

hand of the android she had been working on. She sliced it away with a laser scalpel and brought it.

By the time she returned, August was unresponsive. She tapped him on the face.

"August, wake up. I can fix you," she said. And she could.

August opened his eyes carefully, cautiously. He was sitting up against the kitchen wall, sticky with his own blood and experiencing a terrible pain in all the diodes of his left...wait.

He looked down at his hand, twitched the metal fingers, and screamed.

"You are alive. I am glad," IX said from beside him once his scream petered out.

"H-hand," August blubbered. "Hand?!"

"Yes, that is your new hand. It is an upgrade, I believe."

August whimpered. "Hand?"

"Yes, August. Hand. Did you damage your translation chip when you fell? I can fix that, as well."

"N-no, sorry. Just...shock."

"I understand." She put her hand on his knee in what she hoped was a comforting way. "You will be fine. I must ask, what were you attempting to cut? Cakes do not require cutting until they are complete."

August studied his new hand thoughtfully, turning it around and making it do little things. It couldn't do much yet, but he could twitch it. "There was a dractifly, I used the knife to swat at it."

"And then what happened?" IX pressed.

"I missed, IX."

"I see. Well, you have a better hand now." She smiled at him. "I am glad you survived."

"Oh?" He asked, perhaps a little bitterly.

"Yes, I would have missed you if you had perished."

August smiled, resting his new hand on his lap again. "Aw, you like me. You think humans are cool." He knocked his shoulder into hers playfully.

"I never said cool, you are placing words into my mouth."

"You 'placed' a hunk of metal on my arm. We're even."

IX chuckled. "Happy anniversary, August. Five more orbits and we will be back where we left off." She grabbed an amber bottle that lay on the floor beside them and took a swig, handing it to him when she was done.

"What's this?"

"Vodka. I use it to clean the machines."

"We probably should've just done this in the first place." August drank down the rest of the bottle and promptly passed out on her shoulder. She sat patiently; it was important that he rested.

## THIRTY-THREE
# KINKY

"Took you long enough."

Xan heard the incomprehensibly bored voice even before he'd materialized enough to see her.

It was a voice he knew well. It was a voice he loved. Had loved. Still did, a bit. You never really stop.

For half a second, he felt nineteen hundred again.

"Yvonne!" He launched from the teledisc and trundled into her, trying to lift her into a hug but failing miserably and settling for wrapping around her like a string around a lamppost. Before Xan had a chance to remember that she'd inexplicably abducted humans, stolen teeth, and destroyed the Earth, Yvonne flung him to the wall.

He remembered.

"Blitheon, Yvonne." He rubbed the back of his head where it had hit the wall. "What've you been up to? Last time I saw you, you were all 'let's save the world, I'm an altruist now, war is bad, I don't love you anymore.' And now look at you, burning up planets for kicks? Not like you. The teeth stealing thing, sure, but you used to ask, Yvonne. You've got to ask!"

"Gods don't ask permission, and you've got something I

want."

"A lightbulb? I thought you'd supply your own."

"No, you slorpfignut. You're not here to screw in a lightbulb."

"Oh, you meant sex. Right, well, you could've just asked, no need to get all euphemistic." He stood, stretched, and began tiredly undoing the buttons on his coat.

Yvonne looked to the glimmering spikes twenty feet above her in her office ceiling, praying to herself for strength. "That isn't why you're here, either. I want the probability modifier. Yvonne gave it to you and now I'm taking it back."

Xan re-did the button, watching her cautiously. "Speaking in third person now, are we? Weird. The war must've done a number on you, Yve. You're looking good though, unmentionably so."

"I swear to me, you're the thickest Tuhntian in the galaxy."

He shrugged. "Also, the smartest, seeing as I'm the only one."

"Don't be dramatic. Plenty of Tuhntians were off-world when I destroyed the planet."

Xan's mouth tried to form some kind of phrase. He tried out, "Are you telling me you destroyed Tuhnt?" but only the "A" escaped. He tried, "What are you saying?" but got as far as "Wha" before he choked. He slid down the wall, settled with a simple, "Uh?"

"You must've known the only ship capable of destroying an entire planet was the *Peacemaker*. You really are thick."

Physically, he was there. Mentally, however, he reclined on a surprisingly comfortable beach chair somewhere along the cream shores of Taeloo XII, sipping something sweet and cold which made his head numb. That was nice. Oh! A bird. Interesting bird, a little too fluffy around the skull area, but otherwise pretty good. He sipped his drink, he watched the bird, he tried not to think about where his body was.

Xan shook his head, telling a solid twelve percent of

himself to get a grip, glared at her, and thought of a few horrible names he could call her but wouldn't. "My interests don't really extend to the minutia of military vessels. I didn't realize *you* were capable of that, Yve. What happened to you?"

"Stop calling me Yve," she snarled. "I am a god and you will address me properly."

"A god, eh? Whatever gets you through the season."

She seethed at him. "I *am* a god."

As if to prove herself, Chaos dissolved the floor into a curling meadow of shimmering soot, convinced flowers the texture and color of red gumdrops to spring from ceiling in place of the spikes, called into being a meandering blue sun above them, and spun the walls of her office into soft blue and pink cotton candy which waved in the sudden breeze. Xan scrambled into a tuft of sticky spun sugar and gave a scream which sounded like an urgently deflating balloon as his boots sunk into the curling soot. Above, the gumdrop flora melted and dripped, simmering from the heat of the Stardrive above them, whistling aggressively.

"Alright, great, good to know, you're a god," Xan shouted above the din of the whistling, simmering, melting gumdrop-like flowers above them and the churning grind of the soot below.

Chaos allowed the office to return to a comfortable state of rest, begrudgingly giving the Universe permission to put things back they way they ought to have been. Soon, she'd be powerful enough to keep her illusions until they destroyed the memory of what once was.

Xan kicked a fine dusting of soot from his boots and tried, unsuccessfully, to rub the sticky cotton candy from his gloves.

"Can I, uh, can I speak to Yve, or...?"

"Ha! Even if she was still in here, she wouldn't want to talk to you," sneered Chaos.

Giving up, Xan ripped off his sticky gloves and dusted the glitter from his hands. He was done with her. If Yvonne wasn't in there, this was just a job again. He had a lightbulb to screw in... or something.

"What do you want?" he asked.

"The probability modifier." She held out her hand, in which he placed a confused blink.

"I've no idea what that means."

"The 'piece of the first star ever created.' The 'good luck charm' Yvonne gave you so you wouldn't get killed in the war. You know that was a clever marketing scheme, right? That thing was made in a lab on A'Viltri. It's a probability modifier, it should have a bit of 'good luck' left in it, and I want it back."

"Oh! That probability modifier. 'Course I knew that." Xan groped his own chest for a second before he remembered. He sighed dramatically. Of course. Would *this* have happened to him if he'd had it?

"Slight problem there: I don't have it. But if they're mass producing these things, why don't you go get your own?"

"They haven't produced them in a thousand orbits due to the horrendous repercussions," she spat then launched herself at his throat, pinning him against the wall. "Where is it?" Her nails dug into his flesh.

"Repercussions?" he wheezed, his hands weakly wrapped around her rippling forearms.

"Where is it?" she crushed his throat further and, while this didn't inhibit his ability to breathe, he could barely squeak at her.

"I'll tell you if you lay off," he mouthed, clawing at her hand around his neck.

She released him, having forgotten that mortals needed to vibrate their vocal chords in order to communicate.

"Thanks," he said, straightening his lapel. "I'm not telling you."

"It's on the *Audacity* isn't it?"

"Heh, why would you assume that? I could've thrown it out for all you know. Lost it in a bet, dropped it on some planet somewhere, given it away to someone special—it could be literally anywhere."

"Who did you give it to?" she snarled.

"I never said I gave it to someone!"

"You know, part of the beauty of a luck charm is that it precludes you from losing it. I'm growing tired of repeating myself, though."

All eight feet of her launched into him, pinned his chest under a terribly sharp knee, and punched him across the face. "Where. Is. It?" she asked again, confident he'd tell her.

Had she done proper research, had she really taken the time to sift through Yvonne's memories of their relationship, she would've known better.

Xan laughed, scrunching his nose to be sure it hadn't broken. "Kinky! Are you sure Yvonne's not in there?" He winked at her.

She punched him again. "Where?"

"In there! In you, I mean. Yvonne used to love punching me. Back then it was consensual, of course. Major difference if you ask me."

She punched him again. "The probability modifier! What did you do with it?"

He laughed, tasting blood on the back of his tongue. "Would you believe me if I said I didn't remember?"

She punched him again.

"Thought not. No point in lying, then." His nose was definitely broken now, which was a shame because he used it quite a lot and rather liked how it looked unbroken. Ah well, thought Xan, back to the shores of Taeloo XII.

The bird was preening itself now, which was mildly entertaining to watch.

Chaos was very much accustomed to getting what she wanted. Listay had spoiled her, in that way, catering to her whims and fancies, flattering her from a respectful distance, enslaving the human race. Chaos ground Yvonne's teeth so intensely that she had to stop for a moment to spit out part of a bicuspid. Yvonne's body wasn't going to last her very long at this rate.

She would need another way of attacking this problem. Most of what Yvonne had remembered about Xan had said he was a coward—had said this in no uncertain terms, actually, and with vastly more colorful language. This had led her to assume that getting the probability modifier back from him would be easy as turning an office chair into pie.

"You've one last chance to tell me where it is, and I'm turning this plasma zapper to a random setting and shooting." She yanked a zapper from her belt and, as promised, spun the dial like a roulette wheel before jamming it into his sternum.

"I think you mean 'or.' 'You've one last chance to tell me where it is, *or* I'm—"

She shot him.

THIRTY-FOUR
# CONSPICUOUSLY MUSTACHIOED

"How long," May asked the sponge which perched obliviously on her finger and swayed a little when she talked, "does it take for an alien to screw in a lightbulb?"

Not long was probably the answer, but Osy wasn't offering any useful insights. She petted the top of it with a single finger and it vibrated in response.

Lounging on the couch had become tiresome, lounging at the hover table was uncomfortable, lounging on the floor was depressing, so May lounged in the pilot's chair, watching space-time space-tick away.

Her sense of time had become unutterably distorted, seconds stretched into hours and hours packed themselves neatly into the space of a few minutes. It was driving her mad. So, she watched the clock and tried to suss out the conversions.

If Estrichi time had any correlation to Earth time, which it didn't, May worked out that each blip felt like about the space of a second, fifty blips made a bloop, making the bloop something of a minute, fifty further bloops created a beoop which further compiled into a single rotation eventually, but she hadn't quite gotten there yet. Almost.

He'd been gone for nearly a rotation. A rotation was starting to feel like a day which, May thought a bit dully, made more sense than the word "day" did, anyway. Beoop, though. She would have to speak with someone about the word beoop.

It really should not have taken quite this long. She pulled the good luck charm from between her breasts and watched it spin on its chain for a moment. The charm, she thought, would probably be of more use to Xan right now. Wherever he was.

She could go find him. That option was definitely on the table. But the moment she left, he'd probably turn back up and think she'd absconded with his ship.

Another bloop ticked by on the ship's viewscreen. She'd give it five more bloops, then she'd go looking for him.

To save time, she ran through the ship's teledisc log and found his anchor button coordinates from which she could track him. She understood the coordinates just a touch further than Xan did, in the way that a MySpace user understands HTML coding.

It took two bloops to set the coordinates, now she had three bloops to think about what she was about to do.

Chase after someone who was clearly keeping some vital piece of information from her. Someone who was almost definitely a criminal. Someone who'd supposedly only helped her as a sort of karmic band-aid.

Somehow, she didn't believe that last part.

She hit The Button That Typically Made The Ship Go and she went.

As the *Audacity* neared its destination—a button on Xan's coat—it slowed to allow for safe docking. May peered out through the viewscreen as they approached, looking for a planet or something. It shouldn't be that hard to see a planet from this distance. But it was not a planet the ship had brought her to.

May swallowed. It was not a planet at all. It was a ship.

A very large ship that looked to have been recently patched on one side. A very large ship that looked to have been recently patched on one side due to a retrofitted AMC Gremlin blasting its way through the hull.

A disguise, thought May, would probably be a good idea. In the utility closet, which had become her own personal haven, a bio-hazard janitorial suit had been folded away along with a cap and a set of yellow-lensed goggles. She stepped into the crunchy, cheap feeling suit and zipped it up to her neck, tucking her hair into the cap and allowing the goggles to sit around her neck like a statement piece.

Mounted on the wall, in a red glass case that said "break in case of emergency" with a little mallet on a string connected to it, sat a bushy fake mustache and a bottle of spirit gum. She considered it seriously for a moment, too nervous to think it odd that such a thing would be there, then decided against it. Fake mustaches were always ridiculously conspicuous.

The ship slowed further. It was getting fairly close to its target, and really would've preferred if a sentient being handled the finer details of the landing. May sprung to the control panel and stopped the autopilot, opening the ship's directive log to do some fiddling around. Within blips, she had the ship believing that it was, and always had been, a service vehicle.

She smiled, satisfied that she was cleverly disguised, and began her approach to the docking bay doors. The viewscreen flickered with the image of a green-skinned being whose lips were hidden behind an impossibly thick, black mustache.

"Requesting access to the *Peacemaker*," May said with as much confidence as an earthworm drying in the sun. It was extremely cold onboard the *Audacity*, but May was sweating.

"Directive?"

"Uh, emergency janitorial services." She tried to keep the question out of her voice.

To her relief, the mustache lifted into a smile. "Hey, Sal! They're here to fix the sink!"

"Oh, yeah? Terrific! Get on in here," a more feminine, green-skinned being jogged over, their face also conspicuously mustachioed.

For the ninety-eighth time that week, May questioned her decision making skills.

"I cannot thank you enough for coming out on such short notice. Just ya' see, it's an emergency and all," said the first.

Sweat dribbled down the small of May's back in a way that would've tickled if it weren't so gross. "Don't thank me yet," she had to backtrack a bit, lest she be expected to know what she was doing. "I'm just here to write a quote. They'll be sending in a fleet once I report back to corporate."

"A whole fleet!"

The airlock door opened to admit her; first, the outermost door, which closed behind her, then the inner door. She set the ship down in an empty space between the rows of AMC Gremlins and stepped on the teledisc.

The two beings met her outside the ship, the shorter one offering a hand that she couldn't refuse and pulling her along to a shut and shackled door. An ominous green glow spilled from the spaces around the door which gurgled faintly.

"Oh," she said as they reached the door, hoping they wouldn't expect her to go in. "Um, I have to make a phone call." She excused herself and bolted to a safe alcove in the docking bay. Did they even have phones? Had the word "phone" translated to them at all? She'd have to be more careful, she thought, pretending to talk to someone on her non-existent BEAPER, just in case they were listening.

"This is inspector number 4278965..." she let her mouth continue to spout random numbers as she thought. She was on board, but the ship was enormous and without the ship's computer, she'd lost the trail of the anchor button.

"...06789Alpha. I'm going to need backup." She pretended to listen to a string of alien curses as she continued to work out her next move. "I'll see what I can do," she said to no one and pretended to hang up.

Pulling her sleeve down well past where her BEAPER should've been, May exited the alcove.

"Uh, ma'am?" said the thin one. "Could you come with us? I know this must be terribly inconvenient for you but uh..." They nudged the short one with a boney green elbow.

"It's just you've gotta...well..." They looked extremely uncomfortable. "The Mistress Yvonne would like to see you. I'm sure it's nothing!" they added quickly. "Pro'ly just commending you on how quickly you got here." The mustache smiled, but nervously.

Well, that was that. The jig was officially up. At least, thought May, Yvonne would likely know where Xan was. That was something.

"We don't actually have to...?" the thin one whispered to the short one. The short one shook their head.

"No, no. 'Course not." They eyed May uneasily. "You're, um," they asked her, "you're going to let us take you right? We don't need to," they laughed uncomfortably, "threaten you or anything right? 'Cause I'd hate to do that. Really and truly I would."

"No, I'll come with you. Just trying to do my job," she tried. *They* believed her, at least. The mustaches had faith in her.

The thin one nodded, with a reassuring smile. "It'll be fine, ma'am. Mistress Yvonne can be very reasonable."

The short one squinted at the thin one and whispered, "When has Mistress Yvonne ever been—" The thin one jabbed the short one again.

May followed them to an intershoot which they reached into to type a code before sending her off with two unconvincing smiles under two conspicuous mustaches. The intershoot sent her upwards and, she realized after a moment of vertigo, diagonally into the ship.

If this was a trap, if Xan had been playing some sort of long game to get her back in Yvonne's clutches, she was going to kill him.

# THIRTY-FIVE

# SHIFTY MARACAS

Chaos was waiting for her. As May rose into the Fortress, she came face-to-chest with the towering figure, as tall as IX had been but several pounds heavier in muscle and hair-mass from the looks of her.

"Huh, I didn't think Xan was into short women," was all she said. Something whacked May on the head, knocking her senses off-line.

"Good morning starshine," she heard vaguely as if in a dream.

"Xan?" she sat up, only to be nearly knocked over by the force of Xan propelling himself into her.

He squeezed her tightly. "Zuut, it's good to see you! Wait!" He pushed her away. "No, it's not. What the trok are you doing here? Yvonne's gone nuts! Thinks she's a god! Did she get the—"

"Yep," May said, feeling her chest for the good luck charm.

"Terrific." Xan's face twisted bitterly.

May rubbed her head, worried that Yvonne might've knocked some wiring loose. She was seeing double. No, quadruple. No, infinit-tuple.

"Mirrors," said Xan, noticing her confusion. "Blocks the signal for this," he held up his BEAPER. "Hey, since you're here could you, uh, help me with something?"

She nodded, looking him over now. He tapped his nose which jutted out at an uncomfortable looking angle.

"Would you punch me in the face? But like, the other way? Straighten me out a bit?"

"Oh, I don't know if I could."

"Sure, you can! Hey, uh," he looked at her through half-lidded eyes, winked, shimmied his shoulders a little, "I'm Raskov the Beautiful," he said with what sounded oddly to May like a Russian accent. "Why don't I show you my pipes, babe?"

She punched him, feeling his nose crack back into place as she did.

"Ah, excellent! Thanks, mun," he said, holding his nose as he winced through the pain. "And thanks for looking for me. I really didn't expect you to. Didn't want you to, honestly, but it was a nice gesture."

"Why didn't you want me to?"

"Well, Yvonne's nuts, like I said! You escaped her once, now you're going to have to do it all over again." He leaned back now and sighed. "She's got what she wanted. I don't know what she's keeping us around for, but it's probably going to be more than teeth this time."

"Right, then as long as I have you locked in a mirrored room, you're going to answer a few questions," May said in what she hoped was a serious no-nonsense tone of voice.

Xan's face scrunched. "Sure you wouldn't rather punch me again instead?"

"What aren't you telling me? Those robots were about to arrest you! And the *Audacity* is a military ship reclassified as a racing rocket, why? And furthermore, why was that man chasing us on Platamousse? I don't believe for a second anyone finds you that attractive."

"Alright, well, firstly: ouch, and secondly: *ouch.*" He rubbed his chest as if she had plunged a dagger into it and she noticed that his suit was torn away and scorched in the middle. He stopped talking.

She sighed. "What happened there?"

"Oh, Yvonne shot me. Not much, mind you, it's fine," he shrugged. "I tell you what, though, she really has changed. She would never have shot me without permission before. She said Yvonne's gone but, I don't know about that. Still looks like her. She's got to be in there somewhere right?"

"I don't know. Why did she shoot you?"

"Because I wouldn't tell her that I'd given the good luck charm to you," he said, an accusing edge to his voice. "I was trying to protect you, you know. I'm not evil. Not like Raskov." He tried to laugh; it didn't work.

May groaned. "Yeah, I know. I just wish you'd talk to me."

"And I do! Lots! Tons! An inordinate amount, actually, I love talking. Talking is the best."

"Oh, do shut up." Chaos manifested behind them, duplicating herself into infinity terrifying specters, her silver hair billowing as if a model photography intern were holding an enormous fan in front of her.

She squinted as if the breeze from the fan was irritating her unmentionable eyes. "You fixed your nose. I liked it better broken. Here." She tossed a flashlight at Xan, which he caught, followed by a small bulb. "Make yourself useful."

He unscrewed the head of the flashlight, watching her uneasily as he replaced the bulb, then handed it back to her.

She smiled coolly, slipped the flashlight into her belt, and turned to May.

"I've got time to kill before I enslave Earth, and you can only give a Newton's Cradle an existential crisis so many times before that becomes boring. You're a human, aren't you?"

"You should know, you've got my DNA," May seethed.

"Indeed, I do. Not sure why I did that, but Yvonne so

loved teeth. They placated her." Chaos ground her teeth again, smiling cruelly as another peak dislodged from one of Yvonne's bicuspids. She plucked it out of her mouth and flicked it aside. Teeth were useless to an all-powerful goddess, anyway.

May shuddered; she hated teeth things.

"So," Chaos observed May, "what's the story, here, Xan? Trying something new? Taste for human flesh?"

"No. Don't be gross, Yve."

"Stop calling me that." Without touching him, she flung him against the far mirror, shattering the entire wall. She quickly recalled the mirrors back into being before Xan had a chance to teleport out.

"Hey!" May shouted. "You have what you wanted, let us go."

"Oh, poor Tiny Human—that is your name, right?"

"May."

"Right. Poor Tiny Human May. How long have you been aboard the infamous *Audacity?*"

May thought for a moment; time had really lost track of her. It felt like awhile, at least. "Maybe a month, two?"

Chaos nodded solemnly. "And in all that time has Xan ever told you about Tuhnt? About how he caused the genocide of his own people?"

May had to admit it didn't ring any bells. Well no, it did: alarm bells.

"Stop it. She's just a human," Xan said darkly, picking bits of mirror out of his skin.

Delight lifted Chaos's eyebrows, her face opening in a devilish grin. "Oh, is she just a human to you? Won't mind if I kill her, then, right?"

She casually drew her well-loved plasma zapper. May flinched; Xan sprung. The blast tore into his shoulder with a beam so hot the hole was neatly cauterized. Chaos blew a puff of smoke off the tip of her gun.

"How boring." She glanced at her BEAPER. On Earth, it was exactly one hour and thirty-seven minutes past her promised arrival. She'd officially passed fashionably late and was decidedly chaotically late. "Xan, have fun explaining yourself. I know how much you love to talk."

Chaos and her army of reflections disappeared.

Xan lay on the floor, staring unblinkingly at himself. "Are you alright?" May asked.

"Yep," he said flatly. "You?"

She nodded, studying the hole in his shoulder.

"Doesn't that hurt?"

"Oh well, you know," he sighed, "immensely."

"What did she mean by genocide?"

"May, look. I'm in tremendous physical pain at the moment and while I'd love to reminisce about the past, I just don't think it would help either of us right now. So, could we talk about something nice? Like, I don't know. Congas? How do you feel about them?" He shimmied towards the wall like a drunk sea cucumber until he could prop himself up against it.

May sighed, removed the janitorial cap to shake out her hair, and slid down beside him, resting her head on his good shoulder. "I don't know. There definitely are worse drums out there. Those, um, those wooden box drums that you sit on-"

"Cajons," Xan helped.

"Yeah. Not a fan. It's trying to be a drum and a chair at the same time. What gives it the right?"

"Really? I don't hate any kind of drum, so to speak. I think tambourines are shams but other than that...it's maracas I can't stand. Can't trust a maraca."

"Shifty maracas. How do you know about so many Earth instruments?"

"Lu-"

"Lucy," she cut him off, answering her own question.

They laughed together, and Xan was pleased. For a few minutes there and for several different reasons, he was worried he would never get to laugh with her again.

The pair were silent for a long while, May stewing in the full ridiculousness of her situation as she stared at herself in the mirror. She wondered for a moment, peering inquisitorially into her own eyes, if she wished she'd died on Earth like everyone else, like Kathy and...and her mom. Certainly, it would've been easier, quicker. Less interesting, though. And the past few weeks had been fun.

The last time a "friend" took her to the movies, she'd ended up in the backseat of his car trying to convince herself she was having a good time. Xan wouldn't do that to her. She trusted him. On that front, at least.

She closed her eyes.

"Hey Xan, why did you say I was *just* a human? Is that a bad thing?"

"Of course not! I love humans. Humans are great." He smiled at her. "The most amazing story-tellers, always getting into wacky shenanigans, hungry all the time, so extremely, insanely, ridiculously fragile." He gulped the smile away.

"Not that fragile," she countered.

"Come on, you live like, what, eighty orbits?"

"A little more. I think orbits are shorter than years," she said, defensively.

"Alright, well, we'll see who survives who, eh? Taking all bets." He patted her hair gently. She felt the mirror ripple behind her as he banged his head back into it.

So that was it. She was a pet to him, like a parrot. Only parrots actually lived quite a long time—she was goldfish. A talking goldfish.

"So. Got any ideas for breaking out of here?" Xan asked.

May reached behind her hair and extracted Osy. "One. Have you ever seen *Lassie Come Home*?"

"I'm not an uncultured zoup-nog, May. Of course I have! But that's a tool. It has a very limited understanding of language and even less of loyalty."

She shrugged. "Can't hurt. Osy, get help!" she told the sponge. It drifted over to a seam between the mirror and a row of white lights and rolled slowly along the length of the seam, too large or too dumb to squeeze through.

The mirrored room cast itself into a red glow.

It's important to note that red is not universally regarded as a color of warning, since most species can sense colors much more alarming than red. Explaining the color of Danger Diophalothene, which is something between red and infrared, to someone who's never seen the color diophalothene before, however, is extremely uncomfortable for all parties involved. In truth, the mirrored room cast itself into a Danger Diophalothene glow, but May saw red.

A siren blared. Sirens are universal.

## THIRTY-SIX
# MURDEROUS MUNS

August polished a bit of chrome on the inner wall of the *Robert* with his coat sleeve. He felt it was important to occasionally see how he looked in a mirror, lest he forget entirely.

He peered into the polished metal. Oh, he thought, that's why he never looked.

IX had kept up with his grooming, keeping his beard immaculately trimmed and his hair in shoulder-length silver waves, but Time had taken a ballpoint pen to his face and Time wasn't an accomplished artist. By his count, he was somewhere between forty and forty-five now. Though, due to the difficulties of keeping up with birthdays in space, he decided he might as well stay thirty-nine forever.

He gave himself a half-hearted smile of semi-approval before joining IX in the cockpit of the *Robert* where she'd been carefully combing through a holographic map of the Milky Way which emanated from her BEAPER.

"August, look!" She sounded excited. Nothing got IX excited. This was probably big. He sat beside her and she expanded a section of the galaxy that wasn't terribly far from their current location and pointed to a small, yellow star.

"Is that Earth?" August asked.

"We are mere beoops away. It is perhaps a season past our original departure, but there still may be a chance to save Yvonne. And soon you will be home. Provided Yvonne has not destroyed it, of course."

August nodded. "Right," he said, sitting back heavily in the passenger seat.

They sat in silence for a while.

IX had expected a little more elaboration. He was generally the one who elaborated, and she wasn't sure how to continue the conversation. "I guess," she said, "what I meant to say...or, rather, what I meant to ask is: what will you do? You have spent nearly as much time out here as you have on Earth."

August nodded again. "Yep. Guess I'll figure it out when we get there." He kept his eyes on the screens, knowing he might never see the stars from this angle again. He'd never liked space-travel, but now that he was nearing the end of his journey, he was finally starting to enjoy it. It felt extremely unfair.

"August?" IX asked, her voice quiet.

"Yes?"

IX thought for a moment. She had thoughts and feelings and things she just wanted him to know but the moment she opened her mouth she found no words to express them. Perhaps there weren't any Rhean words for what she meant to say.

The silence dragged on...and on.

Finally, August looked at her. "I don't know if Rheans do this but..." He held out his hand to her.

She smiled. "Of course." She took his hand and they sat together in a silence that felt much, much more comfortable this time.

More comfortable, that is, until the *Robert* lurched and bucked and finally came to a stop. August panicked. "We have plenty of fuel, why did we stop?" He tapped the gauges, thinking it would help in some way.

IX crawled into the backseat of the *Robert* and down the

hatch that led to the engine room. It wasn't so much a room as it was a space. And even then, it was hardly a space. They could both fit in it, on their hands and knees, but August was never terribly happy about it.

Still, he joined her in the space, hoping to be of some use.

"What happened? Was it those damn muns again? I knew we should've picked up the space-cat-thing at the last fuel port."

"It was a kracklepuss. In a ship this small, it would fry us if we forgot to play with it."

"But it would've eaten the muns! And it was cute."

"You are enough trouble on your own," IX teased as she pulled at the engine casing. It came away with a shower of thumb-sized muns that scattered in all directions, squeaking their distress. IX slipped a leather glove on her hand and felt around the generator, extracting a heavy, frayed cable. "They chewed through the generator main line. Do you have the-"

"Electrical tape." August handed the well-used roll of tape to her. They had just enough left to precariously stitch the cable back together. The ship wheezed, coughed, and tentatively turned itself back on.

"C'mon, buddy," August patted the searing hot engine with his metal hand. "Just two more beoops and we'll get you taken care of." He winced, knowing that this would be *Robert*'s last trip. The retro-fitted AMC Gremlin had been forty-four years old when they stole it, now it was nearing sixty-five. The seats and half of the car's steel body were the only original parts left. IX had replaced parts of the ship almost as regularly as she'd replaced parts of August.

IX returned to the driver's seat and quietly rested her chin on her palms, her fingertips lightly dragging on her cheeks. August had never seen her in such an emotional state, he was very concerned.

"Do you think he can handle re-entry?"

IX moved her head ever so slightly. Whether it was back and forth or up and down he really couldn't say.

They stewed in the tension for a while, the lights

flickering at every jostle. Earth appeared through the windshield. They first recognized it at the size of a marble, soon it was a golf ball, then a tennis ball. It continued to increase in relation to Earth ball games until it was all they could see.

IX pushed back in her seat and gripped the foam-vomiting armrests. She turned her head away as if putting off impact by a few milliseconds would help.

The *Robert* entered the atmosphere.

August couldn't really tell if it was sweat or melted skin that was pouring down his face, but he was not ready to give up just yet. The *Robert* plunged towards the ground, all systems down, all shields failing, all hopes actively being dashed.

There was absolutely no chance the *Peacemaker* would pick them up if they sent a distress call. But, then again, absolutely no chance they would be rescued was better than being absolutely certain they would die.

August, with a strength brought on by sheer terror, snapped the pinky off his robotic hand, electricity sizzling from the stub as he jammed it into the distress signal button. Then, he tried to remember the names of every single benevolent god he'd heard about in his travels and dutifully prayed to each of them.

## THIRTY-SEVEN
# BACK TO NORMAL

Yvonne knew how to land the *Peacemaker* without damaging it or the surrounding area. Chaos also knew how to land the *Peacemaker* without damaging it or the surrounding area, but where was the fun in that? Besides, her people would just eat up a starship crash. What better way to announce her existence to a Chaos-hungry populace than to destroy a few blocks of one of Listay's perfectly planned cities?

So, Chaos brought the ship into the Earth's atmosphere and just sort of let it do what it felt was right.

It's difficult to understand what being in a crashing starship feels like if you've never had the pleasure. It's something akin to being inside a cruise liner as it plummets to the Earth at head-spinning speeds, which is also difficult to understand if you've never done it.

The Danger Diophalothene lights didn't make it any less horrific. In fact, it was their singular pleasure to cast an atmosphere of impending doom about the ship.

"What's happening?" asked May, trying to stand up. Xan put a hand on her shoulder.

"Safer down here, mun. Yvonne said she was going to Earth; from the look of those diophalothene lights, she's crashing to Earth. Might want to put on those goggles."

May did, the yellow lenses and the red light tinting everything orange, which somehow calmed her. "We've got to get out of here."

Xan shrugged. "The crash will probably shatter these mirrors, then we can teleport back to the *Audacity* and we're out. All we've got to do now is enjoy the ride. Try to not get too much glass in your face, I don't recommend it." He picked another shard of glass out of his cheek from where Chaos had thrown him into the mirror. "I'll be finding these for seasons," he muttered.

In that moment, May realized humans were, indeed, fragile. In comparison, at least.

"Xan, that will definitely kill me."

He looked at her as if he didn't believe her, or perhaps as if he didn't want to. "Hey, who knows? Might kill me, too. We haven't got much choice, though, so no point worrying about it."

Panic was not something May typically allowed herself to experience. She'd found that, in most bad situations, she usually had some clear course of action to take to keep herself from thinking about how utterly terrible everything was. If she was doing something, she was surviving.

Not worrying at a time like this was not surviving.

"Damnit, I refuse to let you outlive me," she told him, standing now to pat down the thick janitorial suit for something that might be of use. Aha!

"Spanner!" May said.

"Well, there's no need to curse."

"No," she wrenched the wrench out of a tight pocket in the suit and waved it in front of him, "there was a spanner in here the whole time."

"That's a bit too convenient, don't you think?"

She ignored him, flung the spanner into the far wall,

and shattered the mirror. It crashed away to reveal a section of hallway flooded with a diverse array of white-latex-clad beings pelting themselves at the intershoots as they made their way to the docking bay to evacuate the ship.

"Up." She grabbed Xan's good arm and failed miserably at pulling him to his feet; he was much heavier than she had imagined.

"I'm coming, corral your puntls," he said, rolling himself up with a tired groan. He seemed to shake something off his very soul, then said, "Alright! Back to *Audy!*" His face broke into a wide grin again as they teleported onto the *Audacity*.

Back onboard the rocket, May tore off the goggles and crawled out of the janitorial suit, leaving her disguise where it fell, while Xan flew to the control panel and scanned the buttons and levers helplessly. "Think you can shoot a hole in the *Peacemaker* to get us out of here?"

May hopped up to the loft and joined him, grateful to be out of the hot, sweaty suit and in the familiar cool air onboard the *Audacity*. "Oh no, sorry, the Ultra-Ray-Super-Destroyers I installed aren't for shooting. They're for blasting."

It took Xan a long three blips to figure out that she was joking, which was enough time for May to re-open the gaping hole in the *Peacemaker's* hull with the newly installed Ultra-Ray-Super-Destroyers and hurl the rocket through the hole and into the sky.

Xan laughed. "Right, silly me. Thinking the lasers were meant for shooting. Ridiculous."

They sat back in their respective seats and sighed happily as the ship ferried them upwards through the Earth's atmosphere toward the safe, if terrifying, nothingness of open space.

Things were back to normal.

Until a notification appeared on the viewscreen which

May, without reading fully, accepted, allowing a fervently praying and gently sparking bearded man in a long coat and a dusky purple, milky-eyed Rhean to appear on the teledisc.

# THIRTY-EIGHT

# WHOOPS NOT YET

"May!" the scraggly praying man shouted at her. "We thought you were dead!" He moved to hug her, but she jumped up defensively and he paused.

It is always uncomfortable when someone you don't think you know definitely thinks they know you. Fortunately, he explained himself before she had to ask.

"Oh, right. I must look pretty different. It's August. IX and I were sent back almost two decades in that wormhole. Fancy meeting you here in the afterlife. Whose afterlife is this anyway? It's pretty dated."

May waffled between being speechless at seeing him again and feeling a little stung that he'd insulted the *Audacity.* "You're pretty dated," she replied.

August laughed, shrugged. "You got me," he said. "Glad you're alive, kid. Hey, IX, we're in some sort of 70's throwback living room onboard a rocket with May and—" August gestured towards Xan who lounged cautiously.

"Xan," he offered, but only just.

IX's face scrunched. She did a convincing job of looking like she was looking at him. "Xan under Carmnia of Trilly on Tuhnt?"

He rubbed the bridge of his nose. "The very same."

"I am IX, Yvonne's...." She paused. "I am close with Yvonne. She spoke much of you."

"Good things?"

"No."

"Oh."

May studied August, searching for something she recognized in him. "What happened to your hand?"

"Well it's quite a story," August began.

"Baking accident," IX finished. "August, we have a mission, remember."

"Right. May," August said, awkwardly holding his own arm, his hug having been rebuked. "Our ship... he's..." August looked like he might be sick. "We don't have a ship anymore, and IX wanted to try to get Yvonne back, and she thinks she knows how to do that but we need to get back on the *Peacemaker* to do *that*, and it would really be great to have a getaway vehicle, and, if we don't, Yvonne's going to absolutely decimate Earth. Can you help?"

The *Audacity* continued upward. May sunk onto the couch. It wasn't her decision, right? Not her ship, not her decision. Neither was racing, but she'd goaded Xan into doing that. Now she was being asked to rescue Earth and she was hesitating. She glanced over her shoulder at Xan who still sat in the co-pilot's chair, watching her.

"What exactly do you need from us?" May asked.

IX put a hand on August's shoulder to keep him from attempting to give her an extremely incorrect answer. "Yvonne is possessed by an ancient spirit which calls itself a chaos goddess. The *Peacemaker*'s engine runs on energy siphoned from a distant white dwarf star via Stardrive. I believe the spirit attached to the star to survive and lay dormant until it found Yvonne and possessed her. If we destroy the Stardrive, the resulting entropy should cause the white dwarf to collapse, along with the entity."

"And Yvonne will be back to a more normal sort of horrifying?" Xan interjected.

"Precisely. If we do not destroy the entity now, she may become unstoppably powerful."

"It's too late." May said. "She's already taken over Earth. I watched her kill my friend." While Kathy and May had never considered each other friends before, now they each believed the other to be dead, and death changes things.

"That was stage one. Yvonne had, in hopes of recruiting me, shared her plan with me. It was abhorrent, and I declined. She wished to find a willing populace, force them into servitude under a scapegoat, then appear as their savior to be worshipped, feeding off their adoration."

May rubbed her face; it helped her think.

She was not a hero.

She wasn't even a humanitarian, if she were being completely honest with herself.

She wanted to work hard and be recognized for that work and see some degree of success someday, but on Earth no one had ever recognized her for the work she did. It was just slogging through life day in and day out, paying bills and working and sleeping and eating and smoking and...May felt something wet pooling on her bottom eyelashes.

There was a way out of this decision.

She ran her hands over her eyes in a casual, collected sort of way and sniffed curtly.

"Xan, she's your ship," she said, cleverly passing the buck.

This was one buck Xan refused to accept. "Oh, *now* she's my ship." He stood, hopped down from the control loft, and perched on the back of the couch beside her. "You've got a chance to save your home planet from utter annihilation at the hands of an insane god-like-entity and you're asking me to decide what to do?"

"I wouldn't be able to live with myself if I refused, would I?" she asked him.

For once, Xan's mouth was a tight line, his eyes inexpressive. He shook his head, but just a little bit, as if the answer itself was so large it only required the tiniest expression.

No.

No, she would not.

May turned to IX. "You're suggesting we shoot at the Stardrive to destroy the star it's linked to?"

"Yes. Shooting at the drive should cause the star to collapse."

May shook her head. "Ah, damn." She looked at Xan. "We've only got blasting lasers. Is it alright if I blast it instead?"

IX tilted her head almost imperceptibly. "Of course. Those words are synonyms, they have nearly the same meaning."

"I'll make the coffee!" Xan said, launching from his seat on the couch and pulling out four equally chipped coffee mugs.

# THIRTY-NINE

# ALIEN SCUM

Listay loved lists. Not as much as spreadsheets, mind you. Spreadsheets are data-heavy lists and, to Listay, the highest circle of heaven. A clean, simple, one column list was nice, though.

This list, however, troubled her greatly. It was a list of numbers, each number representing a human whose rebellion had so advanced that even the highest zapper setting on the spheres couldn't dissuade them. It was getting distressingly long. She pulled it up on her BEAPER to add another miscreant, scrolling for some time before she reached the end. Perhaps her plan was not sustainable.

A ping on the window which overlooked the city caught her attention. She watched the perfectly paved road far below, and her heart began beating at an extremely inappropriate sixty-two beats per beoop.

Nearly every human on her list, the list of her failures which loomed like a program error code in the distance, had gathered at her control tower. Many held re-programed spheres, wrapped tightly in chefs coats and aprons, sticky with honey and betrayal.

Something had gone terribly wrong with her plan. And things were about to go wronger.

A shadow fell across the perfect city which stretched before her. It was the *Peacemaker*, and the autopilot was deciding which of the two perfectly planned city districts it would be less morally repugnant to crush. It settled on crushing exactly half of one and half of the other and landed with a squeal of buckling metal.

Seventy beats per beoop, now. Listay didn't care. A detailed repair plan began to form in the back of her head. She could have the city back to normal within two and a quarter beoops, provided the angry mob didn't hinder construction.

She felt a slight breeze and a tingle of electricity behind her. Something—someone who had not been there before suddenly was.

Chaos reformed on Listay's desk, her silver hair undulating massively around her face, her eyes doing unmentionably horrifying things, an ugly little chunk of rock glowing gently between her terrifying breasts.

"Thank the goddess you're here, Yvonne. I'm not sure what's happened, there's a mob outside. If I kill them all, I'll wipe out a third of our food service humans."

"Call me Chaos," she said.

"I'll call you whatever you want, but please, I need your help. The spheres are addicted to honey; I can't figure out what's wrong with them."

"Listay," Chaos grabbed her chin in a well-practiced way. Not that she ever had difficulty holding the general's attention. "I'm what's wrong with them. I like them this way; it's more fun."

"You did that to my spheres? Have you any idea how difficult it is to clean honey out of a gyroscope?" Listay said.

Chaos almost jumped out of her skin with excitement. She might have actually, for a moment, before remembering that she still needed to be corporeal.

"That's why I did it."

"You're an evil woman," Listay said, more awed than angry. She was too shocked to be angry.

"Ha!" the laugh was sharp, ear-drum splitting. "Says the enslaver of humanity. How must they feel about you? I would imagine all you are to them is an evil alien overlord."

Listay swallowed, Chaos's fingernails were biting into her cheeks. "I helped them," she said shakily. "I gave their lives order and meaning, I took away all the questions and eliminated all the wrong choices. I gave them each a purpose. They're happy this way."

"Oh, are they? Then why do you have an angry mob gathered below waiting to watch your death?"

"My what?"

Chaos pulled Yvonne's lips taught over her teeth in what wasn't so much a smile as it was a predator showing their prey the tools of its eminent demise. Listay, so enraptured with Chaos's mesmerizing gaze, hadn't noticed the nasty looking Proton Fusion Ray 6000 whose nose was now poking experimentally into the soft space under her ribs.

"But I loved you," Listay whispered urgently, as if it mattered.

"Gross."

Listay felt the blast from the Proton Fusion Ray 6000 push her backwards through the glass window of her office. She felt the glass shatter, the air rush by her unhelpfully, the food service humans part to allow her direct access to the concrete.

A blonde human leaned over her, leaned in close enough that Listay could smell the artificial strawberry flavoring in her lip-tint. "All hail The Mistress of Chaos, you alien scum."

The human plunged a shiv made from a standard issue food tray into Listay's chest. Cheering, several other humans joined the woman, violently venting their frustration upon her like steam escaping a tea kettle. Listay closed her eyes.

She resignedly kept track of her heartbeat, listening vaguely to the insults of the food service humans. Ten beats per beoop, five... three...

She waited.

Chaos watched from above, standing on the ledge of the broken window, Yvonne's hand bleeding profusely as she clutched at the shattered rim of thick glass to steady herself. Once the humans were thoroughly convinced Listay was dead, they turned their attention upward toward their goddess who gleamed unnaturally bright from the window above them, silver hair whipping around her face just as it had in their dreams.

A millennium is a long time to go without having your name chanted by a few thousand of your most pious devotees. But now they chanted, and it felt incredible.

The atoms which built the physicality of the city surrounding her quivered in fear. That was nice. She experimented with them, twisting a few trillion atoms from a nearby bakery into a gurgling bubble-gum-like mass. Not a bad start at all.

"My people." She didn't have to shout; her voice reverberated around the city, emanating from the tastefully manicured shrubbery which separated the road from the sidewalk. "You are free!"

Chaos felt like showing off now. Banks became enormous Hohner melodicas that consumed any confused humans who dared to venture near, department stores were stocked with nothing but warped Pyrex lids and expired Christmas-colored candy corn, and wildly discordant free improvisation jazz began streaming from city rubbish bins, which were looking more and more like standing loudspeakers.

Cheers evolved into screams. Chaos shuddered in absolute ecstasy.

FORTY

# THE PLAN

While the city below dealt with the fallout from Chaos's campaign of degradation, a plan was being formed aboard the *Audacity*. Or, rather, a plan which was already fully formed by IX was being disseminated over coffee.

"Is there any iteration of this plan in which we aren't sucked into a black hole?" Xan set his empty coffee mug on the carpet where he sat cross-legged next to May, facing IX and August who sat at the hover table.

IX had just finished explaining her plan, which did indeed involve being much closer to a collapsing Stardrive than was generally recommended.

"If I get us out of the *Peacemaker* before it jumps across the galaxy but after I shoot the Stardrive, we'll be lightyears away from the blackhole when it forms. Or it'll be lightyears away from us," May said, her tongue gritty from the thick coffee she'd chugged in hopes of psyching herself up. It hadn't hit yet.

"Precisely," said IX. "There will be a .23 blip delay before the entropy of the Stardrive's destruction causes the collapse of the star it is connected to."

Xan looked like a fish trying to climb a tree. "This all

sounds rather needlessly complex. Why can't you set the *Peacemaker* to self-destruct then autopilot it away? Why do we have to manually do the destructing?"

IX tilted her head, her brow working towards a concerned 'M.' "Why would you assume the *Peacemaker* is capable of self-destructing? What would be the point of such a feature?"

"Wha...all ships have a self-destruct, right?" He turned to May. "Right?"

She shook her head. "The *Audacity* doesn't."

"Really?"

"Xan, you've pressed every button and flipped every switch on that console. If she had a self-destruct you would've found it by now."

"Irregardless." IX waved her hand at the pair to dissuade further discussion. "There will be enough time to exit the *Peacemaker* if we disable the *Audacity's* collision cushion. I will set a flight path for the *Peacemaker* to make a hyper jump, then I will return here. We must destroy the Stardrive exactly .23 blips before the *Peacemaker* is set to jump. The Stardrive will release enough energy to jump the ship before it collapses, creating a black hole in an uninhabited sector of the galaxy. The chaos spirit will be drawn into it, theoretically releasing Yvonne and, conjointly, saving Earth from a terrible fate."

"I have something to say," August said importantly. "Are you going to drink that?" He pointed to IX's steaming mug of black sludge.

IX pushed it gently across the table toward him.

August hadn't had coffee in about two decades. August hadn't truly felt completely and totally alive in about two decades. He downed his second cup.

May unhooked the *Audacity's* anchor button from her suit and handed it to IX. "It'll be quicker if you teleport back here after setting the flight path."

"I will give us exactly two bloops before the hyperspace jump," IX told her, accepting the button and clipping it onto her own suit.

"I thought I had the time thing figured out, but

apparently not." May said.

"I can field this one, finally! Estrichi time," said August. "Estrichi is the planet by which all space-traveling peoples keep time. It's about the same size as Earth, which makes the conversations kind of close. Not exact, but you get the sense, at least. You've got the blip," he counted on his fingers now, "the bloop, and the beoop."

"That's horrible," May noted.

"It is. Anyway, a blip is about a second, a bloop is about a minute, and a beoop is a... ah Christ, what's the other one?" he rubbed his face. "This is embarrassing."

"An hour?"

"Yes! Of course. Sorry, it's been so many orbits since I've thought about hours."

"Alright, so we will have about two minutes until the ship jumps and I need to shoot the thing with about a quarter second to spare? Then I've got that quarter second to escape the ship or we're halfway across the galaxy and inside a black hole? Is that right?"

August nodded, then looked to IX for confirmation. IX blinked in agreement.

The *Audacity* beeped tentatively at them; they were nearing the *Peacemaker* again. May rolled herself up and angled the rocket back into the ship, straight through the hole she'd blasted to get out of it minutes earlier.

"What's my job?" August asked, a bit too quickly, two cups of coffee into a raging caffeine high.

"Nothing, August. Your help will not be required for this particular plan. Thank you." IX lifted the corners of her lips in a polite smile. Smiling put August at ease, so she tried to remember to do it with some regularity.

"I've got a job for you, coffee-man," Xan said, hopping to his feet. "We're going to get the good luck charm back."

"Wait, why?" May turned to lean against the console as the rocket settled into the nearly empty docking bay of the *Peacemaker*.

"Listen," Xan leapt up the stairs to join her. "That thing's a legitimate probability modifier which means if Yvonne has it, she's got some massively good luck on her side. We've got to shift the odds a bit."

"But-"

IX rose from the table now, concerned. "If Yvonne has a probability modifier, the probability of us succeeding is greatly diminished. You must obtain the modifier before the ship jumps."

"Oh," May said.

Xan shrugged, smiling. "Occasionally I do know what I'm talking about. Alright," he crouched down just a bit, parking his hands on her shoulders. "I'll see you soon, okay?"

"But what if-"

"Uhp-bup-bup." He put a finger over her mouth. "I'll see you soon?" he asked again.

She sighed and nodded. Satisfied, he took his finger away.

"Yeah, see you soon. Have fun."

"Oh, we won't," he said cheerily. "A chaos goddess would like that too much." He turned to August now. "Are you ready to have a lot of the exact opposite of fun?"

"Yes! No, wait. IX." August held out his arms. "One of us might die," he told her.

"Yes, August. That would be unfortunate. Would you like physical reassurance that I care about your continued existence?"

August nodded. "Please."

IX opened her arms and bent them around him at right angles which felt more like being entrapped by steel girders than wrapped in a hug. She was getting better at it, though.

"Hey, August, do you know how to hot-wire a Gremlin?" Xan asked, already on the teledisc.

"Is there any other way to get one started?" August joined him and the pair fizzled away.

# FORTY-ONE

# A HORRIBLE PLAN

All sentient lifeforms have a sense of style. There are millions of micro-decisions one must make in a survival situation and it has been found that at least fifty-seven of those decisions are related to aesthetics. Even in the direst of moments, when Death's bejeweled fingers tap impatiently on Her scythe, style matters.

This is why, of the hundreds of AMC Gremlins which sat waiting to ferry the endangered occupants of the crashing *Peacemaker* to safety, only a single retro-fitted spacecar remained. Remained a little smugly, it should be noted, because it knew, with the vestiges of consciousness afforded all machinery over a certain age, that while in a survival situation it was too hideous to even be considered a possible escape option, now it was the only choice. And this made it the best choice.

The Gremlin was a dark blue specimen with a dented red door and silver bald patches where the paint had been half-heartedly sanded a decade before. It sat a few hundred spaces away from the *Audacity* in the *Peacemaker's* abandoned docking bay and watched the approaching gangly Tuhntian and tanned Earthling with a kind of eyebrow-raised, "Oh-ho-ho-It looks as if you'll be requiring my services after all."

The pair stopped a few paces in front of it, looked around desperately for a less hideous option, then, resignedly, clambered in. The Gremlin was pleased as punch that it had been chosen and it let them know by being slightly less difficult to start than it could've been.

"So," said August once he'd gotten the engine to turn over and the thrusters to engage. "What now? Seems like you know what you're doing."

"Does it? Excellent. I do not. Glad I could inspire confidence, though," Xan replied, tugging on a seatbelt that hadn't moved freely since the 1980s. August had settled on slipping a single arm through the belt, which was a good way to lose an arm, incidentally.

"Let's see what we're dealing with, then," August said and pulled the Gremlin out of the open bay doors, flinging them into a world that really made them wish the seatbelts were working.

Earth was roiling with activity. Turbulent gusts of something like pollen whipped around them, dusting the remains of the buildings which had been crushed by the *Peacemaker,* and appeared to be sloughing away into piles of lightly seasoned Panko breadcrumbs.

Away in the distance, a single skyscraper remained in something of its original form. Assuming, of course, that its original form involved an enormous neon sign that flashed "All Hail Chaos" and spun dizzyingly from the roof as the silver-haired figure of Chaos stood--no *floated*--atop it.

August and Xan stared for quite some time, mouths slightly ajar, neurons misfiring in time to a cylinder in the ancient Gremlin's engine.

"Alright, okay. So, obviously, we need to get her distracted so I can get close enough to grab the probability modifier," Xan said as they slowly approached the tower, which was now wobbling slightly as if it were really very tempted to devolve into Panko like its counterparts. It had a job to do though, and Chaos would keep it as long as it was useful to her.

"How do we distract her?"

Xan was not used to having to make the plans. August, coincidentally, wasn't either. They stared at each other for a moment, each waiting for the other to take charge.

Outside on the ailing street, the tasteful lampposts which Listay had so carefully designed shattered into assorted hardware. Barrel hinges, padlocks, wood screws, and toggle bolts rolled about the sidewalks, dropping into absurdly clean storm drains and settling in leafless gutters.

"Order!" August shouted at last. "She's a chaos goddess or spirit or whatever, right? If we start organizing that mess, it'll probably annoy her."

"That's a horrible plan," said Xan.

"Then what's your plan?"

Xan blinked, looked over his shoulder at the *Peacemaker* where May would, any second now, be attempting to destroy the Stardrive. He grit his teeth, trying to form a better plan that didn't involve dressing in drag.

"Ah, never mind. Good plan, let's do it."

August brought the Gremlin down in the way that IX always told him not to and they hopped out, setting to work on the hardware that scattered across the sidewalk below the wobbling control tower.

Xan collected every upholstery tack he could find and lined them up in careful rows, glancing up at the goddess occasionally as he did so. August started on the plastic sleeve anchors, cleverly organizing them by color. When the tacks were reasonably ordered, Xan started on the three-quarter inch screws. It wasn't a good plan, but it was their only plan and it would have to work.

High above the city, with the yellow wind teasing her shining silver hair and her feet floating inches above the sign which proclaimed to the world her intentions, Chaos felt a little uncomfortable. It started as a niggle. Like a clothing tag that was twisted the wrong way or an ant beginning to crawl up an ankle.

The niggle grew, though. It was now about as bad as listening to two songs with vastly different beats at the same time. What was it? She searched the city below her until it became properly annoying, like the dislodged rubber bit of a busted windshield wiper as it flaps unhelpfully against torrential downpour on the highway.

At last, she located the source of the disruption and sighed so deeply a small cyclone began curling in the distance, spinning carelessly away and uprooting a field of pineapple bushes which had, until recently, been solar panels. It was Xan. She really ought to have killed him when she had the chance.

She called forth a million copies of her corporeal form from a million other dimensions, found one in which she was already confronting Xan, and jumped into that body. It was a handy trick and, until she really got the hang of being omnipresent again, it did the job. Being omnipresent was unlike riding a bike in that if you go a few million years without practicing that sort of thing, it tends to leave you.

"What are you doing?" she asked. She knew perfectly well what he was doing, but she wanted him to account for himself.

"Just tidying up a bit. It's a mess down here. Have you seen this place? Shambles!" Xan said, not stopping to look up.

"It's not going to work."

"What won't work?" August asked, comparing the size of two bronze eyelets carefully before setting them down.

"Organizing an assortment of hardware is not going to get my attention." She kicked over a neatly stacked pyramid of one-inch bolts and Xan pretended not to notice.

"Hey Xan," August called. "Do you think these metric

washers should stay separate from the imperial ones?"

"Absolutely and without a doubt yes," he said, trying to get a few three-inch springs to stay in a line.

"Don't be ridiculous." Chaos waved a hand and the hardware devolved into uncountable grains of pale gray sand.

The bolts Xan had been holding were no more, and he nearly looked dejected. Nearly. Instead, he turned to August with a wry smile. "You wouldn't happen to have a pair of tweezers and a magnifying glass on you?"

"Never leave without 'em!" August reached into the pocket of his jeans, but paused when Chaos peered into a billion other dimensions and plopped them down into one in which the three of them were far away from anything that could conceivably be organized: the roof of the control tower.

August's head lolled over the edge and he quickly rolled backwards to safety. IX would be extremely displeased if he fell from that height. It would take her beoops to repair him.

The sand in Xan's palm blew away and, at last, he stared up at Chaos. She might have been two or three times her normal size, but her physical appearance was hard to pin down. He could tell it was her--the tinsel hair, the unmentionable eyes--but the lines that separated what was her from what was the sky around her were having a fit. It was extremely difficult to look at, impossible to look away from.

The probability modifier twinkled on her chest, and Xan focused on that as he pressed himself away from her and into an air-conditioning unit. August joined him, both of them trying to disappear into the whirring metal contraption.

From thin air, or rather from air thick with yellow dust, Chaos pulled an enormous flail with something that appeared to be a nastily spiked beachball on the end of its chain. The flail, though cumbersome and surprisingly ineffective due to lack of follow-through, is a terrifying looking weapon. And at that size, in the hands of an ancient evil made corporeal then made slightly less corporeal such that she retained the terrors of both physicality and ethereality, it was extremely menacing. Even before her muscled arms sent it into a wild swing above her head.

Xan tore his eyes away from her; it was just too horrible to watch.

"So, August, you're an Earthling, right? Ever seen 'I Love Lucy'?" Xan asked sweatingly.

August's face was turned away, his eyes shut tight so he wouldn't have to watch himself get mauled. "Uh, yeah. Sure. Some of it. That's the one with the truffles right? Where she's trying to eat all the truffles because she can't make them fast enough?"

"Yeah! *Job Switching*, that one's called. Good stuff. May hasn't seen it, can you believe that?"

"Uh..." August had rather better things to think about, but Xan figured there couldn't be anything better to think about during his last living blips.

They felt a gentle breeze from the spinning flail.

FORTY-TWO
# BUTTON MASHING

"Do you trust him to get the probability modifier?"

"Not... not really, no," May told IX as she checked and re-checked the ship, giving Xan a bit of a head-start.

"Then there is nearly no chance we will succeed."

IX said this very matter-of-factly. May didn't appreciate being told she wouldn't succeed. She didn't appreciate it when her high school literary teacher told her she wouldn't succeed because she'd neglected to finish reading *Catch-22*, didn't appreciate it when the employment agency had told her she wouldn't succeed as an airport traffic controller, didn't appreciate it when that random Sonic customer one ill-fated evening had told her she wouldn't succeed at life in general because she'd given him too much ice.

She stopped fiddling with the rocket's stabilizers and turned on IX, fixing her with a scowl neither of them could see; IX because she was blind and May because it was on her own face.

"What are the odds of being abducted by aliens and immediately offered a chance to escape?"

"Low."

"What's the likelihood of surviving being ejected from a Gremlin in open space?" She leaned in a little closer now, counting her points on her fingers.

"Extremely low. Why do you ask?"

"Last one. What are the odds that I picked up your distress call and just happened to be on a ship with weapons powerful enough to destroy a Stardrive that you wanted destroyed?"

"Absurdly low."

"Great. I'm not too worried about our chances. How do I get to the Stardrive?"

IX conjured a miniature holographic map of the *Peacemaker*'s schematics which spun slowly above her wrist. She flicked at it for a moment, trying to get it to stay still. She ran her finger along the outside of it, then downwards until her finger rested in the docking bay, roughly where they had landed.

"There is a series of service tunnels leading to the Stardrive chamber which the Audacity should be able to fit through. It will be tight." Her finger traced a complex trail through the holographic ship which May tried, and failed, to memorize.

"Can't I use the lasers to blast through the ship to the Stardrive? That will be quicker."

"That would compromise the structural integrity of the ship."

"And I suppose you'd prefer to leave that to the black hole?"

IX was quiet for a moment. "No, I would rather the structural integrity not be compromised at all, but that is unlikely. It may be quicker to go straight through the ship, as you suggested." IX closed the hologram, looking a touch sadder than usual which was somewhere between melancholy and somber. Now she looked positively pensive.

"I'm about to remove the collision cushion," May warned IX, hoping that perhaps IX would stop her. If Xan was to be believed, without the cushion they were destined to perish in a terrible, fiery crash. If IX was to be believed, with the cushion installed they wouldn't have time to escape the black hole and would perish in a terribly underwhelming slurp.

IX did not stop her.

The fiery crash sounded a tad more manageable to May than being sucked into a black hole, at least. She imagined that a black hole would make a sort of slurping noise as it killed her and that was an extremely unpleasant (and, fortunately, incorrect) thought.

She pried open the paneling and tore out the circuit, offering it to Osy who floated nearby. Once they exited the *Peacemaker*, May would have to manually repair the circuit. Osy was useful, but had no sense of urgency, as evidenced by the careful way it curled around the circuit and bobbed in the air before her. Osy ran on sponge time. Sponge time would not save their lives in the event of a crash.

"Are you ready?" IX asked, preparing her BEAPER to take her to the *Peacemaker's* teledisc.

May smiled grimly. "Would it matter if I wasn't?"

"No." IX disappeared.

May waited and shivered a little.

There was, if Xan were being completely honest with himself, one thing that was slightly more important than thinking about 'I Love Lucy' in his final moments. That thing was the probability modifier. Specifically, that thing was taking the probability modifier away from Chaos so that May had even a scrap of a chance of destroying the Stardrive.

Lucy might've had hilariously poor hand-eye coordination, but Xan...well Xan's wasn't great, either. It didn't matter. He, after ages of faffing about alone in space, had something of a purpose.

He focused on the probability modifier again. It still hung around Chaos's neck, resting neatly in her dastardly cleavage.

He needed to grab it. That was all, just leap at it and rip

it off her. Easy. The flail swung away from him...now! Oh no, it was back. He'd hesitated too long. The flail was closer now. It swung towards him and before it had swung too far away, he sprung, reached for the glowing rock, and grasped it as if it were life itself.

A thick iron chain slammed into him, cracking a good two or three of his ribs and bowling him over the edge of the tower.

He shut his eyes tight, positive that whatever the afterlife looked like, he wasn't ready to see it just yet. Metal crunched into his spine, and he felt himself swaying, felt his ribs stinging. What was the swaying about?

"Go!"

"What?" May had been slouched over the console, shakily awaiting IX's return. IX slid into the seat beside her, tapping the *Audacity*'s control panel urgently.

"Go, now. The autopilot was severely damaged upon landing. The ship will jump in forty-three blips... forty-two... forty-one." IX raised a countdown from her BEAPER which took over for her with beeps that rose steadily in pitch and seemed to somehow get faster, as if they were an auctioneer trying to get someone to spend an inordinate amount of money on May's continued existence.

The things that happened next happened in such quick succession and with such ferocity that even moments later, if asked to explain what happened, May wouldn't be able to recount in exact detail. This is partially due to the fact that moments later, May was hurtling towards the Earth in a dead rocket ship with little hope of survival and was, as one might imagine, a little distracted by that.

What happened was this: May engaged the ship's lasers, then its launch, blasted her way straight through the *Peacemaker* in the general direction of the Stardrive chamber, peeled through layers and layers of the ship's ruined interior, got the Stardrive squarely in the crosshairs of all six Ultra-Ray-Super-Destroyers, and shot at it.

And then it began to suck away reality quicker than however quickly the most well-advertised vacuum currently on the market is reported to suck away household allergens.

Fortunately for both reality and May, at the same moment—in nearly the same nanomoment but not quite—the *Peacemaker* jumped to a distant star system and the *Audacity* shot upwards into Earth's atmosphere.

And then the *Audacity* shut off.

The drain of shooting through miles of thick metal ship supports and the Stardrive and the hull of the *Peacemaker* coupled with May's foot pressing so hard on the accelerator that she fractured one or two of her metatarsals had completely and utterly exhausted the rocket. It must be noted that, had the *Audacity* actually been filled with rocket fuel rather than gritty dregs of coffee, the rocket would've had plenty of energy to complete this task and a quick pit stop at the nearest convince spaceport, Lavitry 2 where the plastic bags are stamped with the accurate slogan: 'We've always got what you need, but never what you want.'

Since this was not the case, the *Audacity* was now hurtling to Earth, the immutable law of gravity resolutely not muting.

"Cushion!" May shouted at IX. She tossed Osy, who had been floating near her shoulder and slowly gumming the circuit, at IX as she dove under the darkened control panel and began button mashing in hopes of finding the emergency generator.

It is possible, though difficult, to be very bad at button mashing. There is some skill involved in trying everything in that you must try it with precision and speed but without stopping to see if what you've done has had any effect. This was difficult for May to do, since the effect she was looking for was an important one. Still, her fingers flew over the rows of dials and switches that were embedded in the underside of the console as IX fumbled with the cushion above her.

"May, perhaps it has escaped your notice, but I am blind, and it would be quicker if you reattached the circuit instead."

"Yeah," May grunted as she toggled a sticky lever and waited an ill-advised nanosecond to see if it did anything. "I noticed. Eyesight won't be of much use until I get the lights back on, though."

IX gave her a verbal shrug and began to feel her way around the collision cushion panel. It really would've been much easier if she hadn't lost her goggles along with the *Robert*, but if her hindsight was 20/20, her current sight was 0/0 and her future sight was a solid 10/10.

Outside, the Earth waited patiently.

### FORTY-THREE
# IT WAS KEVIN

Xan peered cautiously around. Oh. This was quite a stroke of luck. The swaying he'd felt was that of a hanging window washer platform which had broken his fall. He lounged a story away from Chaos and her menacing ball.

He laughed manically and spit silvery green blood onto the platform. He was definitely alive. Ghosts didn't suffer internal bleeding, as far as he was aware. The probability modifier was clutched in his fist.

"Not dead!" he shouted at Chaos, immediately realizing that announcing this to someone who *wanted* him dead was a bad idea. She spun to fix her eyes on his. Something suddenly occurred to Xan. "Kevin!"

"Excuse me?" Chaos stopped, perplexed.

"I just remembered! Aimz's ex-girlfriends's brother—his name was Kevin! You remember Kevin of Lipscomb, right? Good times. I think he had a bit of a crush on you, actually. Might've gotten somewhere, too, if Aimz hadn't —" A deafening roar split the air before being hushed by a deafening silence.

Chaos looked as if she had seen the end of time itself, and then the beginning of it, and then realized that they were, in fact, exactly the same and that time was cyclical in nature. Or perhaps more like she'd just heard a strange noise in a large, dark house she thought she was alone in. Either way, she looked spooked.

Her gaze snapped to the wreck of the *Peacemaker*, then her very essence seemed to snap to it too, sucked away as the star, which still held a good chunk of her eternal soul, collapsed in on itself.

The *Peacemaker* vanished, jumping to an uninhabited sector of the galaxy where it could turn itself inside out without greatly disturbing any local populations.

Xan watched, delighted as an orange streak shot into the sky from where the *Peacemaker* had been nanoblips before, then watched, horrified, as the orange streak sputtered out and began to plummet.

Yvonne, small for a goddess but tall for a Rhean, lay on the roof of the control tower. Xan pulled himself up from the platform and back onto the roof, knelt beside her, and tapped her face urgently.

"Hey, mun, are you alive?"

She opened her eyes at him. They were mentionable now. Plain, in fact. A sort of dull greyish purple. "Think so," her brow furrowed. "What are you doing here you spineless wyrntensil dropping?"

"Good." Xan gave her forehead a quick kiss, then sprinted to the roof access hatch and took to the stairs, leaping down them a floor at a time in a way he knew he'd pay for later.

While Tuhntian skin heals relatively quickly, Tuhntian joints, like all joints, are fickle and delicate things.

The city was figuring itself out again. Panko breadcrumbs separated from seasonings and re-became buildings and the tasteful shrubs that skirted those buildings. Lazily traipsing pillars of greasy fur re-became food service workers. Strange, slimy things that crawled bug-like along the gutters re-became politicians. Quails continued to exist but looked strangely out-of-place again.

By the time Xan reached the street, it was about as boring as a street could possibly be...aside, of course, from the absurdly bright neon orange rocket ship that smoked at an intersection and the smattering of quails which pecked curiously at one of its fins.

All that had kept the ship from complete decimation as gravity had intended was the collision cushion, which IX had finished replacing as May's fingers brushed over the switch that turned on the ship's back-up generator, giving it just enough power to manifest the cushion seconds before the ship hit with an indescribably quiet bang, like a fifty pound barbell falling off the shelf beside you but in a parallel dimension which sits directly on top of your own and is like it in every way except that you actually use barbells.

Xan shoved the probability modifier into his pocket, promised himself he'd have it surgically implanted when this was all over, and teleported onto the *Audacity*'s teledisc, startling the quails. This was—the ship being toppled on its side rather than set on its fins like it ought to have been—a bad idea.

The moment he remerged on the disc, he trundled into the glowing orange wall which was now the glowing orange floor.

## FORTY-FOUR
# EXOTIC CUISINE

August was having a lot of awkward interactions lately, which he firmly felt he was getting too old for. It was the only thing about getting older he'd found he'd liked. He now had an extra, subjective excuse to not do something that he could throw around whenever he wanted.

His latest awkward interaction was with the husk of what once was Yvonne and went thusly:

"Uh, hi," he said.

"Who are you?" she said, rubbing her forehead as if she could rub away her brief interaction with Xan.

"I'm, uh, August."

"And?" If Yvonne had ever had a concept of manners, Chaos had boxed that up first and it would take a while to unpack. It was a small box.

"Well, I, uh...I think I'm IX's pet? Do you remember IX?"

"IX!" Yvonne leapt to her feet now, which was quite a task because she hadn't been able to control her feet for a few hundred orbits and they were in impossibly high heels and felt all pins-and-needles. She did it though, for IX. "Where?"

August tried to reach out an awkward arm to steady

her, but she didn't need it—or didn't want it. Awkwardly, August put his arm down.

"In the *Audacity*," he said, watching the orange blur as it began to plummet to Earth.

He went to the edge of the building, closely followed by Yvonne. They stood together in extremely thick and extremely awkward silence as they watched the ship dive into an intersection. They were too far away to notice the quails which gathered round it.

Something landed heavily beside May, taking her out of the warm, hazy unconsciousness she'd been enjoying against the *Audacity*'s wall which was now the floor. She looked at it. It smiled at her casually, as if it hadn't just fallen a good five feet sideways.

"Good morning, starshine," said Xan.

"You could get away with that in space, but I know for a fact it's mid-afternoon out there."

"Details, details." He rolled up, looking around at the mess. The only furniture that had remained where it ought to have been was the hover table and chairs which clung, a bit askew, to the shag carpeting that was now the wall. Xan crawled over May and made his way to the control loft, hopping up and down to get at a particular switch under the console which had been installed, rather annoying he thought, just out of reach of someone who was standing on the wall.

At last he snagged it and a telescoping arm outside began to re-set the ship on its fins. It was a slow and vertigo-inducing process that May did not enjoy in the slightest.

Xan was used to it.

"Is Yvonne alive?" IX asked Xan. She was sitting up on the wall, slowly sliding to the floor in a way that reminded May vaguely of Mary Poppins somehow. Impossibly prim.

"Well, she insulted me, so all signs point to yes. I left her with August on top of the control tower."

"And August is alive as well?"

The ship was upright again, the couch, TV, and coffee table thumping back to the carpet. IX knelt by May who was sitting cross legged on the floor now and checked the usual things she checked for August when he had a near-death experience.

"Yeah, he's fine. Although, I left him with Yvonne so... who knows?"

May felt like a spaceship was parked on her chest and her head was a seething nebula. IX's cold fingers prodded at her, with a silent but understood "Does this hurt?" "Does this hurt?" "Does this-"

"Hey!" May pulled her arm away from IX, holding it like a baby squirrel that had fallen from its nest.

"May, you have a broken a bone. This happens to August frequently. Please allow me to set it. Where is the medical bay on this vessel?"

May groaned, resting her head against the warm orange wall. "I need a cigarette."

"You have also suffered a concussion. Smoking would be detrimental to-"

"I know, I know." She tried to stand but Xan scooped her up before she'd even gotten her feet under her.

"Xan, my arm is broken, not my legs."

"Oh, right." He put her down

"Shit!" Putting weight on her left foot hadn't ended well. She balanced on her right leg. "Okay, fine. Maybe something's broken in my leg, too," she said, letting Xan hoist her up again.

Yvonne leaped over the edge of the building and onto the window washing platform.

"Coming?" she shouted up at August who was still staring, mouth agape, at the wreck of the *Audacity*. He shook his head to clear it.

"Yeah. I'm getting too old for stairs," he quipped as he vaulted over the edge of the building, landing on the platform in a way that made Yvonne suspect that he wasn't, in fact, too old for stairs but that he was perhaps too lazy.

Yvonne let the platform down much more quickly than August would've liked; he had a terrible time keeping them balanced with the other rope, but eventually they made it to the street. Yvonne tore down the normalized street towards the *Audacity,* but August figured he might as well take his time. There was no way he'd reach it at the same time as her so he might as well be a great deal later. To his left, he saw a food service station and wondered if perhaps May liked apples.

"It was incredible, May! A battle of wits, really. I risked life and limb to get the probability modifier back. Yvonne was terrifying—Chaos, I suppose."

IX had forced May to lay down on a table in the medical bay and given her a clean towel to bite down on. Xan leaned over her now, telling her what had happened to distract her from what IX was doing.

"Oh, I wish you'd seen it. A half inch screw there, a wire cap here—it was brilliant. She got *so* mad. She said she wasn't, but I knew she was. You don't manifest a flail the size of a small sun just for the breeze. Which was ungodly, by the way."

Speaking of ungodly, May worked really hard not to punch IX when she set her arm. It would've hurt May more than it would've hurt IX at that point. Now, IX was at her ankle and she focused on not kicking her away.

"Or I suppose it *was* godly seeing as...as she was...are you alright?"

May's face was scrunched with pain; she'd been biting the towel so hard the fibers were lodged like floss in between her teeth while IX gently wrapped something around her foot.

May nodded and pulled the towel from her mouth with her other hand. "Yeah, go on."

"Right, so the flail. It was enormous. If one of those spikes had hit me, I'd have been a rather stringy shish kabob-"

May held a hand up, tilting her head to the side. "You have shish kabob in space?"

"Of course. Why wouldn't we? Everyone's got shish kabob. Anyway, I sprung for the thing—the probability modifier—and I wasn't dead! Just got hit by the chain part. Then *poof*, Chaos is no more, and Yvonne insults me."

May nodded and reached up to pat his face. "Good job."

"Thanks!" He was inordinately proud of himself. Or perhaps ordinately. Heroics weren't really his thing but he'd pulled it off surprisingly well.

A thud echoed from above in the living room.

"IX!" they heard someone shout, extremely muffled.

IX gasped and bolted to the intershoot.

Xan sighed. "Ready to meet the real Yvonne? I must warn you, she's not as different from Chaos as one might hope."

May sat up, studying the rush job IX had done. "Not exactly. How'd she get in without an anchor?"

"Probably scaled the side of the ship and opened the manual hatch."

They were being extremely loud up there. Uncomfortably so.

"Maybe we should let them..."

"Yeah, yes." Xan cut her off and hopped up to sit beside her on the table. After a moment of silence peppered with muffled lewd sounds, Xan decided it would be better to not hear them. "So, Earth's back to normal out there. I suppose you'll be wanting to get back to it." He winced; it was not better.

"Yep. I've got an interview Friday for a really cushy office job with benefits and heaps of PTO. Lady really seemed to like me over the phone, too."

"An office job, eh?" He smiled at her. "You know, sitting all day is murder on the back. I know from experience. You're going to want to find yourself a good bone demangler."

May laughed. "On Earth we call those chiropractors."

"Oh, we have those too, but what you really want is a bone demangler. Trust me." Xan turned to her now, the acid green of his eyes so intense it could've melted May's flesh off. "Honestly, though, I don't want to you to feel obligated to-"

A wet slapping sound interrupted him. A yogurt cup dripped its contents slowly down the outside of the window opposite them in the medical bay. May hobbled over to the window to watch more processed foods, along with what looked suspiciously like quail eggs, pelt the side of the ship. She watched the small crowd of disgruntled people. Disgruntled humans; she wasn't necessarily keen on relating to them right now.

"Look at them," May shook her head. "I don't want anything to do with that."

"May." Xan joined her at the window, watching the food curiously. "I know you have a concussion so let me remind you: Platamousse proper? They pelted us with food, too."

May scrunched her nose at the memory. "Yeah but that was alien food, so at least it was exotic. This is just...well actually I have no idea what this is." She watched a green slime streak lazily by. "Besides, I was just getting the hang of racing. We technically won our last race."

"Technically," Xan agreed. "So...you'll stay as long as we keep racing?"

"Sure. Who knows? Maybe longer." She leaned against him and tried to make out images in the food splatter as if it were a moving Rorschach test. She saw a couple cigarettes, a machete, and a rocket nozzle. Xan saw a tall mixed drink with a salted rim, felt that was a premonition, and told her.

FORTY-FIVE

# AUGUST GETS APPLES

August climbed into the *Audacity's* living room via the manual hatchway just as Yvonne did, but with a great deal less verve and taking more time to puzzle at the quails. When he finally made it up with the sack of apples he'd borrowed from the food service station, IX and Yvonne were entangled in a mess of purple limbs, making out quietly on the askew couch.

August didn't mind. IX had walked in on him plenty of times. It was a nice change of pace.

"Where's May?" he asked the snoggers.

Fortunately, they didn't have to stop to answer. May and Xan appeared in the intershoot, having watched August climb up the side of the ship and feeling bad that he'd also been pelted with foodstuffs by angry humans. Xan handed him the towel May had used to bite down on.

"Thanks. Apple?" He simultaneously wiped some ketchup from his face and held out the sack of apples to them.

Xan took an apple, sniffed it carefully. "I probably shouldn't be eating weird alien foods," he said, and put it back.

May had already crunched into a red delicious, making noises August politely declined to notice. "Mmm. My, God, I've missed apples. All I've had to eat is raw vegetables. What have you been eating?"

"Really?" August asked May, setting the sack down and taking a seat at the hover table to enjoy his ill-gotten fruit. "You know, I've never come across a food I couldn't eat out there. Never came across one I *wanted* to eat, either. But nothing's made me sick and I've tried everything." He looked a little sad at that. "Everything," he repeated, almost as if he wished there was some alien food he couldn't digest.

He sighed and took the first glorious bite of his apple. He proceeded to make noises that he hoped May would politely decline to notice as well.

She did, changing the subject. "Are you going to stay on Earth?"

He shrugged. "Wouldn't be much of a place for me. Not with this anyway." He waved his robotic hand at her. "Besides, IX will probably want to keep me around. Isn't that right IX? You like hanging out with me, right?"

"Yes August." IX broke off the kiss to reassure her human. He liked to be reassured.

August smiled at May. "See! And it'd be so weird going back to my old friends. My gal's still nineteen out there, thinks I ditched her, probably. I'm like...thirty-two now." He began eating a second apple.

May looked at him a bit disbelievingly.

"Thirty-nine?" he tried.

"Maybe. I'm sorry, August."

"Eh, I've had a lot of good women over the years. Good people, I guess. Not all of them were women. Not sure any of them were actually." He shrugged. "I'll be fine."

Xan, feeling a bit left out, stuck a gloveless finger under one of the many new holes in his Fusion Lay-Flex™ suit and sighed at it.

Fusion Lay-Flex™ can take a beating, or so said the third-party digital marketing company based out of a planetoid near A'Viltri. "Make it look sexy, but tasteful," Fusion Lay-Flex™ CEO Gorn McFlornbits had said. The marketing team, having misinterpreted what Gorn meant by "tasteful," went full-on BDSM dungeon culture with the ads, being careful to note in each ad that the liquid fabric came in a variety of "tasteful" flavors.

Fusion Lay-Flex™ did not, in fact, come in a variety of flavors. Its flavor was something between the underside of a gently used shoe and American cheese singles, and this did not bode well for Gorn McFlornbits. Gorn was sacked as a result of the miscommunication and Murb Forngorbits, his successor, quickly re-branded the material for military use and made an outstanding amount of money. Fortunately, the original slogan "Fusion Lay-Flex™ can take a beating" could be salvaged.

And it could take a beating. Just not the kind of beating Xan's suit had gotten in the previous few chapters.

IX and Yvonne tore themselves away from each other, then, holding hands, went to the table. IX nudged Yvonne. "Say it," IX told her quietly.

Yvonne sighed at her, gave Xan a hateful glare, and forced her tongue to work again. "I'm sorry I insulted you. Pent up. Had," she waggled her fingers around her head for emphasis, "things in my head."

"Oh, it's fine! But, uh—and really, I hate to bring up a debt— but you still owe me seven hundred crystals."

"Why?"

"The flashlight. I fixed the lightbulb for you; you owe me seven hundred crystals for that. Those were the terms. Honestly, I wouldn't care, only we really did go through a lot of trouble as a result of that lightbulb."

Yvonne rubbed the bridge of her nose. "Yes, I remember. Vaguely. I'll transfer the crystals to your account."

"Um." Xan smiled uncomfortably. "I don't have an account anymore. Could you just teledisc them to me?"

"Why don't you have a..." Yvonne paused.

A really big box had just been unpacked. A really big, very musty box with yellowed, crinkly tape all over it.

"Oh, Blitheon's stars, Xan. Zuut. I'll send you a little extra. Not that it'll-"

He put up a hand to stop her. "Forget about it. Glad

you're back. Just like the good old days, right? Exorcising ancient evils from one another...flails."

His reminiscing was cut short by a rhythmic clanging from the hull of the ship which was soon joined by a distant litany of curses. Outside, the collection of food service humans whose pent-up rage had to be turned on something, had found the rungs on the body of the ship that led up to the manual hatchway.

May set the remains of her apple on the table and limped up the stairs to the control panel. "Damn humans," she muttered.

"Where am I dropping you off?" she asked no one in particular.

"Wha...me?" Xan asked, worried that he was being kicked off his own ship.

"Not you."

"Please bring us to Clymasir on Rhea I, May. Thank you," IX replied.

"A-hah-uh, no, sorry," Xan interjected, standing now. "Not going to Rhea. Not going anywhere near the Flotluex solar system, actually. Out of the way, you understand. Major inconvenience." He began casually making far more coffee than anyone wanted. "We'll take you to one of the nicer spaceports near there! Just not in Flotluex. Coffee?" he asked, dumping all twelve cups he'd made into the ship's fuel tank and starting another pot.

"I understand your hesitation. Please take us to Tolfy Municipal Spaceport. We can access our accounts from there and purchase a new means of transportation. August, you can get something to eat there as well."

August sat up a little, almost through a third apple. "I've got apples."

"You cannot eat only apples, August."

August bit into his apple glaringly. "Bet I can."

Xan poured another carafe of coffee into the ship and landed in the co-pilot's chair, spinning it around. "Alright." He started chewing on his thumbnail, paused, and rolled his eyes at himself.

This was why he always wore gloves.

"Alright," he started again, his hands firmly stuck under

his thighs. "We'll drop off Yvonne, August, and IX, grab a 'we're not dead' celebratory cocktail, get the gem Yvonne owes me, make new suits...and then?"

He turned to May who pressed The Button That Typically Made The Ship Go. They all ignored a distant scream from outside as the human who had been climbing the ship fell off.

"We race. Let's try Plattamousse again. As long as I don't start from slot three, we're guaranteed to not lose."

"I like those odds!" Xan said with a smile.

FORTY-SIX

# DEAD AND BURIED

"Damn, she's heavy," she heard distantly.

"Come on, we don't gotta drag her far," said another voice, somehow gruffer. She felt nothing, she saw nothing.

"Why even bury her? Not like she deserves it."

"Naw, but I don't want no coyotes and buzzards eating on alien flesh and getting all radioactive, do you?"

"Guess not."

"Alright, lift her up on three. One... two... three!"

Oh, she felt something then. Just a little something. Just the tiniest hint that maybe she was being moved somewhere against her will.

*Of course you are, zoup-nog, they're burying you.* Something thought in her head. Not her thoughts, something in her head and thinking at her.

*Why?* she thought back.

*Because you're dead.*

*Oh.* That didn't surprise her much, what surprised her was that she knew it.

*Hold on, I've almost got you online again. Just try not to freak out the humans or they'll kill you a second time.*

*Okay,* she thought, a little dully. It was okay to be a

little dull though, she was dead after all.

She could feel something else now. A dull thunk in her chest. Oh, that was interesting. She better start counting those again.

# THERE'S MORE WHERE
# THAT CAME FROM!

Go to www.LauraLoup.com
and sign up for my newsletter
to be the first to read

and while you're there, check out *Tarot in Space*, a
78-card Tarot deck inspired by *The Audacity*!

Thank you for reading, starshine. You're the coffee in
my fuel tank, the blueberry in my milkshake, and the
good in my luck charm.

## ABOUT THE AUTHOR

Laura Loup is a very serious humorologist with an extremely impressive BFA in animation that she promises to never actually use and an intense desire to eat orange. Not the fruit, the color. Though the fruit will do in a pinch. She owns a metaphysical shop in Savannah, GA with her husband and is the mildly peckish artist behind *Tarot in Space*.

Connect with me on Twitter or Instagram to see character art, keep up with the process, and get extra content. I'm @LauraLoupArt on both!

CPSIA information can be obtained
at www.ICGtesting.com
Printed in the USA
FSHW011139280919
62435FS